SING TO THE
WESTERN WIND

A Novel

Tariq Mehmood

V

VERSO

London • New York

First published by Verso 2025
First published as *Song of Gulzarina* by Daraja Press 2016
© Tariq Mehmood 2025

The manufacturer's authorized representative in the EU for product safety (GPSR)
is LOGOS EUROPE, 9 rue Nicolas Poussin, 17000, La Rochelle, France
Contact@logoseurope.eu

1 3 5 7 9 10 8 6 4 2

Verso
UK: 6 Meard Street, London W1F 0EG
US: 207 32nd Street, New York, NY 10016
versobooks.com

Verso is the imprint of New Left Books

ISBN-13: 978-1-80429-534-2
ISBN-13: 978-1-80429-536-6 (US EBK)
ISBN-13: 978-1-80429-535-9 (UK EBK)

British Library Cataloguing in Publication Data
A catalogue record for this book is available from the British Library

Library of Congress Cataloging-in-Publication Data

Names: Mehmood, Tariq, author.
Title: Sing to the western wind: a novel / Tariq Mehmood.
Other titles: Song of Gulzarina
Description: London; New York: Verso, 2025. | 'First published as Song of
Gulzarina by Daraja Press 2016.'
Identifiers: LCCN 2024060269 (print) | LCCN 2024060270 (ebook) | ISBN
9781804295342 (paperback) | ISBN 9781804295366 (ebook) | ISBN
9781804295359 (ebook)
Subjects: LCGFT: Novels.
Classification: LCC PR6063.E357 S66 2025 (print) | LCC PR6063.E357
(ebook) | DDC 823/.914 – dc23/eng/20241227
LC record available at https://lccn.loc.gov/2024060269
LC ebook record available at https://lccn.loc.gov/2024060270

Typeset in Electra by Biblichor Ltd, Scotland
Printed and bound by CPI Group (UK) Ltd, Croydon CR0 4YY

Sing to the Western Wind

A NOVEL

Tariq Mehmood

Sing to the Western wind the song it understands

Gulzarina
September 2016

BOOK I

Abroadi

My loose aerial smacks against the outside wall. I turn and face the garden, where shadows race in front of the darkness; where the overgrown rose bush is scratching against the window, its thorns thicker than the veins in my arm, its only flower larger than my trembling fist. The reflection of my withered face, with deep sullen eyes, blurs behind raindrops sliding down the glass. An overcoat hangs on an open door behind me. I pour some whisky and knock it back. My throat burns. The scent of whisky hisses out of my nostrils.

Pushing open the garden door, I step outside. Shadows disappear into the interlocking arms of lifeless conifers at the far end of my garden.

There is no wind and the rain has gone. My new aluminium bin is still in the middle of the garden, where I had left it, full of contents ready to burn. All that now remains is for me to lift the lid, pour the white spirit into the bin and set it on fire.

A powerful security light on one of the houses across the back alley has just come on. I lift the lid off the bin. I have shredded everything that could link the explosives to the friend who got them for me. The shreds are beneath the old clock I bought all those years ago, the one that never worked. The clock is face down on a pile of birthday cards, all marked

'Return to sender' in my daughter Aisha's handwriting. I pick up a returned card and stare at the handwritten words. The curve of the 'R' is a perfect semi-circle that cuts through the left arm of the letter, and its right leg is slightly turned upwards, breaking just before the start of the 'e'. The 't' is crossed with a long cut. The words are close together, in a perfect straight line. There are three large exclamation marks at the end, with their dots dangling below them. The words are underlined with three deep lines, visible from the other side of the card's envelope. I imagine Aisha scribbling these, her eyebrows curling towards each other, just like her mother's used to when she stared unblinkingly at me. I think back to the last time I had seen the silence of those eyes.

Aisha's eighth birthday was in a few days' time. I had a quick pint with some mates and went home early from work. She was squatting next to her mother on a big white rug, leaning against a settee, rhythmically rocking backwards and forwards with a qaida, with which she was learning to read the Quran, repeating a letter and a word in Arabic. Her mother was leaning over an open Quran that sat in a carved wooden holder. When I walked in, she adjusted the dupatta on her head and continued moving her finger along a page, reading aloud.

Aisha looked at me, snapped her qaida shut, shot up and hopped around her mother, who grabbed her arm and yanked her down, saying, 'Never lift your foot higher than the holy Quran.'

'Let her go, Yasmin!' I ordered.

Yasmin ignored me, opened Aisha's qaida and said, 'Repeat your lesson.'

'How many times have I said it's a waste of time reading words in a language you don't understand?'

Aisha looked at me with pleading eyes.

'You can get up, Aisha,' I said.

Her mother glared at her. Aisha opened her qaida.

I smiled at Aisha and said, 'Come, my daughter, let's go for a Chinese and you can tell me what you want for your birthday.'

Aisha snatched her arm free from her mother and ran to me. Yasmin started reciting from the Quran again.

Before leaving the house, Aisha held my hand and took me to the kitchen, where her school bag was dangling off the back of a chair. She rummaged through it and handed me an envelope. It was her school report. I sat down on a chair. Aisha jumped into my lap and stared at me as I read the report: *Whilst Aisha is a bright intelligent child, she gets bored quickly and is often disruptive in class.*

'Have I been a good girl, Abba?' Aisha asked.

I kissed her on the head and said, 'You have been an angel.'

Aisha's face lit up with joy and she vaulted to the fridge, poured some apple juice into a plastic glass, gulped it down and tossed the empty glass into the sink before turning towards me.

As we were leaving the house, I said, 'But it says you are sometimes a bit naughty in class.'

Aisha stepped in front of me, placed her hands on the sides of her hips and protested, 'Dad! You're horrible.'

'But it also says that you are really helpful, and always listen to your teacher.'

Aisha beamed with joy, put her little hand in mine, skipped along and asked, 'Why does Mummy never come with us to the Chinese?'

'She just doesn't,' I said. 'Tell me, what would you like?'

'Why do grown-ups always fight?'

'They don't . . .'

'When you and Mummy are not *fighting fighting*, you're still fighting, just not *fighting fighting*.'

'Come on, what do you want for your birthday?' I asked.

Aisha let go of my hand, stepped in front of me, gave me a great big smile and said, 'I'm not allowed to wear dresses now that I am growing up, Mummy says.'

'If you want a dress for your birthday, you'll get a dress for your birthday. And I'll tell your mother you can wear whatever you like,' I said, grabbing hold of Aisha's arm just as she was about to step off the pavement.

At the Chinese, Aisha sat on one of two tall stools and insisted on eating in the shop. I stood next to her, watching her as she shoved large chunks of chicken breast into her mouth. She bit into a small ketchup packet. It burst open. Some of it dribbled into the takeaway box and some down her yellow flowery frock. Throwing a mischievous look at me, she licked ketchup out of the box.

'That's enough now. Let's go home,' I said, placing the lid back on the takeaway container.

Yasmin was in the kitchen when we came back into the house. Pointing to Aisha's dress, I said to Yasmin, 'You should teach your daughter some better eating manners.'

'What good are manners when you feed my child what you do and bring unclean stuff into my house?' Yasmin protested.

She was a small woman, much smaller than when I had first met her. Her black hair was tied into a long plait that fell over her shoulder. Her eyes were always moist, with dark patches underneath. Even in front of me, she ensured that her dupatta fully covered her head.

Giving me a cold stare, with knotted brows she said, 'How can you give her this meat to eat?'

'And you can really tell the difference?' I shouted.

Aisha snatched her hand away from me, went up to her mother and hugged her.

'Halal meat is halal, my husband.'

'You can taste the difference, woman, can you?'

'The difference is here,' Yasmin said, placing her hand across her chest.

Yasmin picked up a tissue and, wiping Aisha's mouth, added, 'Don't put your dirty sins on my daughter.'

'How dare you insult me,' I said. I pulled a chicken drumstick out of the container, tore some flesh off it, shoved it into Yasmin's mouth and hissed, 'Tell me the fucking difference woman. Tell me the difference!'

Placing her hands over her ears, Aisha hid behind her mother. Yasmin pulled herself away from me, turned to the kitchen sink behind her and spat out the meat. A moment later she vomited. When she had finished, she rinsed her mouth and wiped her face with her green dupatta and said calmly, almost in a whisper, 'Do you do this to your goree, your white woman?'

How dare she bring Carol into this? I thought.

'But then white flesh wouldn't take it like me, eh, my husband?' Yasmin mocked as she went past me towards Aisha, who had stood where she was, mortified. Holding onto Aisha's hand, Yasmin led her past me. 'No one eats in this house because you eat haram and eat that forbidden outsider,' she said quietly.

'And it is called soure, a pig. Yes, a pig and not an *outsider*,' I retorted.

Holding tightly to her mother's legs, Aisha said meekly as she went past, 'Abba, I just want to be normal.'

'You are normal, my sweet.' Tears of frustration burnt in my eyes.

'And you shouldn't do this sort of thing to Mummy.'

Aisha's words hurt me. Taking a deep breath, I said to Yasmin, 'I am sorry . . .'

After kissing her mother on the forehead, Aisha hopped past me and ran into the living room. Moments later the television burst into life. Yasmin closed the kitchen door with her heel and said, 'You may be my husband.' Lifting the lid off a pot of dhal that was simmering on the gas cooker, she added, 'You are not my God.'

She reached up, opened a cupboard and took a bag out.

'I have told you, this stuff will not stay in my house, my husband,' she said, unscrewing a bottle of whisky.

'Don't you dare touch it, you daughter of a blind donkey,' I yelled.

'I cannot sleep with the knowledge that this stuff is here.' Yasmin held her hand over her nose as she emptied the bottle into the sink.

'It is single malt,' I screamed. 'You bitch!'

I gripped her hand with my left and raised my right hand to strike her. She turned to me and looked at me without blinking. I snatched what was left in the bottle, poured myself a large whisky, knocked it back, and thought while going to the dining room at the back of the house, 'I would be better off if the bitch were dead!'

'I beg you again my husband,' Yasmin said, walking in after me a short while later. Placing a tray of food in front of me, she added, 'Do not drink sharab, especially not in front of my daughter and in my house. One day she will grow up.'

Knocking the tray off the table, I said, 'I will drink here and I will keep it here. This is my house.'

I poured myself another whisky and knocked it back in one gulp. The image of the large kitchen knife flashed through my mind. How easy it would be to slit her throat, I thought. The warmth of the whisky filled my stomach. I shook my head, hoping to chase the murderous thoughts away. But they fought back. The knife seemed to have jumped out of the drawer and was floating towards me. I stood up and shook my head again. The knife vanished. I turned to leave and as I opened the front door, she said, 'The stench is bad enough on your breath, but what is worse is the scent of that white woman of yours.'

I did not turn around. I knew she was picking food off the floor. She waited for a response from me and then said, 'You should not have married me when you loved another.'

I walked out into the garden, slamming the door behind me.

Standing outside the door, I thought, how dare she bring Carol into everything? I should have left her in the village. She would never stop.

I was about to go back inside when she opened the door, knife in hand. I stepped inside, grabbed her hand with the knife, put the tip of the blade on my chest and said, 'Go on, do it!'

I was trembling with rage. She stared at me coldly.

'Let go of my Mummy now, Abba!' Aisha said, bursting into the kitchen. She ran at me and bit my leg.

I shook my leg and Aisha stumbled backwards screaming, 'Mummy!'

'Aisha, go into the other room,' Yasmin said.

Aisha went out of the room and shut the door, shouting, 'I hate you, Abba!' over and over again. I let go of Yasmin and pushed her away from me, saying, 'This has to end.'

A screeching white cat with raging eyes jumps out of an overhanging branch close to me, pushing the memory of Yasmin into the darkness. The cat runs up a broken fence and disappears into the shadows of my neighbour's unkempt garden. I pour the whole bottle of white spirit into the bin and throw a lit match into it. The bin bursts into flames.

There is a rage in the sky close by, above a house like mine. It is the third time this week it has been here. Each time it has come during the night, its screaming blades dissecting and re-joining my recurring dreams: fighter planes swarming; a city ablaze; scattered smouldering limbs; Tony Blair showing his teeth; Sarah Ann with her plastic smile, walking her dog.

An arc of light passes over me.

The pulsating hiss of the helicopter gets louder and louder.

Pulling my blue overcoat off the edge of the door, I go to the kitchen and hang it on the back of a chair. Its arm falls across a thick red bible and my mobile telephones, primed for the explosions. The codes I scratched into the body of the phones are just visible. Over the years, I have collected three bibles from Christian evangelicals who have knocked on my door and who, upon learning that a Muslim had left his God, spent many hours trying to convert me to Christianity.

I have had Carol's stone with me all the time this last week, in my trouser pocket. Sometimes I take it out and toss it from one hand to the other, sometimes searching its jagged edges for answers to questions I can't articulate. I have thrown it away many times, only to pick up again.

I place it gently on the table next to my wooden flute and other things loaded with memories, which I will obliterate along with myself. The flute is warm and smooth. It seems to adjust itself to the palm of my hand, pushing itself upwards towards my lips, taking me back to that night before I came to England.

It was a moonless night in 1965, shortly after the end of the war with India. The village dogs, their eyes flashing in the dark, barked ceaselessly at me as I went past them to the crevice in the hills behind my house. Just when I had given up hope of seeing Yasmin, she stepped out of the darkness, through a throng of glow worms, holding a dark dupatta across her face with one hand. Drops of sweat slid down her forehead, down towards her unblinking eyes. She wore a brown shalvar kameez with faded flowers, stopped a short distance from me, breathless, and took her hand off her face. Her dupatta fell down across her breasts.

'It is not that cold. Why are you shivering?' I asked.

'That's the difference between men and women,' she replied.

I felt myself tensing and pulled her closer. She put her hands on my chest and pushed me away. Leaning against the side of a tree, she said, 'And how many times did I look at you in that special sort of way and you did not respond?'

'I was scared you would throw a brick in my face, like you did with Ramzan Jat,' I said, stepping towards her.

'Oh, that bastard—I should have killed him for what he tried to do to me,' Yasmin said, putting her hands on my chest again.

'And everyone else in the village warned me against you. They said, "Keep away from that Massalan. That low-caste has already knocked the teeth out of three men who tried it on with her."'

Yasmin laughed, 'Well, they should have known I loved only you.' She dropped her arms to her sides.

'I didn't know.'

'He didn't know,' Yasmin said, putting her arms around me. 'And that's what I loved.'

'What?' I asked, kissing her.

'Oh, it doesn't matter anymore.'

'Why doesn't it?' I kissed her again, pulling her down to the ground.

I untied her shalvar. She said, 'Promise you won't become like other village men who go to Valait, Britain.'

'I promise,' I said, entering her.

'They say village men can't resist white flesh,' she sighed.

'I am not like them. I am a . . .'

'A teacher from the High School for Boys,' Yasmin said.

'Yes, a teacher from the High School for Boys,' I replied.

'They say even the air of Valaiti, Britisher, gets you high, so high that you forget who you are . . .'

She stopped mid-sentence, pushed me off her, tied her

shalvar, kissed me on the cheek, wrapped her duppatta around her face and ran off into the shadows.

Mother had arranged and rearranged my clothes to ensure nothing was missing. The white shirt with its long collars and embroidered front hung from the back of a chair. A pre-knotted dark blue tie sat alone in the middle of the bed. My dark grey three-piece suit was laid out neatly on the bed next to the tie. A pair of new socks was placed over my shining black shoes.

In the morning, our house filled with people who had come to bid farewell. Dressed in my new western clothes, I felt like an imposter standing in front of everyone.

All the teachers from the High School for Boys stood behind the headmaster, a tall unsmiling man with fierce eyes. As I shook his hand, I promised to send him money so that he could buy himself a desk with a chair.

'And, of course, new reading glasses for you, Master Gulfam. What else for a teacher who was virtually blind but whose cane never missed a mischievous bottom?'

And I replied in a loud whisper, 'And, no, I won't forget you, Taraya. What other school would have a teacher like you, who never raised his voice and in whose company no child dared to misbehave?'

A man lifted my suitcase on his head and walked out of the house, behind my mother.

Holding a stainless-steel glass filled with milk in her shaking hand, mother bit her lip and let out a deep sigh. Her bloodshot eyes stared somewhere beyond me. Her trembling face had become wrinkled, her hair greyer.

I drank the milk, gave her the empty glass and lowered my head. She placed her hand on my chin, lifted my face and hugged me, crying.

'Who knows if I will ever see you again,' she said.

'I am not going away forever,' I said.

My taxi was parked in a field not far from our house. After the driver had placed my suitcase on the roof of his car, I tugged each rope to make sure it was securely tied and then turned to mother, who took my hand and said, 'Come, Saleem Khan, you are going to play your flute for your father.'

All I knew about my father was that I had his eyes and I was as tall him, but not as good looking. People said he had curly hair, unlike mine, and his nose was a lot thinner and, like me, he had a dimple when he smiled, and he was a brave man, as brave as they come they had told me. Mother often said he had been killed fighting in Japan. She did not know why he had fought in Japan, or where Japan was. But there was a letter from the army she had kept for decades. It was in English, and when I got older and read the letter, I discovered that he went missing in action in France and was presumed dead. I kept this from my mother, and let her think he had died fighting in Japan.

Mother had had the letter buried in our family graveyard. She had moulded the earth into the shape of a perfect grave with her own hands, and was waiting for the day when my father's body would finally be sent back home. The path to my father's grave went past the old Sikh houses and what remained of their temple.

Mother stopped outside the ruins of a house, stroked my shoulders and said, 'You were always here, playing with

14

Mangal Singh, just there, where that boy is aiming his catapult up into the peepal tree.'

The barefoot boy released his catapult and a pigeon darted
out of the branches. Mother swore at the boy, who bolted over
the rubble of a wall and disappeared behind it.

I saw my childhood friend's image flash in front of my eyes.
Mangal was sitting on the ground, his hair tied in a bun on
top of his head, wearing only a dirty white kurta, poking a
stick into a hole, oblivious to the swearing of his own mother.
I smiled at the memory of him standing up, with dirt marks
on his bum and bum marks on the ground.

I followed mother to the ruins of the temple. She let go of
my hand as we passed what remained of the gate. I stood
there and watched as she bent down and bowed reverently to
a grass mound just beyond the shade. She kissed the ground
and sat, eyes closed, speaking soft words in a language I did
not understand.

The grass in our ancestral graveyard had been cut down
and the blackening limestone of father's grave had been
cleaned. The taxi with my suitcase was parked on the road
just by the outer wall of the graveyard. After I had offered
my prayers to my father, mother said, 'Play a sammi on your
flute for him.'

I turned away from mother and played the tune. This was
the first time I cried for my father. She pressed on my shoulder. After a little while, she wiped my face with her dupatta,
pointed to my father's grave and said, 'If he has not come back
by the time I die, then this is where you must bury me, my
pardesi, son, my son who will leave for foreign lands.'

'I will come back soon. Soon, mother.'

Mother went silent. She looked away from me for a moment, turned towards me, adjusted her white dupatta across her head and said, 'It is my duty to find you a wife.' She smiled with her cracked lips and her eyes flashed mischievously.

I wanted to tell her I already knew who I wanted to marry, and had thought and meant to tell her once I got to England. I was toying with the idea of breaking the news to her right then, when she said in a heavy voice, 'You should not have taken Yasmin's bangle and sold it to buy your ticket. I saw her grandmother wearing it. No one in her caste has ever had gold before.'

I was filled with shame. How did she know? Yasmin wouldn't have told her or any of my friends. Snatching my eyes free from her, I caught a glimpse of a Rawalpindi-bound bus going past my taxi. Men sat on the roof of the bus and some clung precariously onto the steps that went up to the roof.

Ustad Gama, my driver, a tall dark man, leaned against his car, smoking a cigarette. Cousin Habib, still in his school uniform, was in the driver's seat, pretending to drive. Not far from my feet, a line of ants marched around a small stone. Pointing to the ground past mother's grave space, I said, 'And that is where I will build mine for . . .'

'Shush, now,' Mother interrupted. 'No mother can bear the pain of talking about the death of her child.' She kissed me on my forehead, wiped my face with her hand, and said, 'Come back to me in two years' time. I want to see you married before I die. May God protect you!'

Mother waved to Cousin Habib. He got out of the car, ran up to me, gave me a great big hug and went with mother back towards the village.

Overhead in a clear blue sky, an aeroplane left behind it a long white trail and, below it, I watched my mother walk back to the village, head bowed.

Ustad Gama unwrapped the brown tattered shawl he had around his shoulders and threw it on the back seat as he saw me coming out of the graveyard. He bent down and ritually touched the earth, then his forehead, and kissed the bonnet of the car before getting in. He ran his hand through his long freshly oiled black hair. His was the only car in the village.

I got into the car and looked back at the hill behind our graveyard getting smaller and smaller. Ustad Gama lit a cigarette and talked about the virtues of his car. The engine whined and backfired. 'Don't worry, Masterji,' he said, 'my car loves this hill.' Changing into second gear at the top of the hill, he said proudly, 'Now Masterji will see how my princess can dance.'

I did not answer, and looked away from him at a few villagers who were going into the jungle with their livestock.

'Masterji, when you come back, Ustad Gama will pick you up in a new car.'

I thought of mother. She must have reached home by now.

'And if you remember, Masterji, send me a radio.'

My house will be full of women, sitting close to mother, I thought, dozing off. Sometime later I woke. Ustad Gama was cursing someone in front of the car, 'I will shove a potato up her arse and yours if you don't get out of my way!'

We were in Rawalpindi, stuck behind a donkey cart, not far from the airport, close to the rotting corpse of a dog. A nervous vulture picked on its innards. The emaciated donkey had stopped moving and no matter how hard it was struck by its

17

owner, a bedraggled bony old man, it wouldn't move. The cart was loaded with sacks of potatoes. I was running out of time, so I got out of the car and helped the owner of the cart to pull it to the side so we could get past.

At the airport, I got my luggage onto a trolley and pushed my way towards the departure gate, passing women crying as their nervous men left them, through a throng of charm sellers and beggars, towards eager immigration officers who were opening everyone's luggage. Inside the departure lounge, things were calmer. I had all my documents in place and passed through immigration quickly.

There was only one aeroplane on the runway. It looked like a toy. In a dream-like trance, I walked down the stairs and onto a bus that took us to it. A heavily made-up air hostess smiled at me and pointed down the aisle, telling me my seat number.

As the aircraft got ready to take off, I was filled with fear. I had heard no one survived when aeroplanes fell from the sky. I had a window seat and looked out as the aeroplane roared and took off. I did not know Rawalpindi was so big, with so many roads. We cut through the clouds as my ears popped. I thought of myself sitting next to my mother in my village, looking up as aeroplanes sliced through the sky.

Nothing I had ever heard about England had prepared me for the shock of my arrival. I wanted to laugh when I saw all the white people at Heathrow airport. They weren't white but pink, and had such different coloured hair and eyes. As I came out of the arrivals lounge, I cringed when I saw a woman, with hair the colour of fire, letting a dog lick her face. I was staring at her when I was met by Ajmal Choudry, the agent who had sorted out my visa. He was a huge man, with a thick beard that came down from his bottom lip all the way to his bloated stomach. I got into the van with five other men, who I learnt later had been waiting at the airport since five in the morning for my flight to arrive.

In England, there was no sky, just dark clouds. The world was covered in a thick mist. It was raining, a cold sort of a rain that cut into my face. White people had red noses, ugly big noses.

'This motherfucker is Saleem Khan,' Ajmal Choudry said, getting into the driver's side as I pushed my suitcase on top of the others in the back of the van. 'And you lot can introduce yourselves.' As I was shaking hands with those in the van, Ajmal Choudry said, 'Hurry up and get inside, sisterfucker. I am not your servant and we have a long journey ahead.' As I shut the door, he asked, 'Where are my cigarettes?'

'In my bag, Ajmal Saab,' I replied.

'Why haven't you given them to me?'

'Here, sir,' I said, passing over a carton of cigarettes I had been told to buy on the aircraft.

'I heard you read and write,' Ajmal Choudry said.

'I am a teacher, Ajmal Saab, from the High School for Boys . . .'

'Remember this, motherfucker. Here you are nothing. *Nothing*. No Teacher Saab. No Khan Saab. Nothing. Just a Paki. A wog. OK? If they ask you to clean shit, you say, "Yes, please." You are here to work and pay me what you owe my brother before your mothers die or wives get pregnant courtesy of the barber, or your brothers. Here you will work in the mill, not in a field. You will work by the minute, not by the day. You will earn by the hour. You turn up on time. If you are late, you are fired, thrown out. If you pay me late, I will

19

throw you out and your family will learn that. Just as I can be generous, I can also be angry. So don't tell me this one has died or that one needs an operation until you have cleared your debts. You village donkeys; don't forget that you can't even pray before you pay. Is that understood?'

We all said 'yes' together, and I eventually fell asleep, drifting in and out of dreams, watching the green fields whizzing past, thinking about what would be happening in my village then.

The van slowed down and I woke up. Ajmal Choudry was mumbling, cursing the traffic. Not far from us, behind a fence, cows grazed below a sky with dark rolling clouds.

By the time we got to Bradford it was late, but still not dark. However, there were lights on everywhere: on the roads, in the houses, in the shops, everywhere. Ajmal Choudry pulled up outside a tall house on a long winding street with countless other houses that looked just like each other, all with drawn curtains. There was no one on the street. Two of us got out here. Ajmal Choudry opened the door to the house, saying to someone inside, 'More mothers' sons for you lot.'

I was shivering. The cold air burnt my nose and I could feel it digging into my chest. I dragged my suitcase up a few slippery steps and went inside, followed by the other man.

Inside, there were rows of shoes along one side of the wall of the hallway. In a room to our right, two men were sitting on sofa beds, warming their hands in front of a blazing gas fire. A white sheet hung over the window. The men turned around and smiled at us. One of them, a stocky man with a thick mat of curly hair, stood up and offered his hand, saying, 'Welcome to Valaiti, where the streets are paved with gold and footpaths with dog shit.' His hand was rough and hot.

20

Shaking my hand, he laughed, 'When I was born they called me Waheed Mubarak. There is nothing unique about me.' Pointing to his friend, a nervous little man, he said, 'And this motherfucker was once called Fakhar. He now calls himself Peter. If either of you are called Fakhar, then you'd better call yourself John.'

Peter shook our hands, smiling broadly, and said, 'In this country, you piss in the pot, in the water. It is not a fountain but a toilet. And you leave your shoes out there where everyone else does.'

As I bent down to take off my shoes, Waheed Mubarak asked me, 'With such soft hands you must be the teacher, Saleem Khan?' I nodded.

'I was at the High School for Boys . . .'

'And I am Salamat Ali Teka from Multan, sir. I am planning to leave here as soon as I can with England's wealth.' The young lad who had travelled from London with me placed a hand on his chest and laughed. He had already taken his shoes off and was holding them in his other hand. He had a low, booming voice. The quilt on one of the sofa beds moved and a man's head popped out. He had dark tired eyes. He rolled over the side and grabbed a packet of cigarettes.

Pointing his long finger at a stain running down his white trousers, Salamat Ali Teka said, 'The plane shook and everything went all over me.'

'Salamat Ali Teka from Multan. Turn right out of that door, go to the back of the house and there is our bathroom. Go wash your pants,' Peter said.

Whilst Salamat Ali Teka went to the bathroom, I learnt the rules of the house from Peter. There were four people in each room, each sharing a mattress with another worker who was on a different shift. I was sharing with Haji Khalaq, the oldest worker in the house. The clothes were taken to a laundry on Sundays, where they were washed and dried in machines. There was a rota for this and our names would be put on it. Tea was made in a big pot every other day. Every Sunday, chicken was cooked. During the week, everyone ate at one of the cafés and cleared their bills on pay day. There was a communal 'house fund' with a weekly 'committee' payment of twenty pence per member. Everyone in the house was also signed up to the death committee and should anyone die, the cost of taking their body plus one person home was paid for. Money was collected on each death. There were around three hundred members of this committee, and so far only one person had died this year.

Salamat Ali Teka came back into the room. He had changed into Pakistani clothes and was holding his washed trousers in his hands.

'This is not Pakistan, you son of a mother-in-law,' Peter hissed, pointing to a pool of water behind Salamat Ali Teka. 'You have to wring the clothes out. Go outside and hang them on the wire in the front.'

Salamat Ali Teka went out as Peter shouted after him, 'And when you come back in, you can clean up all the mess you've just made.'

My mattress was in a room in the attic, on the third floor of the house. The window was up in the ceiling of the room. Brown paper had been pinned across it. It was a cold room and I quickly got under a heavy quilt and went to sleep. The next morning, I woke up early from jet lag. The toilet was in the backyard. Footsteps in the frozen ground led to a half-open door. The ground crunched under my feet. Going back inside the house, I heard screaming.

'Look, they have died!' Salamat Ali Teka shouted, grabbing me by the hand and pulling me towards the front door.

'Keep your voice down, you son of a donkey,' someone shouted from one of the rooms upstairs.

Salamat Ali Teka pointed to his frozen trousers on the washing line, and said, 'The sister fuckers are dead!' The trousers were frozen solid.

The next day, Salamat Ali Teka and I were taken by Ajmal Choudry to a textile mill in Shipley. It was snowing heavily by the time we left the house. No sooner had the windscreen wipers cleaned one layer of little white dots when more fell, to loud curses by Ajmal Choudry. Children threw snowballs at each other.

Ajmal Choudry pulled up outside the offices of Shipley Mill and told us to wait in front of a door until called. He sat in the car smoking. We stood outside the door, shivering. We didn't have to wait long before a tall silver-haired white man came out of the snow and introduced himself as Mr Anderson. Salamat Ali Teka stepped behind me. I offered my hand to the white man, who ignored me, looked Salamat Ali Teka up and down, and said, 'You look fit enough for a demanding job. Are you Saleem Khan?'

'I am Saleem Khan, sir. His name is Salamat Ali Teka,' I said, offering my hand again.

'It's good you can speak English. We need more of your sort,' Mr Anderson said without taking his hands out of his pockets.

'Thank you very very much, sir. I am a teacher from the High School for Boys . . .'

'You both start next Monday night.'

When I got back to the house, Peter and Waheed Mubarak were waiting for me with some letters from Pakistan. I was the only one in the house who could read and write.

By the time my first week was over, I had read everyone's letters and written their replies for them. There was this house to build, that sister to marry, an operation had to be paid for, and there were those unending complaints: now that you have become a rich man, you no longer care for us in Pakistan. In the following weeks, I wrote to my friends at my former school and told them how wonderful England was: there was always electricity; there were no flies; there was heating in the houses; all the children in schools sat on chairs and had desks, and they got milk to drink and were given dinners; no one sat on top of buses or clung onto trains; all the houses were pukka and there was no mud anywhere; milk was delivered to the doorstep in bottles every morning; England was really, really green and there was so much grass; no one had the need to go into the jungle to find food for their animals or bring firewood back as there was gas to cook with and fridges to keep food in; the police didn't take bribes and were always friendly; and if you fell ill, you could go to see a doctor or to a hospital and it was all free, and people went for health checks which were also free.

Because I could read and I write, I was moved to a bedroom on the first floor and given the only bed in the house to sleep on. As the other fellow with whom I was to share the bed was away in Pakistan burying his mother, I had it all to myself.

~

On my first day at the mill, I was filled with fear by the noise of the spinning machines, row upon row of them as far as the eye could see. Men moved between them in a grainy cotton mist. It took me a week or so to get to grips with ensuring that the cotton continued to feed the spindles in unbroken lines. By then, I too could talk over the noise of the machines with ease.

One day, I was told to take the empty spindles to the store-room. The spindles were piled into a box that was fixed on to a long trolley. The back wheels of the trolley kept jamming and I had to push it backwards and forwards to free them.

Opening the tall sliding doors, I was surprised by how large the storeroom was. How silent, how calm and beautiful, even with so little light. The shadows in the room reminded me of the trees at the bottom of the hills of my village. Something flashed in the shadows. Tandana, I thought, thinking back to the glow-worms of my village. I imagined Yasmin walking out of the shadows. I took a deep breath, pretending to be inhaling the scent of the jasmine of her hair oil. No tandanas here, Saleem Khan, I thought, looking at the particles of dust floating in a beam of light falling down from a bulb dangling from the ceiling. In the particles, I thought I saw the shape of a peacock's feather, twisting and turning.

'How long has it been since I thought of you Yasmin?' I thought aloud. No, no, I have not forgotten you. It is just very hard to remember you in a place like this.

At the mill, I began to be called Masterji. During the breaks, I often read or wrote someone's letter for them. If anyone had a complaint about anything, they would let me know. Most of the time, we all moaned about white workers getting paid more for the day shift than we did for working nights.

The toilets we used were outside, by the side of an old shed. One of the cisterns was blocked and the flush in the others did not work. The outer door to the toilets was broken and was held to the frame by one hinge. Inside, the doors to the cubicles had disappeared long before I started working there. The urinals were stained and stank. They too were blocked. On pain of sacking, we were forbidden to urinate in the yard and this meant that our urinals were in a constant state of overflow. There were cleaner toilets inside, but these were only for use by the white workers and were locked at night.

One dinner break, as we sat around an overturned crate we used for a table, Salamat Ali Teka came and stood close to me and said, 'Masterji I am really desperate for a shit but the pot is nearly full and I can't do it in there.' He unbuttoned his trousers and ran out. I followed him. He looked around and then sat behind a car. When he had finished, he went into the toilets and came out a moment later shaking water off his hands.

When we got back, three other workers were sitting around our table.

'Masterji, you are the only one who can do this,' Salamat Ali Teka said. 'We have got to make an application for clean toilets.'

I ignored him and sat down. I was not keen to take this responsibility. Everyone looked at me with accusing eyes.

So I wrote an application to Mr Anderson and left it in his office before getting back to work. As he was usually on his rounds and rarely in his office, I did not have to talk to him. I got a message some time later to go to his office at 8.30 a.m. I was relieved by the fact that he had not summoned me during the night as he was in a much better mood in the morning, especially as he was about to go home.

His office was on a raised platform above the machines, past the works office, near the window where we collected our wages. The office staff were just getting to work, some with mugs of steaming tea in their hands. Our wages clerk smiled at me as I went past.

From his office, Mr Anderson could see everything on the shopfloor, but we could not see him. Salamat Ali Teka and a few of the other lads waited for me at the bottom of the stairs as I went up to see Mr Anderson, who was engrossed in paperwork. He threw a look at me and went back to his books. It was not an angry look, so I felt good at having done what I had. I knocked on the door. Mr Anderson looked up and beckoned me in.

'Did I ask you to knock on the door?' he said.

'No, sir.'

'Can't you see I am busy?'

'Yes, sir.'

'Fuck off and wait then!'

I wanted to knock on his door again and take back the application, but there was no way to do that now. Salamat Ali Teka came up and complained, 'Masterji, we are waiting.'

Mr Anderson came out and ordered, 'Follow me.' He was holding the piece of paper I had written the application on.

I stepped out of the way. As he went past, Salamat Ali Teka asked me, 'Masterji, does he mean me as well?'

'No. You should leave,' I said.

Salamat Ali Teka turned around, but Mr Anderson said, 'Both of you. And no Paki talk.'

We followed him, heads down. He stopped by the wages window and said, 'My tea, Carol.'

'Yes, Dad,' Carol said, handing him a steaming mug.

Mr Anderson took a sip from his mug and turned around. He was smiling. The blue of his eyes went cold.

'So, you have written this, have you?' Mr Anderson spoke loudly with a big grin on his face. It was obvious he was doing so for the benefit of the office staff.

'Yes, sir,' I said.

'Read it.'

He gave me the paper I had written on, and I read aloud, 'Dear Honourable Mr Anderson sir . . .'

Mr Anderson interrupted. He raised his thick eyebrows at the office staff and mocked, '*Dear Honourable Mr Anderson, sir.* It gets better. Continue reading.'

I read, 'I, your faithful servant, do humbly and sincerely beg you to consider the very small matter of our latrines. Dear respectable sir, I would be eternally grateful if you could please note that the latrines in which we do number one are very smelly and those where we do number two are not going down . . .'

'Stop. Stop. Stop.' Mr Anderson was laughing hysterically as were others in the office.

'Read that line again,' Mr Anderson asked, wiping his eyes.

I did and waited for him to tell me to continue before reading on. 'Also, sir, I please beg you to notice that we are Muslims and would very much like to have doors on the rooms for doing number twos . . .'

Mr Anderson stopped me again. Everyone was laughing. 'Tell me again who you are?' Mr Anderson asked.

'I am teacher from High School for Boys . . .'

'Well, teacher from High School for Boys,' Mr Anderson said, 'You've got a fucking nerve!'

I stared at him. I could not understand what it was that the white people found so funny.

'You're a cocky one, aren't you?' he asked, putting his cup down.

The laughter stopped. I tried to work out what he meant by *cocky*. Something to do with a cockerel, I thought.

'You shit in the fields where you come from, don't you?' Mr Anderson asked, his voice cold, his face red.

I did not answer.

'Do you think you're on holiday?' I did not answer.

'Who shat next to my car?' Mr Anderson shouted. Oh, God, I thought, it was *his* car.

'Was it you?' he asked, walking towards me.

I stepped back shaking my head.

'Who did it?' Mr Anderson prodded my chest with his finger. 'You know who, don't you?'

I bumped into Salamat Ali Teka. Mr Anderson slapped me hard across the face. And then he slapped me again.

'Dad, stop it!' Carol shouted.

Mr Anderson picked up a heavy cardboard pipe from a pile on the floor and hit me across the shoulders. I was determined not to cry. He hit me again and again until the pipe snapped.

Mr Anderson raised his hand to strike me and Salamat Ali Teka stepped forward and said, 'I shit, sir. I do it.'

'You filthy Paki bastards, always sticking together.' Mr Anderson picked up another pipe and hit Salamat Ali Teka across the face.

Mr Anderson raised his hand to strike Salamat Ali Teka again, but I grabbed his wrist and stopped him. He stumbled backwards.

'It was me, sir,' I said, helping Mr Anderson to steady himself. Carol came out, crying, 'Dad, you're a bastard!'

'You two are fired,' Mr Anderson hissed.

'You do that, Dad, and I'm going to the police and telling them what you did,' Carol said, 'and what you do at home!'

'Carol!' Mr Anderson said, breathing heavily.

'Tell 'em right now they're not fired, Dad.'

'You're humiliating me, Carol.'

Everyone else in the office pretended to be working.

Mr Anderson and his daughter locked eyes for a while and then he turned to me and said, 'I'll see you tonight.'

I turned around and followed Salamat Ali Teka out. Mr Anderson followed me. I could hear him breathing. As I was going down, Mr Anderson pushed me in the back saying, 'I'll always have my eye on . . .'

I slipped and stumbled down a few steps, landing on a metal block. A sharp pain ripped through my back and leg. For a moment I could not move. Mr Anderson stood at the top of the stairs looking down at me. Carol ran past him, swearing at her father, who protested, 'I never touched him.'

She helped me off the metal block, still cursing her father.

'I am fine, thank you. Please don't swear at your father,' I said.

'He shouldn't have done what he did to you.'

'It was my fault,' I said.

By the time I got home, the pain was so intense that I was taken to the hospital, where my hip was X-rayed. I had a hairline fracture, I was told, which would heal with time.

~

I took some painkillers and went to work the next night. I was sent to the storeroom, where piles of empty spindles needed to be thrown into a skip. I was bending down to pick up the first spindle when the tall wooden sliding doors behind me nosily opened and a man's voice called out, 'There are loads more of those in the back room near you as well, brother.'

It was a voice I had not heard before, but one that felt like a voice from my childhood. I stood up from behind the skip, tossed the spindle in my hand into the skip and saw a man pushing the door wider open.

'I said there are more in the back room, brother,' the man said, coming into the storeroom.

He stopped, adjusted a blue turban on his head, stroked his black beard and went silent, his unblinking eyes fixed on me.

'Mangal Singh, you here,' I said, holding my hand out for him to shake.

He took my hand in both of his rough hands, pressed it and said, 'And you here, my brother.'

We hugged and cried. I had not seen him since the day the Sikhs left my village.

Stepping away from me, Mangal Singh nodded to my hands and said, 'First time they have done real work, eh.'

I laughed.

In the short time he was with me, we talked excitedly. I told him about who had been born and who had died since he left the village. We agreed to meet after work.

As he was leaving, he asked, 'And who lives in my house now?'

'No one,' I said. 'It is still waiting for you.'

'You never could lie,' Mangal Singh said, leaving the storeroom, 'and I never did stop thinking about our pigeons.'

As I threw spindles into the skip, I thought back to before I was separated from Mangal Singh, and our first pair of pigeons. The birds were white. One of them had a black circle around its left eye. It was a restless bird that tried to escape even when there was no chance. We sat under the shade of our favourite banyan tree. Holding a bird each, we stood up and stepped out of the shade. Mangal Singh kissed his bird and tossed it up as high as he could, and I did the same. Our birds went up and opened their wings, flipped in midair, before swooping over the tree and turning towards the hills. They became tiny dots and then disappeared into the hills. It was the first time we had flown our own birds. Mangal Singh held a hand over his mouth as tears rolled down his cheeks.

We were scared lest the birds did not return to the khudla, the underground hole, their home in Mangal Singh's house. We ran to Mangal Singh's house as fast as our feet could carry us. When we got there, we hugged each other with joy; the pigeons were sitting close to the mouth of the khudla.

We had dug the khudla under the shade of a peepal tree. It was four and half feet deep and two feet wide. We had finished the job off by plastering the insides with gara. We did this with our bare hands. The mixture of buffalo dung, hay and mud had squelched between our fingers.

We were admiring our work when Mangal Singh's father, Chacha Hari Singh, came. The elders in our village called him Comrade Chacha Hari Singh. His sweat-drenched clothes were stuck to his small thin body. He was, as usual, carrying a cane basket on his head. It had rocks in it. Mangal Singh bent down to pour his father some water. I stepped forward to help Chacha Hari Singh lower the basket to the ground. Chacha Hari Singh smiled as I took some of the burden off his head. Even though he held most of the weight, I felt my legs buckling. Putting the basket on the ground, he sighed with relief, saying, 'Be careful not to scratch yourself. That crazy mother of yours will never let me rest.'

As Chacha Hari Singh sat down on a manji bed, Mangal Singh said, 'We have a pair now, Abbaji. We will not let any cat come near them. Our birds will lay eggs and soon we will have lots and lots of pigeons.'

'Our birds are going to be the best birds in the world,' I added.

'We will take our birds to the Khari mela next year and win the competition,' Mangal Singh said.

'You daft boys, have you not heard of Sheikh Chilli?' Chacha Hari Singh shook his head incredulously. 'He was taking eggs to sell at the market one day. On the way there, he sat down and started dreaming. He was going to sell the eggs and buy more chickens. Then he would have more eggs and more chickens and he would sell these and buy a goat. He would raise more goats and then buy a cow. He would raise cows and build himself a great big mansion. In the mansion, he would stretch his legs and live like a king. When he stretched his legs, he kicked the eggs and all of them broke.'

We had heard the story of Sheikh Chilli umpteen times.

'Well, Chacha, you are right. We don't want to be fools like Sheikh Chilli,' I said, 'we will first make sure we breed the pigeons.'

'God will protect our birds, Abbaji,' Mangal Singh said.

'Our birds will live and breed, uncle,' I insisted.

'We will go to the mela in two years' time, Abbaji,' Mangal Singh said.

'In three years' time, if we have to,' I added.

Chacha Hari Singh just sat there rubbing his heel on the ground. He pursed his lips and brushed the dust off his beard with his hands. After shaking the dust out of his turban, he wrapped it round his head and nodded to the space next to himself, saying sorrowfully, 'Come sit my sons, sit.'

We sat on either side of him on the manji.

'Sometimes, dreams of childhood remain just that, dreams . . .' Chacha Hari Singh said.

'Chachaji, we are only going to breed some pigeons,' I interrupted, worried lest it was one of his long talks which might end with 'No pigeons in my house'.

'It does not matter what we dream of in childhood,' Chacha Hari Singhsaid in his deep voice. It was as if the very hills around him were speaking through him. 'It is the right of childhood. There is no past or present without these. And without these, there is no future. I dream of protecting your dreams. But sometimes, childhood is stolen. And sometimes, even doves are slaughtered for the crime of singing.' Chacha Hari Singh took a deep breath and started singing verses from 'Saif-al-Maluk', his voice lifting into the wind.

Then he continued, 'The white man's rule is coming to an end, and like its beginning it will be drenched in blood. But this time much, much more blood will be spilt. It will be our blood.' Pointing to the hills behind his house, he said, 'My childhood dreams will be ripped out of my hills. I do not know if the birds of your dreams will ever fly over these, my son.'

'There you are, you little rascal,' my mother cried, stepping into the courtyard. She was accompanied by Mangal Singh's mother. 'And don't you know it is getting dark?'

Tears were running down Chacha Hari Singh's face.

'Ever since he heard the mention of Pakistan, sister,' Mangal Singh's mother said to mine, 'he has stopped putting new rocks on the wall. In all these years I have been married to him, he has raised the wall a little bit each day. But now he just brings rocks and piles them over there. And you know how much he hates the English . . . but sometimes, now, I think he wants them to stay.'

'You know, Kamli Kaur, that is not true! It must end. Those robbers must go back to wherever they came from, but what is it they are leaving behind? A land of broken men and stolen dreams, drenched in their own blood, wrapped in religious hatred.'

'Brother Hari Singh, thieves come and thieves go. We have had our backs broken by whatever our elders borrowed from Ram Kataria. And if God wills, let us get free from the never-ending burden of this debt,' Mother said, putting a hand on my head. 'Tell me, elder brother, when did our comrades start worrying about God and godly things?'

'Don't start him on this comrade thing, sister,' Auntie Kamli Kaur laughed as she poured some water into a bucket for Mangal Singh to wash with. 'He had left them, but you know he is now fully back with those comrades of his, and the last time they came here, they did not stop talking all night and I did not stop cooking for them. If he starts . . .'

'You were given the right name, Kamli,' Chacha Hari Singh said. 'I left because the Party wanted to get their Muslim comrades to work in the Muslim League for Pakistan. Maybe they were right, but in my heart of hearts I know that if God does exist, then He has made all our blood red. There is no space for green or saffron. I went back to them because they realised they had made a mistake. But for me—India, Pakistan—what does it matter? And does it matter if it is Bhagwan, Rab or Allah?'

'Elder brother, I don't understand all these big things, but all I have seen throughout my life is that even after all of us have spent night and day working, we have still had to borrow from the Katarias. Each morning I take my animals into the jungle, each night I bring them back. Will I not still be doing this after the English leave?'

'The animals of the poor care not for flags, sister,' Chacha Hari Singh said, 'but the books of the moneylenders are always written in sweat and closed in blood.'

'My brother Mohammed Ishaq did go to some big meeting where some trouser-wearing babu spoke about this Pakistan.' Mother tugged on my ear, forcing me to stand.

'Ishaq the hoodlum went to the meeting in Jhelum to listen to Jinnah, did he?' Chacha Hari Singh asked in amazement.

'Have some food with us before you go?' Kamli Kaur asked, lighting some firewood.

'You do not need to offer food to me, Kamli. By eating with us, you have come as low as us,' my mother said. 'Even your own family doesn't think you are proper Sikhs.'

'Well, they should not have married me off to a Comrade Singh then!' Kamli laughed, kneading the dough.

'May the Almighty bless you, Kamli.' Mother pushed me towards the door. She turned towards Chacha Hari Singh and said, 'Ishaq didn't understand a word. The babu spoke in English.'

'I think the Ishaqs of this world understand more than we think,' Chacha Hari Singh said softly, 'but remember, Kamli, I will let no one chase me out of my house and my village. Not Pakistan. Not India.'

'Brother Hari Singh!' Mother paused. 'Who is chasing you out of your village?'

Chacha Hari Singh did not reply. I waved to Mangal Singh who was standing close to the khudla. I knew he was imagining the baby pigeons cooing in there.

The big door to the storeroom screeched open behind me and took me out of my childhood. Mangal Singh stepped in and asked, coughing violently, 'And do you remember my pigeon, Saleem Khan?'

'No.' I wanted to go back into the waves of stubborn memories rising inside me.

Mangal Singh dumped a few spindles on top of a pile and left.

I had held Mangal Singh's beloved pigeon's lifeless body two years before his letter arrived in 1949. The letter had been brought to our village from India by a dark-skinned man with bloodshot eyes. He had come to our house and shouted my name. He was dressed in rags. I was sitting watching over Mangal Singh's bird. Its broken wing had still not healed properly. The bearer of Mangal Singh's letter said, in a Punjabi accent I had not heard before, 'I promised your friend's father that if I lived, I would deliver this letter.'

He turned around to leave as soon as he handed me the letter. I said, 'Uncleji, have some water.' He waved his hand in a gesture I did not understand and went away.

My name was written in great big letters. It was a thick envelope stuck down with flour paste. I carefully opened it. Mangal Singh's neat handwriting spoke to me in Pothowari:

Saleem Khan, my brother,

I hope this letter reaches you. I miss you very much. I think of my village and my house every day. I hope you and all your family are in good health. I have given this letter to Ghulam Mohammad. He is leaving for Pakistan with what is left of his family. We are living in their house. My father has promised to look after it for them until things get better and they can come back.

I have been writing this letter to you for a long time. Sometimes, I cry so much the paper gets wet.

My mother does not speak much nowadays. The last time I asked her to say something, she replied, 'Corpses do not need words.'

My Abbaji asks for you every day. He says give his Salaam to your mother.

Abbaji wants to know—what did his buffalo give birth to? Was it a Katta or a Katti? If it is female, you can keep it. If it is male, then give it to the butcher, Raju Jat.

I looked away from the letter, and remembered the last day in the life of Chacha Hari Singh's shining black buffalo. It was the summer of 1947.

Soldiers had surrounded our village. All the Sikhs were ordered to assemble in our school. No one was allowed to move. We were told that anyone else who came out of their houses would be shot on sight. We were kept like that for many hours and we saw the Sikhs being driven away in army trucks. Just after they left, many men turned up from God knows where. There was shooting around the Kataria house. It was the biggest house on the edge of our village. People were fighting to get into it. I ran to Mangal Singh's house. There was no one there. Smoke was coming out of the tandoor. I bent over it. Auntie Kamli had not managed to take the roti out. A bit of it was still stuck to the tandoor. Then lots of men, most of them strangers, burst into the house. They grabbed whatever they could. One man grabbed a sack of grain and ran out. It was spilling behind him. I ran and lifted the lid of the khudla and the birds flew out. Two men ran towards the buffalo. They pushed each other away from the creature. Then more men came, all of them claiming the buffalo. I begged them to leave it alone. I told them it was Chacha Hari Singh's. But they did not listen to me. The men started fighting with each other. One of them hit the other with a stick. Somebody among them spoke: 'We should all share it.' He took out a great big knife. The other men quickly brought the buffalo down and tied its legs.

I yelled, 'No it is pregnant. It is forbidden to halal a pregnant buffalo.'

The man with the knife said, 'Allah O Akbar,' and tried to slaughter the beast. It kicked and freed itself and stood up, its head dangling. It looked at me with big unblinking eyes as it fell to the ground. A fountain of blood spurted out of its neck. The men jumped out of the way as the buffalo turned this way and that before dying against the rocks piled close to the wall. The pigeons came and settled on the tree above. I tried to shoo them away, but they would not move. Someone hurled a stone and hit Mangal Singh's white pigeon. It fell to the ground. I ran forward and took hold of it in my hands while, behind me, the house burnt.

I turned back and read more of Mangal Singh's letter.

Abbaji wants to know if Master Tara collected the books from our house. And he wants you to look after his books and he says you can have the buffalo as long as you promise to read the books. And he wants you to go to Pir Jamali's shrine and tie a green ribbon on the tree, the Thursday after you receive this letter.

My Abbaji wants you to go to the house of Bava Boota and touch his feet and say, 'Hari Singh begs your forgiveness, Bavaji, for not wishing you farewell. But God willing, one day, I will come, Insha'Allah, I will, and sit by your feet myself.

And when you are leaving Bava Boota's house, when you are out of the reach of his walking stick, please tell him that it was you and I who stole his watermelons and not that squint-eyed Shamu Jat. And if he does not go mad, then tell him that they were the most beautiful watermelons in the whole world, and I would give my heart for just one more of them.

Yesterday Abbaji left this world, Saleem Khan. He is no more. Before he died, he cried like a baby. He wanted to die in his village, in his own house.

Today your Chacha Hari Singh was cremated in a stranger's field, in a strange land.

Your Chacha's last words were those from the 'Saif-al-Maluk':

Baghay andhr hik bulbal aalraan payee see banaani.
Ajay na charya thour Mohammad, Ur gaee ay kurlaani.

In the garden a nightingale was building its nest.
Before reaching her destination, she flew away screaming.

And did my pigeon flap its wings when you threw it up in the air, Saleem Khan?
And did you take it to the mela, and did the dhol play for us when you won . . . ?'

The flapping of a piece of cardboard covering a broken window brought me back from my childhood. I had put hardly anything into the skip and didn't know how much time had gone by. I began to hurriedly throw the spindles in.

There were hundreds of us on the night shift. Apart from the white overlookers, the rest were Asian. Had it not been for Mister Anderson's daughter, Carol, the union might have remained white. I was standing in a queue waiting for my wages one Thursday with Mangal Singh who, unusually reserved for a pay-day, said, 'Yaar, did my father not spend his life carrying rocks on his head and trying to better the life of all workers? And did he not teach us to question our conditions and existence?'

I was close to the counter, with only one person before me taking his wages from Carol. Carol smiled at me. I lowered my head but stole a quick look at her. Her face turned red. My body tingled.

Mangal Singh said, 'Why should white workers work on the day shift and get more than us working the nights? Even white women are paid better than us. We should all get the same pay, and those who work nights should get a night allowance, like they do in the factories in Birmingham. But there they are all in the union.' The only English word Mangal Singh used was 'union'.

Handing me my brown envelope, Carol said, 'See you next week, Saleem. And, yes, you should join the union. Anyone can.'

I looked up at her and grinned stupidly. Mangal Singh shoved me out of the way, 'Have some shame, Saleem Khan, looking like that at such a pretty woman.'

'But I have said nothing,' I protested.

After collecting his wages, he patted me on the shoulder and said, 'It is not what you said but what you desire, and the last person who desired her had his legs broken.' He coughed, and added, 'And he was a gora,' he laughed. 'And what do you think her father will do to you? He is the regional organiser of the National Front and if you saw the size of her brother, you would keep away from her—otherwise you will be going back in a box much quicker than you think.'

I kept quiet.

Walking out of the mill gate, Mangal Singh said, 'But, you know, Saleem Khan, if a man doesn't try, how does he know he will fail?'

'I'm not thinking about her.'

Carol drove past us in a blue Ford Cortina, smiled and raised her eyebrows at me, brushing her shoulder length curly brown hair away from her face, and waved at me.

'I know, my friend, I know,' Mangal Singh said. 'And she—'

'Leave it, Mangal Singh,' I said, quickly walking in front of him.

Slamming his heavy hand on my shoulder, he said, 'And did you see those glowing blue eyes . . .'

'She's a goree and that's that,' I said, moving my shoulder away from him.

'And that's that then?' Mangal Singh said, putting his arm around my shoulder.

'That's how it is,' I said.

Mangal Singh and I began to share a car to and from work with three other workers. Getting into the car, Mangal Singh said, 'Dyers and Bleachers belong to us. We should join the union. What do you say, boys? I have the forms right here. We get everyone to sign up at the same time.'

'Whatever you say, Sardarji,' the driver said. He was the youngest in the car.

The others nodded. I kept quiet.

'Carol wants you to join,' Mangal Singh teased.

The lads in the car hooted and shouted. I looked out of the window.

'I have already talked to all the lads on the night shift and everyone will join,' Mangal Singh said. 'And there are a few white lads who are with us as well. They want us to join.'

I kept quiet all the way back. As I was getting out of the car at my stop, Mangal Singh gibed, 'Just go down the Lane if it gets bad. It'll only cost a few bob and you'll feel better.'

I slammed the door in his face.

Ten of us turned up at the union offices and handed in our membership forms; everyone had signed up. When we finished work the next morning, a handful of white workers looked stiffly at us but the rest clapped their hands. Carol was there, twirling her finger through her hair, her head tilted, smiling at me. I looked away from her and left as quickly as I could.

We soon started earning the same as white workers. As I could write in English, I started contributing small pieces to the works' magazine.

The Asian workers were united on almost every issue at work. We got the canteen opened up for the night shift. Though our wages went up, we were still not paid any night shift allowance, but we were happy.

Mangal Singh and I were the only two Asians who regularly attended union meetings. I went along not so much out of any commitment but because I did not want to disappoint my friend and, besides, I enjoyed the post-meeting debates in the Mucky Duck, where I learnt about the world of socialism: where God only served to justify suffering and the priests served the bosses; where workers had nothing to lose but their chains.

It was in the Mucky Duck that I had my first taste of bitter, which Mangal Singh had proudly put in front of me, slapping the table with his hand as he had done this. He'd laughed when he noticed me staring at the brown liquid below the white froth which dribbled down the sides of the glass. I was trying to work out how to drink the stuff without it touching my moustache. Rolling his own between his thumb and forefinger, first in one direction across his lip and then the other, he picked up his own pint, downed it in a few gulps, burped and said, wiping away the froth, 'Just like this.'

It was also in this pub that I was picked up by my first white woman, a small round woman, who loved curry and for whom I was her first Pakistani.

When I first started work at the mill, I felt a sense of humiliation, which I hid even from myself: it felt demeaning, doing the dirty jobs like everyone else. After all, unlike the other illiterates, I was a teacher from the High School for Boys. I was special. I was me. I had become a Paki; even when sworn at, I lowered my head. I quickly learned from other workers that it was best when the over-lookers swore to just smile stupidly. I hid myself in my world of doing as much overtime as I could get and spending as little money as I could, and sending as much as I could to Pakistan.

Sometimes I would cry on my own, despising myself for what I had become. Surely this was not meant for someone educated like me. I was no longer shedding light into the eyes of the future, just making something that made no sense to me, to which my only connection was my wage.

But joining the union began to make me proud of being a worker, of being one of those who made things, especially during the discussions about what sort of world we could build: a just world, a world without war, where there was no hunger and people had what they needed and worked to their abilities, where colour was not an issue and everyone had rights. But we had to fight to get this world, I learnt. We had to snatch it from the rich. Before long, the day shift ceased to be all white, but the mill would close down one year and three months later.

The unity of the Asian workers at the mill came to an abrupt end in 1971 when the Pakistani Army tried to put down the rebellion in East Pakistan. Bengali workers from East Pakistan started collecting money to send to the Mukhti Bahini fighters demanding an independent Bangladesh, and the West Pakistanis condemned the Bengalis for being traitors. Many people from my village were in the army, including Cousin Habib who had been posted to Dacca in East Pakistan. Mangal Singh declared his support for Bangladesh, proclaiming that every nation had a right to self-determination.

I didn't notice the years passing until the end of the Bangladesh war in 1971, when my mother passed away. My housemate, Peter, came to the mill at around 4.30 in the morning with the news. He embraced me, and said, 'It is the will of Allah,' and gave me a piece of paper. It was a telegram from Pakistan. It said *Mother dead. Your permission for funeral.* From the office telephone, I made a call to Pakistan and sent a message that the funeral should go ahead and that

I would be on the next available flight, which was the following evening.

After making the call, I went back to work. The worker who had relieved me had not kept his eye on an oil leak and now there was a puddle on the ground. I was wiping it off the floor when Mangal Singh came and embraced me, crying like a child.

'I have told them so many times to get this fixed but no one does anything about it,' I said to Mangal Singh, pointing at the leak.

'Allah decides who lives and dies,' Mangal Singh said. 'I wish I could have said farewell to Auntiji.'

'Look at this floor, someone could slip and get killed,' I said.

'Yes. Yes. It must be fixed,' Mangal Singh replied.

When I got to my room later that morning, I counted the money I had hidden inside the mattress. I had more than enough to pay for everything. I warmed some water in a big pan, filled the bucket in the bathroom and had a wash. As I was getting dressed, Peter came into the room and gave me my air ticket, saying, 'Masterji, death committee buys your ticket.'

This was my first trip back to Pakistan and I made a list of all the people for whom I was to take presents. There were my friends from the High School for Boys and there was my Cousin Habib and Auntie, then there was Abbi, and there was Yasmin. Mother had always wanted a red Valaiti jumper and brown leather shoes. I went and bought these for her. I bought lots of socks from the market and some cloth as well, as someone or other was bound to be getting married. I bought a big torch for Mother, which was like a lantern but worked on batteries. I could see her cooking in its light.

After packing my suitcase, I rushed out to a shop and bought four cans of baked beans and shoved them into the suitcase as well. I was sure my old mates would love to have a taste of white man's food.

Mother had been buried where she had wanted, in the space reserved for my father. Standing in front of the fresh earth, I held my hands up in prayer and looked out at the long line of tali trees across the road that ran alongside the graveyard. Behind the talis, on a small hill, stood the ancient peepal, the oldest tree in the village, which some said had been there for over a thousand years. Behind the tree, above the hills awash with all shades of green, flew a flock of birds. They were high, higher than the dark mountains behind the hills, through which ran the dried river, past which were the snow-capped mountains of Afghanistan.

As the birds disappeared into the mountains, I thought back to the machines in the mill. They would be turning right now, the men shouting at each other over the noise of the machines, and Mr Anderson looking down at the shop floor from his office.

I don't know how long I stood with my hands held in prayer, but when I turned around many villagers were standing close by. I recognised the faces but could not put a name to any of them. Some of them were crying. They told me it was God's will. Whatever he wishes, they said. I walked up the hill, along the snaking path, past a dead cow, bloated and stinking in the heat, and went home.

The house was full of women, some wailing. Even those who mother hated and who hated her started crying when they saw me. I looked around the house. It was indeed now a pukka house, as she had told me in her letters, but much smaller, nothing like what I had imagined it would be. I shook a few hands and agreed that it was His will and, going over to the outer wall where food for the mourners was being prepared, stood on some logs and looked over the wall. The dirty gutter was still there, in the middle of the small gali that led to the road. I had sent Mother money for this to be covered. The money had been spent, but the gutter had not been touched.

After changing out of my English clothes, I sat down with the men, nodding an acknowledgement whenever some-one offered condolences. Abbi the carpenter walked into the room. He was drenched in sweat. His brown kurta was stained with dirt and ripped at the shoulder. He was a tall man with sharp lively eyes and a mischievous smile. I stood up and embraced him. I had not smelt this sweat mixed with earth since I left for England.

I remembered it was my turn to deposit the money for the gas bill in Bradford. They had sent a second reminder.

'God's will, Saleem yaar,' Abbi said, 'that's if you still believe in God.'

'Why do you ask this, today of all times?' I shook his hand.

'Let's pray for Auntiji.'

After he finished praying, I asked, 'How is your mother?'

He laughed. 'She's dead.'

'I am sorry. I didn't know.'

He smiled back at me and said, 'Valaitis forget themselves, how can they remember the dead?'

Abbi stayed with me until the other men had gone and then we walked out towards the hills at the back of our house. It was a cool evening with a pleasant wind. A line of soldiers was marching away towards the Grand Trunk—GT—road. Abbi pointed to them and said, 'Motherfuckers, wrecking our fields and pulling their pants down in front of the Indians in Dacca, ninety thousand of them. And it's not just your cousin who is an Indian prisoner. Every other house is in mourning. No one knows who is dead or alive, or who got injured.' Abbi was squatting on the edge of a newly sprouting maize field. I tried to do the same but could not get comfortable. He looked at me and said, 'Six years and your arse has forgotten this earth.'

It was only when I spoke to Yasmin that I remembered I had forgotten when I had last thought about her. I didn't notice her at first among the women cooking for the endless numbers of people coming to pay their respects to Mother. Putting a tray of food in front of me, she looked at me with trembling eyes and said, 'Has your blood turned so white you have no feelings for me?'

'I am here, am I not?' I said, pulling the table closer to me. I thought about the trams in Bradford, running down towards the city centre with sparks falling on top of them from the overhanging wires.

'This is for your obligation,' Yasmin said, pouring water into a glass.

I remembered I had forgotten to tell Peter where the bus pass was.

'Do white men not cry at the passing of their mother?' Yasmin asked.

Her dupatta had slid off her breasts. How much larger her nipples are, I thought. Her moist lips looked as though she was wearing lipstick.

Yasmin leaned back against the door, covering me with her shadow. 'You did forget all that you said you would remember.'

For a moment she stood where she was, and became a memory at the end of the shadow, a cold wall between us, going all the way back to England. I wanted her to leave and take her shadow with her. Has my blood really turned white, I thought? Have I really forgotten who I am? Who she is? How I used to long to hear her voice, to hear her laugh, her whispers and her curses.

'I never forgot our crevice,' I said.

'It is still there,' Yasmin said.

That night, when the village was asleep and the stray dogs were barking at the creeping shadows, Yasmin came to see me in the crevice in the hills. We made love.

Lying with her head on my chest, Yasmin said, 'Your heart doesn't beat like it used to.'

A bird fluttered in a bush somewhere. Crickets sang around us and glow-worms flashed and Jackals howled in the hills. We listened to the music of the night for a while and Yasmin said, 'Have you forgotten anything?'

'How could I do that?' I said, putting an envelope in her hand.

'What is this?' she asked, sitting up abruptly.

'Enough money for you to buy six gold bangles.'

Yasmin opened the envelope and looked inside. She stood up and tied her hair back. She smiled and took the money out of the envelope. Throwing it at me, she said, 'I am not a whore!'

In the morning an old woman came into the house. She was barefoot and walked slowly, placing her walking stick firmly in the ground in front of her. Her dark face was zigzagged with wrinkles. A pair of silver earrings flashed in the sunlight. Holding on to the walking stick with both her hands, she squatted close to the gate and stared at me silently.

'You are my mother's friend,' I said, emptying my cup on the ground, 'and you are going to tell me how good a person she was.'

The old woman brushed a fly from her face and stared at me. The fly buzzed around her head and came back again. She brushed it off again and said, 'You were born in my hands. You cried then,' she said, 'just like now.'

'I am not crying,' I laughed.

She took her walking stick and stood up to leave.

'Mother, wait,' I said.

The old woman turned around and walked towards the gate.

I went into the house and opened my suitcase. In it there were still the presents I had bought for Mother. Apart from my things, I shoved everything else into a cloth bag and went back outside. The old woman was leaving. I called out to her to wait. She was stepping over a small open gutter that ran along the back of the house. She did not stop.

'Here, Mother, take this,' I said, running up to her and offering her the cloth bag.

She smiled and shook her head.

I opened the bag, held up the torch and showed her a small bundle of white socks, a pair of brown shoes, a piece of light green cloth with large roses for a kameez and a dark green piece for a shalvar and some dupattas.

She started singing in a language I didn't understand. She walked on, still singing.

She took something of me with her when she left, or left me with something I had lost. I felt so utterly alone, living in the midst of where I had been born, where I knew the names of every plant and every tree, and every hill and the bends of the streams that snaked through the hills in whose cusp my village sat. I waited for her voice to fade, went back inside, threw the bag into a corner and decided I was not going to stay in Pakistan for forty days as expected of me.

The next day I went to Rawalpindi. I booked myself on the next available flight, which was in three days' time. Here I bought the returnee presents: Pakistani cigarettes, a lota, a water container, for the bathroom, a hooka, a shalvar, kurtas for Mangal Singh and Peter, and an assortment of sweetmeats.

Later that day, as I was packing my suitcase, the old woman turned up. She squatted by the door as she had done the previous time. She was holding something wrapped in a cloth.

'Come inside, into the shade, mother,' I said.

With moist faded unblinking eyes fixed on me, she shook her head and adjusted a white duppata with purple circles over her hennaed hair.

She shook her head, held out a little bundle and asked, 'Will you take this to England?'

With all the presents people from my village were sending to England for their relatives, my luggage was overweight.

'I can only take things for Bradford.' I didn't want to disappoint her. 'They will have to collect from there.'

'I thought you were going to England,' she said.

'Bradford is a town in England, mother,' I said. 'That's where I live. They will have to come and collect your stuff from Bradford.'

'Who will?' she asked.

'Whoever you are sending this to,' I said, pointing to her bundle.

'It's panjiri, a sweetmeat,' she said. 'It is for you. Your mother would have made it for you.'

'I will take it on one condition,' I said, picking up the things I had shown her earlier, 'if you take these.'

She started humming.

Letting out a laboured breath, she stood up and hung the bundle she was carrying on the branch of a tree nearby.

'I am just a poor woman. I have no need of Valaiti things,' she said, 'but you must stop crying.'

'I am not crying!'

'You can't stop crying until real tears fall,' she said, walking out of my house.

On my way to the airport, I went and prayed at Mother's grave and left the bundle with presents for her by its side.

Ustad Gama, who was taking me to the airport, came into the graveyard and raised his hands and prayed with me.

After I had finished praying, I nodded to the bundle next to mother's grave and said, 'Take this bundle, Ustad Gama.'

Placing his right hand on his chest, Ustad Gama bowed. He bent down, kissed Mother's grave, picked up the bundle, placed it on top of her grave and walked out of the graveyard.

He still had the same car, but now it had no rust and a new engine. There were two side mirrors on either end of the bonnet of the car and one on either side of the front doors. He had tied black ribbons on the front mirrors. I caught a glimpse of myself in the inside mirror. My hair was going grey. My face was hard. I had aged more than my years.

Ustad Gama put his foot down on the accelerator and said, nodding to the hill in front of us, 'This time, Masterji, I will go up in top gear.' When we were halfway up, he changed down to second gear, saying, 'If they fixed this road, I would show you what my princess can really do'.

I leaned against the window and thought of England. Peter would come to collect me from Heathrow. We now had a hooka, and a lota, a water container, for the bathroom, and panjiri, sweetmeats, and baryaan, cooked dried lentils, and could enjoy the taste of home in Bradford.

The Peter that came to collect me from Heathrow airport was not the same man I had left. His shining brown skin looked dark, darker under his sullen eyes. It looked like he hadn't shaved since I left.

'We're on three-day weeks now, brother,' he said as he greeted me.

'Allah Malik, everything is his, he will look after us,' I said. 'I had heard rumours before I went, but didn't think it was going to be so soon.'

'Yaar, I know you don't believe in God.' He smiled falsely.

'Yaar, you know,' I tutted.

'Two years at the most,' they said, 'it's going to close down. They are all closing down, all over, and I have so much debt to pay back.'

'Don't worry. You'll be OK, my friend.'

Taking my trolley from me, he said, 'And did you get a chance to say farewell to Auntiji?' Before I could reply, he said, 'And was the first roti okay; and how many people came to the funeral?'

'Everything went well, Peter, really well.'

~

The mill closed down after my return from Pakistan. For a short while, I found a job in a small aluminium foundry in Bradford and Mangal Singh went to London, where he worked in a bakery. After a while, we lost contact with each other.

Pakistan began to become a fading memory; but one in which I still lived, to where I wanted to go, in which I was Saleem Khan and not just a Paki. I signed on the dole and did odd jobs here and there on top. I drank when I had money, and when I was short I borrowed till the next dole day. I don't know how he found out that I was unemployed and signing on, but one day Mangal Singh called me and asked me to come to London to look for work.

We met in a bar. His beard was much blacker then when I had last seen him and he had lost a lot of weight. His beard was cropped, clearly showing his square dented chin. He wore a starched black turban. As soon as I walked in, he winked at me with his mischievous eyes. He was sitting next to a small plump blond woman. I recognised her from the mill, and Carol was there as well. She looked at me with her deep blue eyes. On one side her hair was tucked behind her ear and on the other it flowed down to her shoulder. Her diamond shaped silver earring glittered.

'I thought you would never make it,' Mangal Singh said in English, putting a round of drinks down in front of us. 'And you must remember Donna from the office?' he said. 'No, you only had eyes for Carol.'

Donna laughed loudly. Carol's round freckly face turned red. She turned away from me and whispered into her friend's ear. I kept quiet. The women got up and went to the toilets.

When they were out of earshot, Mangal Singh said, 'Gal kar, talk to her, you daft git.'

'Who?' I asked, downing a pint.

'Mother Teresa!' Mangal Singh laughed.

Ignoring Mangal Singh, I rolled a cigarette. He snatched it from me, lit it, took a big puff and said in between coughing, 'You've spent years dreaming about her and look at you now, like butter.'

'Do you want me to get a round in?' I asked. 'I've got enough.'

'Are you a man or a mouse?'

I looked away towards the toilets and smoked.

'What is it?' Mangal Singh asked.

'I don't fancy her, you know.'

Mangal Singh put his face close to me, looked me straight in the eyes and said, 'You've never done it, have you?'

'If you don't shut your trap, I am leaving right now.'

'You should have asked her out for a drink all those years ago.' Mangal Singh curled the tips of his moustache.

Carol and Donna were back. Donna quickly turned around and went back to the ladies. Carol looked nervously around and whispered loudly at Donna, 'You cow.'

Mangal Singh got up, put his arm around Carol and said, 'I'll buy you another drink, Carol.'

'I haven't finished the last one,' Carol replied.

Carol put her bag next to me, straightened her brown skirt and sat down. She tapped on the table with the fingers of her left hand, let out a loud breath and, crossing her legs, turned towards me. She had a little mole on the right-hand side of her small nose and piercing eyes. I looked into the froth at the bottom of my pint and watched the bubbles popping.

'I don't want to sit here anymore, Donna,' Carol said, as Donna came back.

'Why don't you two go for a walk? We have a few things to sort out,' Donna said. Carol picked up her bag, put her coat on and waited for me.

'Go, you sister-fucker,' Mangal Singh swore in Pothowari. 'Go!'

It was cold outside. London's traffic hissed slowly by. I put my hands in my trouser pockets and walked silently with Carol.

'You stupid git,' Carol said. 'Give me your hand.'

I felt the warmth of her hand before it touched mine.

'I'm sorry, Carol,' I said, as she put her fingers through mine.

'What for?' Carol asked.

'Just sorry, you know. Just sorry!'

'Why didn't you ask me for a drink all those years ago?'

'I didn't drink.'

'He didn't drink, he says.' Carol kissed me on the back of my hand. 'Why didn't you just ask me out?'

'Out to where?' my voice cracked.

'Out to where, he says! Every time I saw you, I smiled. And I just blushed, you know.' Carol said. 'Couldn't you see?'

'But you smiled at everyone.'

'But not like I smiled at you.' Carol squeezed my hand.

I laughed. 'I didn't want my legs broken.'

'That bloody Donna. She spread all sorts of rubbish around. And that Jack Filkins, he was after anything in a skirt. He got what he deserved, the bastard.'

The road ahead of us wound away to the right, past rows of red-brick apartment blocks spread out on our left.

'Where are we going?' I asked, crossing the road after Carol.

'Oh, just there and back to see how far it is,' Carol replied. Stepping onto the pavement, she said, 'Can't you put your arm around me?'

'In public!' I was horrified.

'In public, he says!' Nodding to a couple on the other side of the road, who were walking arm in arm, she asked, 'Who cares if *they* do?'

'I've never done it in public,' I said.

Carol teased, 'Never done it in public, he says.'

I saw Carol every day for the next week. I was floating in a dream, dreaming of being with her when she was away. We walked up and down Oxford Street and laughed at all the things we could not buy. We went into museums and cinemas and one day, when we were walking past Camden Market, she suddenly stopped speaking, placed a hand on my face and kissed me on the lips, whispering, 'And how long do I have to wait to be kissed?'

It was a quick kiss. I started crying.

'I'm so sorry,' Carol said, pulling away from me. 'I didn't mean to make you cry.'

I couldn't stop my tears.

'You've got a girlfriend and you're feeling guilty, aren't you?' Carol asked.

'No.'

'No, you haven't got a girlfriend, or, no, you're not feeling guilty?'

'I haven't got a girlfriend.'

'You've got a wife in Pakistan?'

'No,' I said, wiping my face.

'Then what the hell is your problem?'

'I don't know.' I said. 'What are *you* crying for?'

'I must be happy.'

For a while, I shared Mangal Singh's room in East London and saw Carol, who lived in a bedsit in Stoke Newington. The bedsit was made out of a huge room, with polished floorboards and a very large three-windowed alcove. There was a dark oak folding dining table, with three chairs, near the central window. Both of the other alcoves extended out onto the windows of the floor below. One had been partitioned into a bathroom and the other into a kitchen.

I am not sure when it happened, but we started living together in her bedsit.

I never knew I could miss someone who was still in my arms and how empty I would feel when she wasn't close to me, how just the sight of her with her chin resting on the back of her hand, with her hair flowing over one side of her face and the other tucked behind her ear, would remain ingrained in front of my eyes, sometimes even when she was asleep next to me.

I got a job as a driver for a small bakery and Carol worked in a supermarket. I left for work at 5 a.m., Monday to Saturday, and Carol worked shifts. I would work as much overtime as I could get, as I needed to ensure that I had enough money to pay the contractors who were building my house in the village and for the other responsibilities to my family over there, some of whom I helped to find work in England. Sometimes, especially if I got overtime and Carol was on her late shifts, we would hardly see each other awake.

When I came home one Saturday night after a long day at work, Carol was sitting, where she often was, on her favourite high-backed settee, her head on her shoulder, a book in her lap, but she was still awake and reading a novel. She threw a cold look at me and continued reading.

'Love you, too,' I said, walking into the kitchen with two bags of fresh vegetables. I came back out, took off my brown duffel coat, hung it by its hood on a coat rack near the front door and asked Carol, 'Want a beer, love?'

'No.'

I got two cans from the fridge and went into the living room. I smiled as I remembered it was that time of month.

As I entered the living room, Carol crossed her legs and continued reading. We had a pair of red, two-seater, high-backed settees facing each other, with a long oak coffee table in between the settees on a rectangular rug with blue, green and white interlinking square shapes. As I walked around it towards Carol, stepping slowly on the polished wooden floorboards, she lifted her feet and placed her legs on the settee.

Saleem Khan, I thought, better sit on the other sofa and wait for the book to come flying at you for not turning the kitchen light off, or maybe doing something as outrageous as not drawing the curtains in the morning, leaving it for her to do all the time.

I opened a can and placed it next to a plate with a half-eaten cheese sandwich and pushed the can towards Carol.

'I said "no", didn't I?'

Leaning back into the settee I waited, ready to duck, but she carried on reading. It was clear the book was staying where it was, as was I.

This is not like the normal monthly moods, mate, I thought, you are in real trouble today. You need to do some TLC, Saleem Khan.

Turning on the best charm I could muster, I said, 'Bad time of month is it love?' Even as the words were coming out of my mouth, I knew I should just have kept quiet.

Carol slammed the book shut and flung it at me, swearing, 'How dare you?'

Placing my beer can on the table, I quickly moved out of the way of the incoming book, but it came with such force that it clipped the side of my face before landing behind the settee.

Carol got up quickly, picked up the book, came back to the settee and held it up for me to see. The cover was ripped.

'Look at what you made me do,' she said, her flushed red face almost hidden behind her hair.

'Sorry.'

Placing the book gently next to her, she pushed her hair behind her ears, patted the book and sighed, 'You could think a bit before you open that trap of yours, you know.'

'I know, sorry.'

'And no, it's not what you think,' Carol said.

I took a swig of beer and said, 'Well, Carol, I need a real job. I am so tired of working at Paradise Foods. I can't do this for the rest of my life. I don't get a chance to read a book, I am always so tired.'

Carol frowned and then she picked up the book and started reading again.

'It must be a really exciting novel, that one,' I said.

Carol's bottom lip quivered as she looked at me with trembling eyelids and a distant but questioning look. 'It's not the book, is it? But you never really see what it is you should see. You're in your own world!'

I tried to work out what it was I had done.

'I know what you're thinking, and it isn't about what you've done. You left your world, but I know you can't really. It can't leave you, I know. But we have our world now.'

'I love you and you know that.'

'You know what this is about. Why don't you be man enough to face it?'

I freed my eyes from her, looked down and said, 'I'm not ready for kids.'

'With your white whore,' Carol smiled, her face a ghostly white, 'your goree, eh? Well let me tell you. It isn't always about what *you* want. No. It's not always. We can't get what we want. We get what we get.' She stared at me with an intense bitter gaze. 'I got the results today.'

She put her hand into the back of the settee and pulled out a packet of cigarettes and a lighter. She lit one and inhaled deeply.

'We need to talk about this more.'

'There is nothing more to talk about.'

'Carol, please . . .'

'There is no danger to the baby,' she said, rubbing her hand across her stomach. Slapping her stomach with the palm of her hand, she added, 'And you really care for my baby, eh?'

'Maybe I have just done everything wrong.' I stood up to hug her. 'But I love you.'

As I bent down towards her, she pushed her long finger into my chest and laughed falsely, saying, 'Liar, liar, your pants are on fire.'

I stepped back and Carol said, letting smoke out of her nostrils, 'Your pants are on fire.'

She shoved her cigarette into my beer can, lit another one and said, 'This goree is not pregnant, you do not have to worry.'

I didn't know what to say to her and sat down.

'She can never be pregnant. Never! She's barren, completely barren.'

We sat in silence for a while, Carol chewing her teeth and digging her fingers into a hole in the upholstery of her settee. Me, vainly trying to avoid questions. How come I had laughed off her suggestions about having children by saying we would never be able to agree on a name? How come I didn't know she was having these tests? Where did I go when I came home?

Without taking her eyes off the hole she was making she said, pulling some yellow stuffing out, 'I should never have let you buy this settee, it was not worth it. And I hated it from the moment it came here.'

'I thought you liked it.'

'It always had this hole in it,' she said, making it bigger, 'but you never did notice it, did you?'

'How did you find out?'

'How did *I* find out, he says,' she said, leaning back into the settee. She untied her hair and shook her head. 'It was obvious. It was worn out, probably picked up from a skip. You only needed to see.'

'Please answer me, Carol.'

It suddenly struck me that she had not worn the short-sleeved purple blouse since she had left Bradford, nor the brown silky skirt or the square silver ear-studs that her mother had given her, which Carol hated.

She adjusted the folds of her skirt and wiped invisible dirt off it with her small hands, her silver nail varnish shining under the ceiling light.

'We can get another settee, there's money in the bank and you can choose any colour you want and I won't say anything,' I said, trying to catch hold of her eyes, which moved away from me as soon as we made contact.

Carol threw a searching look around the room and said, 'You never can see, can you?'

I looked around. It was much cleaner than usual. There were fewer books on the bookshelf. She can snap and go off on tangents, like she was another person, but today was different. How different I was about to find out.

'Stop looking for answers in things,' Carol said in a voice filled with pain.

You're blind Saleem Khan, I thought, as I realised what was happening. All the books were mine. All of Carol's photographs were gone.

I went into the bedroom. Three suitcases were packed and stacked on top of each other, along with a pile of boxes. When I came back into the living room Carol was talking to someone on the telephone. Putting the receiver down she said, 'Our Jack'll be here tonight to pick me up.'

I hugged her. She kept her arms dangling down her sides.

'We can work this out,' I said.

'Work what out?'

'This. You leaving.'

'Me leaving isn't the issue, it's us. We're not working. We're just not working, are we? I don't want to be your white bit on the side.'

'What have I done for you to say this?'

'Why is it always to do with what *you've* done?' she whispered, putting her arms around my neck.

I pulled away and looked into her shining moist eyes. I tried to work out what she meant. It didn't make sense.

'Not really good enough for your lot, am I?' she said, walking towards the sideboard next to the bookshelf. 'You never could manage, could you?'

I don't know how to tell you, Carol, I thought, as she opened and shut one drawer after another. She turned around, folded her arms across her front and waited for me to answer, tapping her right foot on the naked floorboard. Her face suddenly flashed red, her eyes burning.

'So you think I wouldn't understand, eh? So you think your white bit doesn't understand you lot only do girlfriends, eh? Just fuck us and marry your village virgins. Isn't that it?'

We'd often joked and laughed about how I was always nervous if I thought anyone from my family might see Carol and me together, but I hadn't realised until today that Carol wasn't laughing.

'I've got a few old uncles and aunts here, that's all,' I said.

'And one is called Abdul Karim and he comes from Pindi, and there is an aunt of yours from God knows what you call the place . . .'

'Khevara.'

'Yeh, Kewara, that fucking place . . .'

I laughed at Carol's mispronunciation. She stopped mid-sentence, took a deep breath and said quickly, 'I have a barren relationship with you. I know you will leave me for a village girl, especially now. You always wanted children and now what good am I? Not that I was any road. In your heart of hearts, you know you're just passing your time with me. That's why you've never taken me to meet your relatives or anyone from your village.'

'Don't leave. We can work this out.'

'How?'

'Tell me when I can meet your family?' I said.

Carol burst out laughing, 'They're a bunch of racists.'

She stepped forward, grabbed my hand, pulled me towards her and kissed me, as she went down towards the floor. She unzipped me and then said, 'Put "Tubular Bells" on.'

'What, now?' I panted.

'Now!'

'Put it on, or else.'

I rushed to the record player and put it on. When I turned around, Carol was naked to her waist. As I bent down to kiss her, the music cried off the walls of the living room.

Getting dressed, she looked at her wristwatch and said, 'Jack'll be here soon.'

'And what we just did?' I was shocked.

'It doesn't change anything,' she said coldly. 'As I'm taking my things, you can stay. But I don't want a scene between you and my brother, so leave now.' She waited for a moment and then cried, 'Please leave, for me, just leave.'

I didn't move. I didn't know how to. I was in complete denial. Deep down, I told myself this was just one of those moments, be calm, it will be OK, but the mention of Jack shut this door.

'And I know he's full of shit, my brother, but he's got a decent heart, he has.' She paused and added, wiping her eyes with the back of her hand, 'Sometimes you need to look to your own.'

I wanted to cry but could find no tears and remained silent.

'Before you tell me he's just a racist pig, I know that. But he's my only brother and I still love him,' Carol said. And then she went silent. A deep, deep silence.

I walked slowly out of the room and put my overcoat on, all the time hoping Carol would call me back. But she just stood where she was, silent.

As I was walking out of the door, she shouted, 'Make sure you have your keys.'

I slammed the door behind me without answering. The keys were in my hand.

I headed towards my local on the high street, trying to work out why Carol was leaving. She was right, I didn't know how to introduce her to my relatives; how could I take a girlfriend home? Was this really the problem, or was it because I was working all hours? But she knew my responsibilities in Pakistan, and I always gave her everything else apart from what I sent back home and could not remember her once complaining about money. She wanted to marry me, but from the day I arrived here my heart was set on earning as much money as I could and going back to Pakistan, back to my village. How would she fit into that life? She just couldn't. And why the hell did I care what *they* thought? And I didn't know she was being tested to see if she could have children.

'Why didn't you tell me, Carol?' I said aloud. 'Why?'

An old woman in a long black coat, pulling a shopping bag, threw a worried look and stepped into the road. A white van screeched to a halt, narrowly missing her. It took a few moments for me to recognise that it was Carol's brother, Jack. He showed her a piece of paper and she pointed towards our road, walked in front of the van and crossed to the other side, unconcerned by the honking of a bus coming from the opposite direction.

Jack would have to drive round a one-way system in order to get to our road. I took a short cut through an alley, rushed back and hid behind an old Ford with flat tyres. Carol was looking out of our bedroom window which overlooked the road and turned around when she saw Jack's van. I didn't want Carol to see me spying like this and went to the local and drank till closing time.

When I got home, I looked up at the bedroom window. The lights were off, curtains drawn. As I opened the door, I almost called out to Carol, before remembering that she had gone.

The usually overflowing coat rack to the left of the front door had only two of my raincoats on it. I could smell Carol in the thick silent air.

I walked around the room searching for something; I didn't know what. I went to the bedroom, the floorboards creaking nosily, competing with my pounding heart. Carol had made the bed and left a glass of water covered by a saucer on a small table.

Sitting down on the bed, I cried in Pothowari, 'You didn't have to take the plants, not my plants, why my plants? Why the Yucca we bought together, it was ours, not yours.'

I fell asleep fully dressed and woke up sometime in the early hours, filled with dread at something wrong I had done, and then a moment later I realised that Carol had left me.

Carol had left the Yucca in the kitchen, next to the sink.

I tried to call her in Bradford but I never got past her mother.

It took me nearly three weeks to realise that Carol was really not coming back. I was drinking so much at night that I found it difficult to get up the next morning, but somehow I managed to get to work and get through the day, all the while thinking and hoping that maybe Carol would just turn up and everything would be back to normal. But she didn't.

After Carol left, I lost my job as a driver but found one at a fruit and veg shop. One day when I turned up for work, my boss, a fat-bellied man with a hennaed beard and thick-lensed spectacles called Mohammad Farooq, was there before me.

Placing an envelope in my hand, he said, 'My nephew has come from Pakistan and . . .'

'God bless you, Farooq Saab,' I said, taking the envelope.

I turned to leave and Mohammad Farooq said, 'Saleem saab, you misunderstand me.'

I thought I understood pretty well and turned around and was about to swear at him when he said, 'My nephew is open-ing a Taxi Base in Manchester and I said you are a really good worker, and the money in here is for your ticket to Manchester.'

'Manchester, Farooq saab, just what I need—to get out of this city.'

I rented a two-bedroomed house in Chorlton, Manchester, near the taxi base for which I drove a minicab. My house in Pakistan was finished a few months later, and I began to save money and soon had enough to put a deposit down on a three-bedroomed house. When I bought the house I wrote a letter to Carol and asked her to forgive me.

She didn't reply.

And then, a year later, when I was in bed with flu, Carol knocked on my door. At first I thought my eyes were playing tricks when I saw her standing on my doorstep, staring at me with shin-ing eyes. She was much thinner than when she had left. A taxi from our base, a Nigerian student driver, was parked on the road.

'Carol!' I coughed, moving away from the door.

'You've lost so much weight,' she said. 'Well, aren't you going to say anything?'

'I don't know what to say.'

'He doesn't know what to say,' Carol said. 'How about asking me in?'

'Please,' I said, waving my hand towards the living room.

'Please what?'

'Please, come in.'

Instead of coming in she turned around and went to the taxi, and a moment later I heard her arguing with the driver. As I stepped out of my front door, he got out of the car and laughed, waving at me to go back in: 'Keep your germs away from me.' He placed Carol's bag on the pavement, got back into his car and drove away.

Flushed with anger, Carol said, 'What does he think I am?'

'What happened?'

'He wouldn't take any money from me.'

'He can't,' I cleared my throat, shutting the door after her, 'we work together.'

'I don't want charity, and sit down before you faint,' Carol said, walking into the living room.

As soon as she stepped into the living room, she put her hand over her mouth, aghast, and then ran her fingers across the brown high-backed three-piece suite, saying, 'You bought my favourite colour,' before walking over and touching the leaves of my tall Yucca, 'You really did love Yuccas, eh, Saleem Khan.'

'No, only this one.'

'Only this one, he says,' Carol was blushing, 'don't tell me.'

I nodded and asked, 'How did you know I was in?'

'Your base told me,' Carol said, flopping onto the three-seater.

'How did you know where I worked?'

'I was nearly a Pakistani once,' she laughed.

'How did you know I wouldn't be with another woman?'

Carol stood up, folded her arms across her chest, tilted her head and smiled, 'Who would have you?'

'Why did you come back?'

'Do you want me to leave?'

'No.'

'Then stop asking so many questions.'

When I recovered, I realised she had brought her plants back.

'I thought you'd like these,' she said as I looked around the room. 'You always did, you pudu.'

'It's *pindu*,' I laughed, correcting her. 'That's a swear word. It means . . .'

'Pin-du,' she said. 'Do you want to keep them?'

'As long as you come with the deal.'

'On one condition.'

'What?'

'We go to Bradford and sit under the weeping willow.'

'When?'

'Whenever,' she said, touching my hand with the tips of her fingers.

We quickly slipped into a routine, shopping on Saturday mornings and cooking for the week in the afternoon before she went to Bradford for the rest of the weekend to stay with her family.

Once, on a freezing February evening, I gave up on waiting for fares for my taxi and came home early. It had been snowing non-stop for hours and cars had skidded into each other here and there. It was almost impossible to walk on the pavements, so people walked in the middle of the road along the tracks created by cars.

Ours was the only house in the street with its windows open on a night like this, with a song by the Beatles blaring out. I stamped my feet on the step in front of the front door to shake off the snow before going in. Just then I heard a rumble on the roof and before I had had a chance to open the door a soft white avalanche crashed around me. I got inside as quickly as I could and shook the snow outside.

The door to the living room was open and Carol was laughing at me. She was in a brand-new blue jogging suit, her hair was tied in a ponytail behind and she was tying the laces of her white trainers. Behind her, our long green drapes trembled with a chill wind that cut through the room.

'Have you lost your marbles,' I said, pulling my green anorak tighter around me.

Carol threw her head back and smiled, blew me a kiss and put her other foot on the chair, tied her other lace and wiggled her bum to the music of *Sgt. Pepper's Lonely Hearts Club Band.*

'This is a no-smoking house from now on,' she said, coming towards me, her eyes beaming and with a mischievous smile on her face.

'You'd better not have done what I think you've done, Carol.'

Putting her warm hands on my cheeks, she pulled me towards her, kissed me on my lips, and just as our tongues met she pulled away, stepped back towards the window and laughed, 'That's how it is.'

As she stood against the open window, the world behind Carol with the falling snow, the white covered roofs with icicles pointing downwards and hungry birds landing and taking off, was that of a beautiful picture postcard. The freckles on Carol's reddening face looked larger than they had ever done before. Her square silver earrings glittered. I wanted to have her and felt myself tensing.

'And you'll get nothing till we go on a date,' Carol said, swinging her arms one way and then the other.

'You barmy git, have you forgotten we live together?'

'Maybe,' Carol said, stretching down to touch her toes.

She ignored me and touched her right foot with her left hand and the other with the opposite hand a few times and then placed her hands on her hips and twisted a few times. As she did this she locked her eyes on mine and said very slowly, 'No date, no mate.'

As Carol continued with her warm-ups I went around the house, shut all the windows, drew the curtains and put the central heating on.

'How are you going to jog out there?' I asked, taking my coat off.

'I'm going to the gym, took out family membership,' Carol said, stretching and leaning back on one leg whilst keeping the other straight.

'I'm not going to any gym . . .'

Walking out of the house, Carol waved a hand in the air saying, 'No fitty, no bitty.'

After Carol left, I realised there were no ashtrays around the living room. I rushed into the kitchen and opened the cupboard where we kept the duty-free cigarette cartons I got when someone came over from Pakistan.

They were all gone.

'You can't have thrown them away,' I said, searching through one cupboard and drawer after another, but they were all gone.

I was on my knees rummaging under the kitchen sink when the front door slammed shut.

'Bey Sharam, shame on you,' Carol said in bad Punjabi. She held something in her hands behind her back.

'I thought you'd gone to the gym,' I laughed, getting up.

'It's bloody freezing out there,' she replied.

She stepped closer, till our noses touched and chuckled, 'I've chucked the death sticks away.'

'You're fibbing, you couldn't,' I said, rubbing my hand down her long arm. 'And what are you hiding, you daft git?'

Carol shrugged her shoulders, stepped away, brought her hands forward with the cigarettes from my coat pocket and crushed them.

'And there's none anywhere else either, not even a frigging dog end,' she said.

Pangs of nicotine withdrawal rushed through me. My head suddenly felt heavy, as if someone had put a clamp around it, and my throat dried.

'No father of my children is going to be a smoker,' Carol said.

I was about to snap, You can't have children, Carol, but the sight of her chewing her teeth and her trembling eyes stopped me.

After a while she sighed and said, 'Miracles can happen you know.' She smiled and added, 'We've got Jesus.'

'For God's sake Carol, you're off your head,' I said.

Carol untied her hair and shook it free.

'Besides, we're not married,' I said.

Carol frowned.

'I've not proposed to you, yet,' I said.

'Who said I would accept someone like you?' Carol's voice suddenly aged. 'Besides, if I had left it for you to ask me out, you would still be trying to work out how to do it.' She went silent for a moment, took my hand and kissed it in the palm.

'Well, propose to me then.'

'You have to convert.'

'To what?'

'Islam, like,' I said, swallowing a lump in my throat.

She laughed, 'Great. OK, I'm going to convert to a beer-guzzling Muslim just like you.'

'You're making me look stupid. You know it's not like that.'

'But you want me to convert and become a Muslim, yes?'

I kept quiet.

'OK, let's do it. But tell me, Saleem, how are you going to manage without your grilled bacon butties?'

'It's not just that, is it,' I said, 'I've got to sort stuff out with me family, like, you know.'

'He's got to sort things out with his family,' she said coldly, throwing her hands up in the air in exasperation, 'Saleem Khan, your mother and father are dead. You have no brothers or sisters.'

'Maybe I'm not ready for this,' I said, 'besides, your family won't like it like this.'

'They can fuck off,' Carol said, unzipping her jogging suit top. She took it off and tossed it onto the back of a chair. Her white T-shirt was stuck to her body. 'It's not my family that's the problem, is it?'

She turned around and went into the bedroom, slamming the door behind her with such force that the wine glasses on top of the dining table jingled.

I paced about in the living room for a while, thought about going out to buy some cigarettes, but went into the bedroom instead and we made love.

~

A few years later we made our first trip back to Bradford and went to the hill past the mill and sat together under the weeping willow, looking at the scene below.

Chewing a blade of grass, Carol lay with her head on my lap, looking up into the swaying branches of the tree. A gentle breeze blew her hair across her face as it whistled through the grass on the hill. I told her how I loved sitting here, looking down at the waters of the canal flowing round the mill. I told her I loved these hills. She nodded. I said that they reminded me of the hills around my village, which came out of the earth in waves, each with its own colour. Our hills are as tall as your mountains. Sometimes they were green, all the shades of green, I told her. She sighed. Sometimes they were burning with the colours of wild flowers covered with butterflies and, just after the rains, with little red insects that were so fragile they died almost as soon as they were touched. And after the monsoons, the smell of the earth as the rains hit was so rich that the taste of it stayed in your mouth for days. And the rains were not like the rain here, which could sneak up on you from cloudless skies. At home, angry winds and raging thunder announced the coming of the monsoons; hills shed streams of foaming red earthy water into the mighty River Jhelum. Life over there, especially after the rains, even with all its hardships, was very beautiful.

Someone was calling Carol. It was a man's voice, coming from just below the dip past the old stone wall.

'Ignore them,' Carol said, spitting the grass blade out of her mouth.

The man called out to her again. Four white men climbed over the wall and came towards us.

'That's our Jack on the left—thick as two planks—and the other three are me cousins—not a brain cell between them.'

'Let's get away from here, Carol,' I said. 'I don't like it.'

'It's me family,' Carol said, sitting up.

'That's where you are, you slut,' Jack shouted, walking towards us.

Two more men came from behind us. They had sticks in their hands.

'Fuck off, Jack, and take these morons with you,' Carol said.

'Margaret said you'd be here with your wog,' Jack said. 'She said to make you see sense.'

We were encircled.

'Don't bring Mum into it,' Carol said. She had no fear in her voice.

'You could have had anyone you wanted, you could, Carol. And you went for a Paki,' Jack said.

Carol pointed to the two who had come from behind us, 'You call the Flanagan twins men—they only get a hard on when they see sheep!'

'Come on then, you slut, I'll show you right here. It'll come out of your nose,' said one of the Flanagans, a big fair-haired man, holding his groin.

The other Flanagan came towards me shouting, 'I'll sort the Paki, our kid.'

Carol bent down, picked up a small stone and threw it at him. It hit him in the head. He held his head and screamed.

'I'll have you for that,' the big Flanagan said, going towards Carol. She bent down and picked up another stone.

'Kevin Flanagan, you touch our lass and I'll have you,' Jack said, rounding on the Flanagans.

Carol clenched her fist with the stone in it. Throwing the stick onto the ground, Kevin Flanagan said, 'You got Pakis in your family, not me. You sort your shit out,' and left.

'Well, Carol,' Jack said, after the Flanagans had gone. 'Look what I've done for you.'

'You came here to do me boyfriend over,' Carol said. 'You want me to thank you?'

'You're me little sis,' Jack said. 'Don't call a Paki your boyfriend.'

'He's me boyfriend.'

'He's just a fucking dirty slimy coward,' Jack said. 'He's not said a word.'

'He's me boyfriend. And I'm coming home to sort this shit out with Mum.'

They stared at each other for a while and then Jack and his cousins went over the wall and back down the hill.

After the boys left, I said to Carol, 'I wouldn't have let him touch you, Carol.'

Giving me the stone she held in her hand, she smirked, 'Here, keep it, in case they're waiting for us.'

Carol put her head in my lap, closed her eyes and said, 'You know Saleem . . .'

'What?'

'Oh, nothing.'

There was a slight smile on Carol's lips, a sly sort of a smile behind which something was hidden, waiting to come out.

'Aren't you wondering why we came here?' she said, her eyeballs rolling behind her closed eyelids.

'It's our special place, innit,' I said.

'No, I mean today.'

'Cos you wanted to.'

'Yeah, but I also want something else.'

I thought for a while, bent down, kissed her on the lips and remembered where she loved to go in Bradford. 'You want to go to the Taj. And I'm so hungry I could eat a horse and chase the jockey.'

'Well, yes, but I also told Mum you were coming round tonight to our house.'

'Your house!' I protested, 'and does your dad know I worked for him?'

Carol sat up and pressed my hand. 'It'll be alright, I promise.'

'Please, Carol, no.'

'You've got to come round one day. There's only going to be Mum and Dad.'

'No.'

That night after a meal at the Taj, we went round to Carol's parents' house for the first time. They lived in a tall double-fronted house in a long tree-lined street in Shipley.

Carol opened the stained glass door and went in, tugging my hand as she did. Two Staffordshire bull terriers, their angry eyes fixed on me, ran down a tall winding staircase. The door to the living room to my left was ajar and people were talking loudly. Carol pointed at the dogs and ordered, 'Stop!'

They stopped in their tracks, their eyes still fixed on me.

'They know you're scared,' Carol said. 'They're really soft, don't worry.'

Carol led me towards the room to the left. As soon as I took a step, the dogs came down a step as well. Carol looked at them and they stopped.

Walking into the living room, Carol said loudly, 'We're here . . .' and it went silent.

I followed her in. It was a large square room with dark brown four-seater settees against three walls and a three-seater in the bay, which overlooked the street through stained glass windows. Carol's mother and father sat in front of the window with Jack, who was perched on the arm of the sofa next to his father. I nodded to her father. He stared stiffly at me.

'Uncle Tom and Uncle Willy,' Carol said to the two men who were sitting on a four-seater close to Jack, their arms folded in front of them, 'what're you doing here?'

There were others in the room, glaring at me.

'Thanks for the warm welcome,' Carol said, her voice trembling.

The dogs came into the room and growled at me. Carol's father snapped his fingers and the dogs ran to him, turned around and stared back at me.

'What you all doing here?' Carol asked. No one answered.

I looked at Carol's mother, who nodded and smiled at me. I nodded back and quietly said to Carol, 'Let's leave.'

'No,' she said, holding my hand. 'Mum we're going into the other room, and we're going to sit down to have a drink and then I'm going to my home. You want to talk to us, you come in there.'

As we walked out, I said to Carol, 'I'm leaving right now.'

Carol swung round, locked her eyes with mine and said, 'You do that and I'm staying here.'

'They might set the dogs on me,' I said.

'For fuck's sake,' Carol hissed. 'Get real.'

'It's horrible.'

'It's great for me, you know,' Carol said, nodding to the other living room. 'Mum and Dad'll come over in a minute, just wait and see.'

As soon as we stepped into the room, Carol hugged me and burst out crying, 'I'm really sorry for this Saleem. I really didn't know they would all be here, honest.'

'It's alright,' I said, kissing her on the head.

Carol pulled away from me as she heard her father's voice throwing obscenities at her mother and said, wiping her eyes with her fingertips, 'Do you really want a cup of tea here?'

'I'd much rather have a pint in Manchester.'

'Yeah.' Carol smiled.

As we walked out to leave the house, Carol's mother came out of the other living room but stopped in her tracks when Carol's father shouted, 'You're not going to meet that Paki.'

Carol's mother turned around and said softly, 'What you going to do, beat me again, right here, like you've done all your life.' Turning to me she said, 'I got some Yorkshire pudding in the oven.'

'We've eaten, Mum,' Carol said and ran to her mother, kissed her on the cheeks and said, 'Thanks Mum, thanks.'

I nodded and walked out of the house.

Had it not been for the airmail letter from Cousin Habib in Pakistan, with the words *Remember Me*, my life with Carol would not have ended the way it did. Habib's two words made me really homesick.

Carol was still in bed. I took the letter and a cup of tea up to her. She was fast asleep with her arm slung over a pillow on the side of the bed I had slept on.

After placing the tea on the bedside table on her side of the bed, I went over to my own and sat down.

'Did you bring me two cups or one?' she asked sleepily.

'One.'

'You're mean.'

'I got a letter from Habib.'

'What did he say?'

'Here,' I said, giving her the letter.

'Very funny,' she said, rubbing sleep out of her eyes. She looked at the letter, which was in Urdu, and said, 'Very funny.'

'It's been a long time since I've been home.'

'This is your home . . .'

'And that,' I said, pointing at the letter.

'You're not going there.'

'Why?

'You know why. You'll just do what your other mates have done, get a village girl.'

'I'm not like the others,' I said.

'Men's promises are as reliable as their dicks—always letting you down.'

'OK, if that's your worry, that I'm going to do something stupid like that,' I said, 'why don't you come with me? We've got enough money and we could live out there for a while. It'll make a change and it's not that bad.'

'OK, Saleem Khan,' Carol said almost immediately, 'let's go. I feel like a change and I've had enough of Manchester's rain.'

'Well, it's not that simple,' I said. 'We can't just live together like we do here . . .'

'Why not?' she asked.

'We have to be married.'

'Well, I thought you'd never ask.' Carol kissed me. 'You could have made an occasion of it, though.'

I didn't say anything. Carol stopped smiling and said bitterly, 'We could pretend we are, couldn't we?'

'Yes, we could,' I said.

'Who wants to marry a bum like you, any road?' Carol said resentfully.

Whilst we never went back to Carol's parents' house in Bradford, her mother, Margaret, came to our house occasionally, always with a basketful of food. I was trying to have a nap on the living room settee when she next came to visit us, just after we had decided to go to Pakistan.

Mother and daughter were in the kitchen and I could hear them clearly.

'You are not married and in Pakistan they have this law there. You can't do out there what you do here. You can't just live together like here.' Margaret said, 'I've been reading all about it.'

'Mum, I'm not a kid.'

'You can live in sin here, against the wishes of your old mother, Carol,' Margaret said. 'Over there you'll be stoned to death.'

'We've already told everyone in Pakistan we're married,' Carol said.

'Carol, how could you get married without telling me?' Margaret sobbed.

'I wouldn't do that to you, Ma. But in the eyes of God, I am married.'

'You don't believe in God, Carol.'

'Alright then, Ma, we're just going to pretend,' Carol said.

'Oh, God,' Margaret cried, 'now you are going to lie that you are married and live in sin, and over there at that.'

'It's only a sin if you believe it is, Mum,' Carol said, giving her mother a tissue.

'They stone you to death for that in Pakistan,' Margaret said.

'Oh, Mum, you worry too much.'

Blowing her nose, Margaret said, 'And what is a drunk like him going to do out there? They flog you in public for drinking. I saw it on the news.'

'They've got to catch you first,' I said. 'And you have to be so poor you can't afford a bit of a bribe.'

Carol laughed as her mother blew her nose again.

Before leaving England, I had told my relatives in Pakistan that I was coming back with my wife. Carol and I moved to Pakistan in late August 1982.

Cousin Habib was waiting for us in the middle of a crowd of people, all pushing each other to get a better glimpse. At first I didn't recognise him amidst all the moustaches and smiling faces. He was thinner than I had imagined he would be. He had a thick black moustache and his hair was oiled and neatly combed. His light brown face was a little browner than the last time I had seen him. He waved at me, disappeared behind the crowd and then reappeared close to me and hugged me, whispering sarcastically in my ear, 'New *sister-in-law* is beautiful.'

On the way back to the village, as he drove he talked non-stop about my new house, making sure I translated what he was saying to Carol: it was the only house in the village with a toilet in all the bedrooms, and even had Valaiti seats and Muslim toilet showers; the grill on the veranda had flowers carved into it and there was special wire meshing which meant no flies or mosquitoes could get in.

When we got to our village, Habib parked the car near the wall of a house I had not seen before. He got out and shooed a flock of barefoot gaping children blocking our way into the village.

Opening the door for Carol, he said, 'Tomorrow I find cleaner cook for you.'

'Tomorrow I will find a cook and a cleaner for you,' Carol corrected Habib, getting out of the car and speaking slowly.

'Yes,' he laughed.

'Saleem and I can clean and he is a great cook,' Carol said. 'Aren't you, Saleem?'

'This is not England, we need help.'

The children made way for us to pass in between them.

'Why are they staring at me?' Carol asked.

'Never seen a goree before,' I replied.

'Oh, God, can we hurry up,' Carol said.

When I got home, I was awestruck by the beauty of my new house's brown-tiled walls, its tall wooden doors and the water tank on top of the house in the shape of a large swan.

My house was at the bottom of the village, overlooking two hills through the centre of which ran a large stream that cut its way down into a gorge and fell into a cave. Above this stood the dark rocky mountains, alongside which Karachi-bound trains could be seen slipping in and out of the breaks in the hills.

Seeing me cry, Carol asked, 'What's up, Saleem?'

'He miss mother,' Cousin Habib answered.

Carol spent the first few hours jumping up and down at the sight of every flying insect, zapping flies during the day and mosquitoes at night, much to the amusement of my family, who came in an endless stream to see my new wife.

I am not sure who cooked or where the food came from, but in the morning Cousin Habib arrived at some ungodly hour and knocked on the door shouting, 'It's the middle of the day. Get up cousin, I have tea for you and my sister-in-law.'

'Send him away, Saleem. Whatever it is can wait,' Carol moaned, pulling a white sheet over her head.

'Two cups of garam, garam, hot, tea; drink before lachis, cardamoms, drop in,' Cousin Habib said loudly.

'What does he want?'

'He's got tea for us and says we should drink it before flies fall in.' Carol curled up under the sheet.

'You can't sleep with your wife during the day, cousin. It's not England.'

Carol grunted angrily, 'For God's sake.'

I looked at the time on my watch. It was 6.30 in the morning.

I got out of bed and went outside into a blazing morning. I felt like wiping the beaming smile off my cousin's face but took a cup of tea and went back into the room, covering the cup with the saucer and placing it on a carved bedside table.

'What's the time?' Carol asked.

'Six thirty.'

'For me, back home?'

'One thirty a.m.'

'Oh, God,' Carol groaned.

I went back outside, walked off the veranda and sat down on a manji next to Cousin Habib, under the shade of our baeri tree.

Handing me my tea, he said, 'I've been to every house in the village. Can't find anyone to come and work here. Not even a toothless buddhi is available until the Jat wedding is over in three weeks' time,' he said, nodding back towards a woman who was standing just beyond the shade of the veranda, her head lowered, her dupatta covering her head.

'She's all there is,' he smirked. 'She makes good food and is good at a lot of things, as you know. You loved her once, but what's a dark girl compared to a goree, eh, elder brother.'

It was Yasmin. She was much darker than I remembered and thinner. I felt deeply uncomfortable and ashamed, and didn't want her in the house with Carol. I felt the bitterness of her accusing gaze, *has your blood turned white, that you've brought your white woman here*.

Carol came out wearing a short-sleeved kurta over blue jeans, with her camera dangling off her arm. 'Oh, God, it's so hot.' She slapped her arms to swat a fly and asked, looking at Yasmin, 'Why is that woman standing like that over there?'

'Habib's found a cook for us, but I think we should get someone else.'

'Why, what's wrong with her?' Carol said scratching her arm. 'And for God's sake, why is she standing in the sun like that? Tell her to come here.'

I hesitated and called, 'Come here.'

Yasmin came into the shade and squatted a short distance away, her head still lowered.

'What's her name?' Carol asked.

I didn't answer and Habib said, 'Yasmin.'

'Yasmin,' Carol repeated.

Yasmin lifted her head.

'Why is she crying?' Carol asked. 'Maybe she doesn't want to work here.'

'Stop crying,' Cousin Habib ordered her.

Yasmin lifted her head and looked at me with flaming eyes.

Carol looked at her and then me, hesitated for a moment and said, 'Tell her to start, Habib.'

After saying this, Carol went around the house taking photographs. She took a photograph of me yawning on the veranda and of Yasmin sweeping the yard with a long jahroo.

An endless stream of beggars seemed to pass through my house after we arrived. The first few sentences Carol picked up after arriving in the village were obscene curses, which she heard from me each time I swore at a beggar, but Carol would go inside, get some money and give it to them. I tried to explain to her that this meant more and more would come. But she ignored me.

Early the next morning while Carol was still asleep, I went for a walk and ended up at the shrine near the railway line, listening to the wind singing through the hills. A train whistled behind me.

Unlike most other shrines around, there was no grave here. It was said that a Holy Man had stayed here on the top of this hill and preached love. He had over a hundred thousand followers who came with him. Every Thursday night, the hills came to life to the sound of beating drums and singing. The followers danced through the night. I sat for a while, thinking back to the Thursday nights of my childhood when I used to follow the drummers from our village out here and wait for the rice to be cooked, eat as much as I could and wrap as much as I was allowed in my kurta to eat on my way home. The shrine was as clean today as it had been the last time I had seen it, before I went to England.

I waited for the whistles of the train to fade, and then stepped across the boulders into the waters of the stream and crossing it walked barefoot on the cool dry sand. Birds were flying out of nests in the sides of the hill, below which tall blades of grass swayed in an easterly breeze. Then I went back to my old school. It had a new board with the words 'High School for Boys' written in English. It had changed a lot since I had taught there. It had an outer wall now and the trees which we had planted in a long line in the middle of the school had grown tall. I imagined rows of boys sitting under them, reciting loudly; a teacher, cane in hand, walking up and down the lines. Most of the classrooms had roofs and there was even a well and a water tank.

Later that day when I was alone in the house, Yasmin brought me my lunch but stood in front of me, head bowed.

'What is it?' I asked.

'Is the food as you like it, sir?'

'Yes.'

'Shall I make some more roti for you?'

'No.'

'Shall I make tea for you now?'

'Why are you wasting my time with these questions?' I said, not looking at her. 'You know what I like and when.'

I ate my lunch and went to sleep. The electricity had come on and the ceiling fan was keeping the flies out of the room. I dreamt I was asleep and Carol was asking Yasmin, in English, 'Is there something going on between you and Saleem? Is there something going on?'

'Why do you ask, madam?' Yasmin replied in Pothowari.

'I am a woman,' Carol said.

Yasmin did not reply.

'Your eyes . . . so sad,' Carol said.

'I have lost my world, madam,' Yasmin said.

'Where did you leave my world, Saleem Khan?' Yasmin asked me. Here words were riding towards me on raging waves, devouring the hills around my village. I was drowning, trying to hold on to somewhere, just out of reach.

Carol woke me up, sprinkling some water on my face. 'Where is everyone? I nearly broke my leg jumping over the wall.'

Later that night we returned to Rawalpindi. As Carol went past Yasmin, Yasmin lowered her head. Carol stared at Yasmin for a moment and was just about to say something to her but then seemed to change her mind and walked out of the gate. As I drove out of the village, Carol asked, 'Why is there so much pain in Yasmin's face?'

'Didn't she just tell you?' I asked.

'When?'

'When you came in,' I said.

'I was going hoarse calling for someone to open the gate.'

'I was asleep.'

'You never locked it before.'

'Yasmin must have done it and gone out over the roof.'

'Anyway, why is she always so sad?' Carol asked. She looked at me, then away, and said, 'You know, don't you? You villagers know everything about everyone. I know that if nothing else.'

Carol squeezed my hand and kissed me on the lips.

'For fuck's sake, this is not England,' I said, pushing her away. Carol laughed.

The first time Carol went into the bazaar in Rawalpindi, she saw a cow sitting in the road. To the amusement of passers-by, who pointed at us with big evil smiles, each time we tried to cross the road we ran back for fear of being hit by a rickshaw, tanga, bus, van, truck, motorcycle or some other mechanical monster. Throwing caution to the wind, I stepped into the road. She dug her nails into my arm and followed. Other than the smoke from the exhaust of a rickshaw, nothing hit us. As we got close to the cow, it stood up and Carol screamed, 'It's alive!'

'It's a cow,' I smirked.

'It moved,' Carol said.

'It can't help itself.'

'They just let a cow sit in the middle of the road?' Carol asked.

'Cows here don't ask for permission,' I said.

'Is it because the people think it's a God?'

'That's in India,' I laughed. 'We eat them here.'

One day, an old man with long unkempt hair and bloodshot eyes, a professional beggar I had known from childhood, came early in the morning and continued to stand in the doorway even after Carol had given him twenty rupees. I got up, went and slammed the door shut and said to Carol, 'You've handed so much money out to this scum, we've hardly got anything left.'

'You're not the man I knew in England. You're so cold towards all these people. You even walk differently here than you did there. What's happened to you, Saleem?'

I was taken aback and looked at her. Her face twitched. Maybe she is right. It's because I'm no longer a Paki. I've become a saab, a babu, a sir, with a big Pukka house and servants. Is this really me or was that me? Without waiting for an answer she turned around and ran inside.

She began writing to her mother every day. She would sit on her own, looking silently out of the window.

One day, giving me a letter to post, she said, 'I want to go home. I have had enough.'

The tone in her voice left no room for discussion.

'When?'

'As soon as I can.'

I nodded.

'I know you want to stay longer,' she said. 'It's OK. I'll send you some money when I get back.'

'No, there's no need. Cousin Habib has asked me to help out with his business. He is about to make a big deal and wants my help.'

'You didn't tell me,' she said.

Yasmin went past with a cane basket loaded with rubbish.

'But I guess you don't tell me much, do you?' Carol said. 'And do you think I don't know?'

'Know what?' I asked.

'Oh Saleem, just go and sort out my ticket.' Carol waved her hand and sat down on a white plastic chair.

I should have told her, I understand it is hard for you. Pakistan is a hard place, and it's not just because of the flies and mosquitoes. It's hard for Pakistanis. I wanted to tell her, I know you really tried, you came out here for me, into this world, which sometimes just makes no sense to me, how could it to you? I should have told her, I love you, stay with me a little while longer. I should have told her, you are so full of love and warmth for all these people, but instead I replied, 'If that's what you want?'

She was silent for a long time and then sighed, 'Yes, Saleem, that's what I want.'

I was regretting not going back with Carol when Cousin Habib took me to his office and insisted I work with him. A wedding party with drummers and two men playing the

Shehnai had just passed Cousin Habib's office, which he called the Adda—the Kamal Goods Forwarding Agency. It was not too far from Rawalpindi, where I had now moved to a flat after Carol left. The Adda was north of the city, further up the GT road towards Peshawar. It lay at the foot of the Margala hills, next to a fruit and vegetable market. To get to the office you had to cross an open sewer. The Adda was below the Awan Hotel, the only one that remained open during the holy month of fasting (for travellers of course, where everyone ate). The only furniture in the Adda was a three-legged desk propped up with bricks, a backless swivel chair and two broken plastic chairs for customers. Because the room was below the hotel and out of direct sunlight, it was beautifully cool during the day and night and tired truck drivers slept in there on some crumbling straw mats with faded darrees spread out on them. The pillows were stained black and were infested with nits and other creepy crawlies. Each time someone asked Cousin Habib to get some new pillows, he would reply, 'Not until they walk out of here on their own.'

I started to learn the business of the Adda. Cousin Habib had orders to supply limestone for road and building construction and cement factories. Trucks would fill from the Margala hills and mostly go south. The drivers would pay a small commission to the Adda, as would the people who placed the orders. It took me a couple of weeks to learn about the negotiating habits of the drivers. They would come with tired red eyes and oily clothes and stand just past our two broken chairs and ask, 'Order-shouder anywhere, Habib Saab?' Cousin Habib would tell them what orders he had and how much the transportation fee was. He told me that if the driver scratched his groin, we would not get the job and the driver would have to move on to another Adda. If they sat down on the chair, that meant they had already been to other Addas and they were ready to pay the commission.

The Adda never closed; drivers could turn up at any time. I enjoyed the company of the regular drivers, many of whom turned up stoned and continued to smoke dope until they passed out, somehow managing to make sense right up to the last moment. Austad Aurangzeb, aka Kala, a lightskinned, short, round man with permanently bloodshot eyes who drove an old Bedford truck, ensured everyone around him knew that he had arrived. He was the first one from my village to call me Britisher, one of the few English words he knew. I had told him I was still the same man, but he had dismissed this with the words, 'You've become theirs now, you don't sit, shit, walk, talk or even laugh like us. You are a Britisher. You are an Abroadi.'

He was Yasmin's uncle and lived in a new settlement on the outskirts of our village. He was the only loyal driver of our Adda. Whenever he came round and saw me in the office, he drove his truck to the edge of the gutter, revved the engine a good few times and stuck his thumb up at me to show that he understood how to greet Britishers. I saw him as he jumped out of the truck, still holding his thumb up for me to see. He wore a greasy old vest with lots of pockets and a lungi around his waist. He went around the truck followed by two young assistants, slapping each tyre with the palm of his hand.

When he had finished inspecting the truck, he asked the assistants, 'How many of them need more air?' The boys looked dumbstruck. They looked at each other for help. I

94

knew what was coming and got up, but by the time I got to the gutter he had slapped the first one saying, 'You were not paying any attention, you motherfuckers.' The other lad ran towards the market. Kala ran after him. I ran after Kala. Drivers and stallholders started clapping and laughing. I caught up with him without much difficulty. He had not gone far and was out of breath. Pointing at anybody and everybody he thought was laughing at him, Kala said, 'May the devil fuck your mothers.'

Regaining his breath, he wiped the sweat off his face with a corner of his lungi and then took my hand. Holding it tightly, we went back to the truck. 'What am I to do with these tyres?' he said. 'They burst on feathers. And even if they were new ones, what would we do?' Nodding to a large Mercedes Benz truck, he said, 'The Afghans get those German ones free from the motherfucking Americans. And the police don't stop them. They pay no fatigue, not like us. We have to work free for them, by giving them one day's work as fatigue every month.'

Kala came into the office, lit a cigarette and sat staring at his truck. Black ribbons were tied to the side mirrors. Two eyes with long lashes and eyeliner were painted on the bonnet.

On the days that I came and sat in the Adda, Cousin Habib ensured that there was always an English newspaper for me along with his regular Urdu daily. When there were a lot of drivers, the pages of the Urdu newspaper were passed around, the literate ones reading and the others looking at the pictures. Kala picked up my English newspaper.

'Read the Urdu one,' I said, 'what will you understand of this one?'

'It's all the same to the blind,' Kala laughed, looking at a picture of a burnt-out bus.

'Sixteen people died in Pir Vadahai,' I said. 'The picture is of the bus where the bomb went off.'

'Twenty-three,' Kala said, 'not sixteen, Saleem Saab.'

'It says sixteen,' I said.

'It may say sixteen,' Kala said, 'but I'm a GT road truck driver and what do I not see? And what do we not hear? A bomb here, a bomb there. This bazaar, that station. Government blames Indians, Afghans, terrorists.' Kala placed his hand across his chest. 'This is Pakistan. Our rulers know how to get fucked by the Americans and they know how to fuck us. They know we can't digest our food if a hundred people don't get killed. Bomb blasts here, Saleem Saab, hathowra group, hammer group, there Saabji, jumping into people's houses, smashing their skulls in with a hammer and then disappearing in the morning. A big game, sir. As Ustad Daman says: *Pakistan de dho khuda*, Pakistan has two gods, *hik tey rehndha arshaan uttay*, one lives in the heavens; *dhoja rehnda farshaan uttay*, the other lives on the ground.' Pointing to the sky, he continued, '*us dha naan eh Allah meaan*, there His name is Allah,' and he then pointed to the ground, '*is dha naan ai General Zia*, here his name is General Zia. *wah ji wah, General Zia, Koan Kehndha tennu ithoon ja?* Oh wondrous General Zia, who asks you to leave this place?'

He saw one of his assistants and stopped mid-sentence, flicked the cigarette into the gutter and went off towards the market, swearing, 'I'll break his neck.'

It was a particularly hot day and the gutter stank far more than usual. There was a light wind that brought in the stench of rotting fruit and vegetables from the market, mixed with that from the gutter, and pushed it inside the Adda. The electricity had just gone off and the flies were having a field day. Cousin Habib had been dropping hints here and there that he was onto the big deal, but wouldn't tell me much more than this.

Though a lot of cash passed through his hands, not much stayed in them and even less came to me.

The scent of spicy frying meat wafted in from the Afghan kebab place next door. I swatted a fly on my arm, closed my eyes and thought of kebabs being fried. I could hear the sizzling oil, the rotis slapping around in the hands of the worker on the tandoor, the momentary silence in which he bent down to look into the hot oven, pulling cooked ones out and slapping new ones back in again. The crisp scent of the tandoori rotis was making my mouth water. A young boy was shouting orders. He was eight years old. I had seen him here every time I had come. He ran from customer to customer, who sat on wooden benches a few yards from a large pan half-filled with black oil in which chappal kebabs were cooking. The boy ensured the wood was continuously burning during the busy times and shouted orders to the chef and the tandoorchi.

A stallholder in the vegetable market burst into song, praising the virtues of his aubergines, potatoes and tomatoes. Buses and trucks went past noisily on the road beyond. Someone shouted at the little boy to put some music on. He shouted the demand to his boss. A moment or so later, a Pushto song rang out over the traffic noise. I thought of England. It appeared to me in my dreams as a land of order, a land of ease, where everything worked as it should. But despite all the hassle of power cuts and flies and running short of money, I was at peace, I felt I was someone, and I wasn't a Paki taxi driver smiling through insults, nodding at jokes of drunks or listening to their arguments about which curry house produced the hottest vindaloos and how they suffered the day after.

Cousin Habib's *today-is-the-day-for-the-big-deal* finally arrived when he came back from wherever he used to go, waving a piece of paper. He lifted his kurta, showed me a wad of money in his vest pocket and said, 'I have got a big order, cousin, a big, big order.' He limped over, lit two cigarettes, giving me one, and slammed the paper in front of me. 'Now I really need your help.'

The order was written in English. It was from the National Logistical Agency and was for the supply of trucks required for the transportation of goods from Karachi to Peshawar.

'Are you going to work for the Army now?' I asked.

Rubbing his hand across his injured leg, Cousin Habib said, 'Most countries have an army, but here in Pakistan the army has a country. They do everything and have their fingers in everything. They build the roads—I supply the rocks. Now they want trucks for another job; they don't tell me what the job is. I give them trucks. The man who gave me the order was my colonel in 1971 and I saved his life in Dacca.'

'I don't feel comfortable about working for agencies, cousin,' I said. 'You know what they say about them: they have no mothers and fathers.'

'That's because you have the comfort of your British passport, brother,' Cousin Habib said, waving at a worker who was carrying a tub on his head. The worker came into the Adda and placed the tub in the far corner of the room. It was full of Murree beer bottles in icy water. That evening, just after sunset, we started drinking.

'This is the first night since I opened the Adda that the door will be shut,' Cousin Habib said.

The drunker he got, the more he cursed the army. 'If I were Bengali, I would shoot them for what we did in '71. I would shoot me as well.' He went quiet and stared at the wall, as if he could see through it. 'They told me we were going to teach the Bengali traitors a lesson,' Habib said. 'We would change their dark-skinned race for ever. We would plant Punjabi seeds in their women. But I couldn't do it. She was only a girl. The unit had had her mother and then shot her dead. The girl had hidden behind a buffalo. The buffalo stood up. She cried and she begged. The colonel said I wasn't a man. The unit laughed at me. The little girl jumped out from behind the animal and lunged at the colonel with a knife. I pushed the colonel out of the way and knocked the knife out of her hand. She tried to run away but I caught her. She looked at me—and those eyes—I can see them even now, they were full of a fire I have never been able to put out. I let her go. Others ran after her and caught her, but I let her go.' Habib talked and talked until he fell asleep dead drunk.

We slept in the Adda that night. Mercifully, there was no load-shedding and the fan kept the mosquitoes at bay. Cousin Habib was up early the next morning and woke me with a breakfast of steaming hot cholay and naan, saying, 'I have already sent Kala to Peshawar and he's got so many trips he won't be back here for a while.'

As I was getting up off the floor, he said, 'And soon we have to see someone, cousin. I will need you with me.'

'Who?'

'Big order, yaar, big people at the ice factory,' Cousin Habib said. 'Just speak lots of English with Colonel Duraid Shah when you meet him and leave the rest to me.'

After breakfast I rode on the back of his motorcycle and we went off for our meeting at the ice factory. I had gone past it many times and seen ice blocks being brought out on carts pulled by donkeys. I had not thought much about the wooden barrier that let the cars in and out.

At the gate were two guards: a bored youth with a thin moustache under his long nose, who threw me a suspicious look; and a strong old man with a shining white beard and a loosely wrapped turban on his head. Two Kalashnikov rifles rested against a tree behind the guards. The older guard placed some snuff between his teeth and his bottom lip. He had a cigarette in between the fingers of his clenched hand. He looked at me suspiciously and then placed his lips around the top of his fist and sucked hard. The tip of the cigarette glowed.

'My cousin from England, Chambail Chacha,' Cousin Habib said, pulling up.

'Mr Habib's cousin from England, do they believe in God over there?' Chambail Chacha asked, snapping his fingers to flick the ash from his cigarette.

I was searching for an answer when Cousin Habib smirked, saying, 'Chambail Chacha, would *you* have any need to believe in God over there?'

Chambail Chacha waved us through. We dismounted a short distance away in the shade of a peepal tree and Cousin Habib said, 'Just about everyone works for either the Americans or the Russians. Chambail Chacha is with the Russians and the other one is with the Americans.'

Rows of donkey-pulled carts with their bedraggled owners sitting patiently on them, some smoking, others looking blankly on, inched towards a platform with blocks of glistening ice stacked on top of each other at the mouth of a large shed. Workers dug metal hooks into the dripping blocks and dragged them onto the carts. The sides of the shed were lined with poplar trees. We walked in the shade of the trees and went down a path which opened up into a massive courtyard. Newly built blocks of houses were straddled along one side of the perimeter wall. On the other side, across an open ground with chalked lines, were much older houses with tiled roofs.

'I have heard so much about you from Habib, Saleem Saab,' Duraid Shah, an unshaven shaven man with deep penetrating black eyes, said, as soon as we walked into his office. He stood up, adjusted his black tie and shook my hand warmly. Smoke rose from a pipe in an ashtray on a table overflowing with documents.

'And he has told me how you have cared for him, Colonel Saab,' I replied.

'Oh, yaar, leave the Colonel bit. Just Duraid is good,' Duraid Shah said. 'I like meeting face to face with my business partners.' Switching to English, he said, 'And tell me, how are you finding Pakistan?'

'Well, Duraid Saab—'

Cousin Habib poured a glass of water from a water cooler and eyed me mischievously.

'Saab, sounds so un-English,' Duraid Shah interrupted.

'I feel I should never have left Pakistan,' I said, looking around the room. Rows of silver trophy cups were locked up in a glass cupboard and a great big picture of Mohamad Ali Jinnah hung on the wall behind Duraid Shah's chair.

'Abroadis always say this,' Duraid Shah laughed, 'and us desis all want to leave.' He looked at a photograph of a four-year-old boy dressed in Army shorts and T-shirt posing stiffly in front of the camera, and asked me, 'How many children have you got?'

'I don't have any,' I replied.

'And I heard you had an English wife.' Duraid Shah gave me a dirty look.

'Well, she . . .' I looked at Cousin Habib, who turned his face away. How could he know the truth? I had told him that I was married to Carol.

'It's OK. I understand. You English get married every weekend, eh?' Duraid Shah winked. 'Habib told me everything. You, I can understand, Saleem Saab, but what I *don't* understand is why your cousin won't get married.'

'In Dhaka, sir, in '71 when I was an Indian prisoner, I swore I would never go near a woman,' Cousin Habib said, rubbing his chin. He often did this when something was troubling him.

Duraid Shah and Cousin Habib went into a heavy silence for a moment, excluding me from that world.

I looked at a dusty ceiling fan turning awkwardly above us, jerking noisily every now and then.

Duraid Shah broke the oppressive silence, 'It looks like it will fall from the ceiling, Saleem Saab, but it is only playing with us.' Turning to Cousin Habib, he sighed, 'Well, what does a soldier not see, eh?'

'I am not a soldier, sir,' Cousin Habib said.

'And I am not a soldier either, but we have to eat and live,' Duraid Shah said. 'And this Pak land, this special land of God, has never seen peace. We are just doormats of history. But we are not here to discuss history, though I love history. Let's make some money.'

Duraid Shah lit his pipe. A plume of smoke from the pipe was dispersed towards me by the noisy ceiling fan.

Duraid Shah sat back in his chair and went into deep thought, puffing on his pipe. After emptying its contents into an ashtray, he placed the pipe on a small tray with other pipes, rubbed his hands on his immaculately combed greying hair and went over the details of our job. We were to supply a variety of transport which would include trucks, buses as well as smaller vans to transport men and supplies from different parts of Pakistan, from the south to Rawalpindi and from here to Charsada in Peshawar and some to Muzzafarbad in Kashmir. On the 21st of each month the accounts would be settled for payment due on the 1st of the next.

At first the jobs we did were much the same as those the Adda had always done: we gave the drivers a bilti, a receipt on which we wrote what they had to collect, from where, which address to deliver to, and the cost of the truck. The major difference this time was that we deducted our commission from the drivers as well as paying them for the cost of the fare of the truck, often part up front and part on return from the jobs. We transported rocks from the Margala hills to the crusheries. From here we took crushed rock up north to towns towards Peshawar and supplied the building materials for the extension at the back of the ice factory. Sometimes we moved livestock, but during times of high demand drivers were loath to take animals, especially when an animal died en route. Some of the best paid jobs were those where we transported sealed boxes of donations from western countries to Afghan refugees, whose camps were spread all the way from Rawalpindi to Peshawar.

Hundreds of thousands of rupees were passing through the Adda and for once we were making a lot of money as well. Usually, on Fridays we were entertained with Russian vodka by Duraid Shah. Duraid Shah had a special room for guests in a bungalow at the back of the office. He drank vodka in large glasses and knocked it back like it was water. After the second glass he talked in English, often about the time he had been invited to Buckingham Palace but had refused to go. Sometimes it was Queen Elizabeth who had invited him and sometimes it was Queen Victoria herself. After the third glass he cursed the queen, passed out and snored so loudly that we often went back into his office to finish off the booze.

One Friday night, we were very drunk and hungry. Crisp hot naans had been dropped off by an Afghan boy from the local tandoor. Just before he took the second glass of vodka, Duraid Shah realised he had forgotten to order kebabs and now everything was closed. Feeling ashamed of himself, he quickly moved on to a third glass which he raised in the air and mumbled, 'Pakistan Sheikh Reganji your friend General Zia saab, great man, hangs man who promoted him.' He thought for a moment and then made his toast: 'Almighty, cursed be Chambail Chacha's cockerel which shits on my car . . .' He was snoring before the end of this sentence.

'Why don't we eat one of Chambail Chacha's chickens?' Cousin Habib suggested.

'That is such a nasty thing to think,' I said. 'He loves them.'

'A chicken is a chicken,' Duraid Shah said, suddenly sitting up, 'and Chambail Chacha has gone to his village. We have roti, but no boti. What good is bread without meat? I have my honour. Meat you shall eat.'

Cousin Habib added, 'No one will suspect a Britisher of stealing chickens.'

'No.'

'No Pathan would be scared of catching a chicken,' Duraid Khan said, pouring himself another vodka.

'If I get the chicken, who will slaughter it?' I asked.

'It is a job for men,' Cousin Habib boasted, emptying what remained of a large bottle of vodka equally into two glasses. He knocked one down and said, 'I am a man.'

'Sharpen your knife,' I said, knocking my glass of vodka down in one gulp. It hissed out of my nose as I set off to get a chicken.

The chickens were kept in a small shed close to the front gate. I grabbed the first one that came to hand, held it tightly by the neck so that it would not make too much noise, shoved it under my kurta, looked around to ensure the coast was clear and ran back to the bungalow. Duraid Shah was snoring. Cousin Habib was sharpening a very large knife on the side of the wall.

'It is a chicken, not a bull.'

'You can't take risks with these things,' Cousin Habib replied.

'Have you done this before?' I asked, handing him the bird.

'Have I done this before?' Cousin Habib laughed a Punjabi drunk's laugh. 'And this is not a chicken. You brought the bloody cockerel. Chambail Chacha's cokker.'

'It is a chicken, that's what it is.'

Cousin Habib had hardly put his hand on the bird when I let go. The bird flew noisily out of his hand and landed on top of Duraid Shah, who sat up and said in English, 'My lords, ladies and gentlemen, it gives me great pleasure to go teach the Russian bear a lesson. Let us toast to victory.'

'Shut the motherfucking door,' Cousin Habib said.

I kicked the door shut with my heel as Duraid Shah

continued his speech. Cousin Habib ran at the bird, swearing and cursing. He dived at it. It flew up and landed on the desk. Cousin Habib hit the bed and said, 'Turn the motherfucking light off.'

'And Maulana Reagan, thank you for giving us this squint-eyed man,' Duraid Shah said. Turning to the picture of Mohammad Ali Jinnah, he said, 'And when you didn't know how to pray, how come you gave us this country, eh?'

I made a dash for the bird but it jumped up and hit the light bulb. The bulb crashed to the ground plunging the room into semi-darkness.

'Ha, ha, there you are, you bastard,' Cousin Habib panted, pointing to the corner of the room where the bird was sitting.

'If I was the president of America,' Duraid Shah said, 'I would push a bottle of vodka up General Zia's behind and then make him drink what came out.'

'We should get a sheet and throw it over the chicken,' I said.

'What do you Britishers know?' Cousin Habib boasted. 'It is not a lion.'

He dived at the bird and banged his head into the wall, but a moment later he panted triumphantly, 'I got you, you son of a chicken.'

'Wait, don't move! Let me put a new bulb in,' I said.

'Watch you don't fall off the chair,' Cousin Habib said. 'You are drunk.'

When the light came on, I saw Cousin Habib's faced covered in blood.

He was leaning against the wall with his legs spread wide apart, holding the chicken by the wings with one hand and the knife with the other. Duraid Shah was standing in a corner talking to the wall.

'To your health ladies and laydas,' Duraid Shah raised his glass.

'You could have killed yourself with the knife,' I said, looking for some tissues.

'We Punjabis know how to handle knives,' Cousin Habib slurred.

Cousin Habib pressed some tissues into his scalp for a few moments. Duraid Shah was mumbling something unintelligible to his shadow. Cousin Habib waited for the bleeding to stop and then we went outside. He placed the bird's legs under his right foot and was about to cut its neck with the knife when I said, 'Wrong way round.'

Cousin Habib looked at the knife and said, 'You've had too much vodka.'

I pointed to the chicken, 'You are holding its neck the wrong way round.'

Cousin Habib bent down to check and turned the bird around, placed the knife on the neck and said, 'I have never taken a life. I just can't do it.'

I said, '*Allah O Akbar,*' grabbed the knife out of his hand and slit the bird's throat. A jet of the bird's blood hit Cousin Habib in the face. He vomited. The bird slipped out of his hand.

'You lion of Punjab! Look over there, it's still running,' I said.

Cousin Habib looked at the bird, its neck dangling about. The bird dropped down dead. He vomited again.

'You take it in, yaar,' Cousin Habib said in between vomiting. 'I can't do it. Chambail Chacha loved this bird.'

I picked up the bird and took it into the kitchen. Cousin Habib followed a few moments later. A once-silver two-ringed cooker, now black, was placed on a dark brown marble worktop. The sink, a deep cemented bowl with a large tap, was overflowing with dirty plates. We stood staring at the bird.

Duraid Shah had stripped down to his shorts and was doing sit-ups.

'What have you done?' Cousin Habib said.

'You wanted to eat?' I said.

'It's not halal,' Cousin Habib said.

'I said the takbir, God is great,' I said.

'You did it all wrong,' Cousin Habib said.

'Where every halal is haram, then haram is halal,' Duraid Shah said in between press-ups. 'My wife will cook it for us. We will enjoy it.'

'You didn't wake your wife up.' I said.

'No, I told her before.'

'Before we caught the chicken?' I asked.

'Ya Allah. He understands nothing.' Duraid Shah threw his hands in the air. 'I am a Pathan. I told her last week that I was going to go to England to meet the Queen.'

Duraid Shah went into a contemplative silence.

Cousin Habib lit two cigarettes. He gave me one and said, 'Let's get Chambail Chacha another cockerel before he gets back.'

A few days later, Cousin Habib bought a new cockerel and quietly released it among Chambail Chacha's hens before he got back from his village.

In the coming weeks, I managed the invoices and Cousin Habib was mostly out of the Adda, coming back with piles of paper every now and then which I logged in a ledger. I lost all track of time.

Sometimes, I used to go to my house in the village to sleep. Yasmin would be waiting at my house, usually with her brother or some other member of her family. I rarely said anything to her other than an order. Usually, she slid past me in the shadows of the house.

One day when I walked in she was alone. It was hot. She was sweating. Her kurta was stuck to her. Usually when she saw me, she pulled her dupatta across her breasts, but this time she didn't. Her hair was tied behind her in a bun. Drops of sweat trickled down her face and neck. She stood motionless, staring. I felt tension in my groin.

'Come here, Yasmin,' I said, sitting on a bed on the veranda.

She put one of her bare feet on top of the other and said, 'You remember my name, sir.'

I wanted her badly and said, 'Didn't you hear what I said, Yasmin?' 'Is that an order, sir.'

'Order?'

'I am but a slave, sir,' she said.

Is she playing with me? I thought for a moment, getting more aroused.

'If that is what you would like to hear,' I said.

'Then who am I? Who is this small dark massalan, who is no better than a donkey. Ride her if you will sir. How can she say no? But my duty is nearly done for today.'

Yasmin stared at me, knotting her eyebrows. She knew how to humiliate me, I thought, but she is right. I remembered my promise to her, in that bygone world of mine, before I became an Abroadi. A promise I had made to her with the words of a poem, *Ishq na puchda zaatan*, love does not care for caste.

'You never did love me did you, it was all a lie?' she asked.

'I did.'

'Then what happened?'

I shook my head.

'And then you hated this dark-skinned woman and just wanted white flesh.'

'No.'

'And then what happened?'

I kept quiet.

'Do you know what your mother said when she found out you were going to marry me? When I told the world I loved you?'

I was about to tell her, that was enough, when she interrupted my thoughts and said, 'Don't tell me to stop. I know you can. And I will obey.'

I kept quiet.

Yasmin continued, her voice trembling, 'And do you know what I told my own mother. I told her, that Saleem Khan did not win my love with his looks, no, but with his tender heart, a bright heart, in this village of darkness. A heart that does not beat to the rhythm of his caste, but to the rhythm of our love.'

She paused, took a deep breath and continued, 'And my mother told me, the upper castes don't have hearts.' Yasmin stopped again looked at me and said, 'And let me tell you what your mother said to me. You might be surprised by what such a respected woman of your caste might have really said.'

Again I was about to stop her when she interrupted my thoughts, 'No, you don't believe your mother would say bad things to me, to this low-caste lover of her son. But let me tell you what she said. She swore such words at me, and I ask God to forgive her, and then she said, "He is all Allah has given me, don't humiliate me, you are not worthy of him. You can never be worthy of him. He will marry you over my dead body."

'I fell at your mother's feet and kissed them and said, "Auntie, my love for your son is so pure, so pure. And, I don't know how to unlove."

'Your mother kicked me away and left in a taxi to phone you from the city.'

Yasmin paused to wipe her eyes. I remember the day well. Mother telephoned me in England. It was a quick call with just one question, 'Are you in love with a low-caste massallan?'

I felt my eyes fill with burning tears, as I remembered my answer to my mother. But Yasmin was unremitting . . .

'I saw your mother come back to the village in the same taxi after she talked to you.' Yasmin said. 'She was carrying something in her hand. She had two of your relatives with her. Two men. I was at home looking over our wall. My mother, who was sitting in front of the gate of our house, all the while looking out to see when she would return, kept on telling me how the high castes will kill me rather than see their man marry one of us. When my mother saw your mother walking towards us, she told me to run and hide and save my life. I told her, no man was going to touch me. No high caste woman. I would not hang from any tree. No one was going to burn our house. No one will come into our house, whilst I had breath in my body.

'When your mother got closer to our house, she told the men to stop. She walked up to our door and asked, "Can I come into your house, Yasmin?"

'I stepped back. She came up to me and put her hand on my head and told me what you had said to her from England, "My love for Yasmin was made in heaven by Allah, and He sees no caste."

'Your mother took a red bridal suite out of the bag she was carrying gave it to me and said, "No one will stand against the

111

will of the Almighty. When my son comes back from England, I will have the biggest wedding this village has seen and take you home in a doli, a bridal carriage."'

Yasmin stopped and after a pause asked, her voice suddenly cold, 'So what happened to us, Saleem Khan?'

I shook my head again. I closed my eyes. I could feel her gaze. I could hear her bitter breaths, which stopped suddenly.

'Would you like me to come to you before I bring you your food, sir? Or do you want to hear what I have to say? And before I say what I want to say, there is another letter from Madam Carol for you. I have put it on the table inside. She wants to know why you are not replying to her letters.'

'You bitch, you have been reading my letters,' I snapped.

'She wants to know if you are fucking me,' she said calmly.

'How dare you read my letters . . .'

'I am illiterate, master. I am a woman.'

I stood up, stormed into the bedroom, looked at Carol's letter, put it back on the table and came out.

Yasmin had adjusted her dupatta across her breasts.

'I am not hungry. Go home now.'

'I have something to say.'

'There is nothing for you to say to me. The past is done. Dead! Understand. Gone!'

'What has happened to my uncle Kala? He has not been home for a long time. It is not like him.'

'To hell with Kala. Now get out of my house before I throw you out.'

She lowered her head and walked away.

The next morning, I left before she was due to come to work and when I got to the Adda Yasmin was standing with a small dark woman squatting by her feet. I ignored Yasmin and walked by, but felt the glare of her eyes on the back of my neck. After opening the door of the Adda, I looked across at her. She was glaring at me with accusing eyes. I turned my back on her and started reading an old newspaper.

The sun was already out and getting hotter. I could feel my neck burning. I read the activities page and tried to work out the chess puzzle. I was hoping they would leave but the women were still there.

'Everyone asks me for money and the bitch is not going away till I give her some money,' I said, crushing the newspaper into a ball. 'Come here,' I called her over with a wave of my hand.

Yasmin stepped forward. Her eyes were fixed on me.

When she was close enough to hear me, I said, 'Understand this once and for all. Whatever happened between you and me happened a long time ago. A very long time ago,' I paused and looked at her. Her unblinking eyes were looking past me. I asked her, 'How much do you want?'

She lowered her head. Drops of sweat fell onto the ground. She said, 'I want nothing from you, Saab.'

'Do I not pay you enough?' I laughed falsely, tapping the wallet in my pocket. 'What else do you do there? You want nothing from me!'

'Saabji, I am your servant, but today I have to come to ask a favour of you . . .'

I had never wanted her to work for me, and now just the sound of her voice was throwing me deeper into a rage, 'I owe you nothing, do you understand, nothing! I have paid you back for what you gave.'

Yasmin looked at me with anxious eyes, adjusted her weight from one foot to the other and said, 'Uncle Kala should have come home last week.'

'Truck drivers can't stick to time,' I said.

'Even when Uncle Kala didn't come home, he always sent money.'

It was just a charade to get some money out of me, I thought. Pakistanis never give up. They come at you from a different angle every time.

I didn't see the other woman move. She was now squatting close to Yasmin.

'Uncle Kala worked for you. Where is he?' Yasmin asked dryly.

'I will find out,' I snapped. 'Now go.'

Nodding to her auntie, Yasmin said, 'Come, let's go.' Yasmin held her auntie's hand and helped her off the ground and the women disappeared into a throng of excited school children walking past the Adda.

After they left, I flicked through the receipt books to try to work out Kala's movements, and Kala should have indeed been back over a week ago from his trip to Peshawar. As he was owed a lot of money by our Adda, he should at least have been in contact with us, even if he went on another job on his way back down.

Later that day the owner of Kala's truck, a brooding old man by the name of Haji Akber, turned up at the Adda. He plonked himself down on one of the chairs and started stroking his hennaed beard. I buried myself in the paperwork and instinctively swatted a fly every now and then.

'You know, Saleem Saab, times are hard for us owners and it been a long time since Mister Habib has made any payment to me.'

We never paid him, but his driver. I was about to say this but then realised he knew that and kept quiet.

'I don't know where that bastard Kala, my driver is . . .'

'I have had a message from Kala. He has had a tyre problem and then some engine problem. I have sent some money to Peshawar so he can buy some new tyres, and you know we have connections and we will get them at a better price than anything you can get,' I lied.

'But I have no money to pay for any new tyres, Saleem Saab.'

'Uncle, we will pay and you know how sharp Kala is. He will make double sure he gets the best deal.'

This cheered him up and he left. I leaned back in my chair and watched him shaking hands with people as he walked off towards the GT road. What had happened to me, I thought? Why didn't I care what happened to a driver, especially someone whom I knew?

It being a Friday and as Cousin Habib and I were on our way to meet Duraid Shah for our next drink up, I said to Habib, 'We have to find out what has happened to Kala.'

'There are lots of Kalas in this world. He will turn up when he turns up.'

'What if something bad has happened to him?'

'So, if he dies, what is it to us?' he replied. 'Drivers, dogs and donkeys—'

'We owe it to his family to find out,' I interrupted.

'Just think about us, elder brother.'

'No,' I insist, 'we will find out what has happened to him and even go to where he went.'

'You're such a gora at heart, brother Saleem'—Habib laughed—'such a gora. Duraid Shah will know.'

We turned up a little early for our drinking session at Duraid Shah's. Chambail Chacha, with a Kalashnikov in one hand, was feeding chickens with his other. There were four hens and one rooster in front of them, which was pecking the ground and calling out to the hens. The hens ran towards the food. The rooster opened its wing and turned towards a hen. It sat down.

The rooster was about to mount the bird when Chambail Chacha said, 'Nothing is safe nowadays, khour ghoud, sister-fucker.'

'Chambail Chacha, I heard the thief gave you a cockerel back,' I said.

Chambail Chacha spat at the rooster, which jumped nois-ily out of the way.

'Only a God-fearing thief returns what he stole, eh, Chambail Chacha?' Cousin Habib said.

'If you say so, sir, if you say so,' Chambail Chacha said. Then he added quickly, nodding to a group of bearded youths who had pulled up in front of the gate in a jeep, 'The morning azaan of my cockerel is sweeter than their barking.'

A tall young man with a loose flowing beard, wearing dark sunglasses and a keffiyeh, sat on the front passenger seat. His leg was dangling out of the door of the jeep. His leather boots went up to his knees. Tossing the chicken feed to me, Chambail Chacha whispered, 'The Sheikh is back for the second time this week.'

Cousin Habib took a handful of feed out of the bag and we fed the chickens. I asked Cousin Habib, 'When did the Sheikh come here?'

'I have been coming here for three years and he was here before I came,' Cousin Habib said. Throwing feed to the chickens, he added, 'Mind you, the Americans fly him home to Saudi Arabia for breakfast whenever he wants.' Cousin Habib sighed. 'Rumour has it that Regan's Nancy has a fancy for him.'

Chambail Chacha lifted the barrier and the jeep went through and stopped in front of the management offices that were located around the back of the ice factory. The Sheikh stepped out. His armed escort jumped out and stood around him. One of the men standing close to the Sheikh was unarmed and dressed like a Pir, a Holy Man. He had shoulder-length black matted hair and a thick wild beard. His kurta was made of a patchwork of old cloth. A green scarf dangled off his shoulders. A thick loose turban sat on his head. He held prayer beads in his right hand, which swayed to and fro. He took two cigars out of a packet, gave one to the Sheikh, put the other into his own mouth, flicked a cigarette lighter and offered the first light to the Sheikh. The Sheikh brushed the keffiyeh back over his shoulders, bent forward, lit the cigar and surveyed the surroundings, blowing a plume of smoke out of his mouth. He nodded an acknowledgement towards Cousin Habib and me.

'Pirs of Pindi smoke Cuban cigars,' I said to Cousin Habib under my breath.

'Some say he is from France. Others say he is from your country,' Cousin Habib whispered, stepping towards the Pir.

The armed guards looked suspiciously at us. Chambail Chacha had slowly made his way closer to us.

'Such is life, Chambail Chacha,' the Pir said to him in Pushto.

Chambail Chacha bowed respectfully and moved away a little. As the Pir shook Cousin Habib's hand, the Sheikh placed his own right hand on his chest, bowed respectfully and walked off towards Duraid Shah's office, leaving behind him a trail of cigar smoke.

The Pir asked in Urdu, 'Why so much sadness in your eyes today, Habib Saab?'

'French Holy Men smoke cigars in Pindi and we watch chickens being fed,' Cousin Habib said.

'And would an American Pir be more to your taste, sir?' the Pir said in English with an American accent, offering me a cigar.

I refused the cigar.

'Saleem Saab, it is rude to refuse a gift,' the Pir said in Queen's English.

I was taken aback by the fact that he knew my name and I replied, trying not to betray my feelings, 'I dislike their taste, Pir Saab.'

Cousin Habib stepped forward and took the cigar. The Pir smiled at me, bowed humbly and said, 'Pir Daniel J. Steigler at your service, Saleem Saab. And you may call me Pir if you be so pleased.' Throwing his head up towards the sky, the Pir said, 'And such are the ways of the Almighty. Fate never lets the believer down. Soon, very soon, Insha'Allah, very soon, the Red invaders are going to learn a lesson of history. No one can conquer the Afghans.' After saying this, the Pir walked off in the same direction as the Sheikh.

Cousin Habib had emptied the contents of the chicken feed and was crumpling the bag when Chambail Chacha came up to us and said, 'Saleem Saab, you are new here and you don't know, sir, that you can't trust anyone in this place. Look how quickly the cockerel has adjusted here. But the last one, the one stolen from me, that I raised since it hatched, was better. And may God punish the bastards who took him.'

Cousin Habib looked away. I was filled with shame and fidgeted with some coins in my pocket.

I suspected Chambail Chacha thought I was somehow connected to the disappearance of his cockerel but never made a direct reference to this. He was a thin, sixty-year-old man, who was usually chewing on a paan or sucking on snuff. He was forever turning around, sometimes in mid-sentence, to spit out the residue of whatever was in his mouth. If it was paan, it came out like a jet stream and left a red splodge on the ground; and if it was snuff, it came out in a small ball. He turned to some chickens behind him and expelled a reddish jet of spit, then said, 'Do you call that a cockerel? Look at him.'

I looked at the cockerel while Chambail Chacha refilled his mouth. It was standing on its own, looking nervously around.

'Punjabi cokker,' Chambail Chacha hissed.

'Why Punjabi?' I asked.

'Do you think a Pathan cockerel could be like that, when so many beautiful chickens are around?' Chambail Chacha asked.

'Does that cockerel speak Punjabi, Chambail Chacha?' I asked.

'The motherfucker does not speak or do anything he is meant to do. Not even what you call a baang. But come, let us go and pray. It is time,' Chambail Chacha said. The loud-speakers of the mosques had burst into life.

'Not today, Chambail Chacha,' I said.

'Ah, you Englishmen, you only turn to God when you are old and good for nothing. Until then you have your hooris, eh, Saleem Saab?' he winked.

'Chambail Chacha, for a moment I thought I saw years fly off your face!' I said.

Chambail Chacha stood up, spat on the ground, laughed and went to pray, slapping me on the shoulder as he went past. Just as he stepped over a small puddle of water, a motorcycle backfired somewhere on the road beyond the barriers.

When Cousin Habib and I got to Duraid Shah's office there was a note on his desk for us to meet him in The Royal Club.

It was early evening. There was a beautiful cool wind rustling through the leaves of the tree-lined avenue. The tall poplars, the base of their trunks painted white, led to the foyer of The Royal Club. It was a large hall with a bar in one corner. A huge chandelier hung from the ceiling in the centre of the foyer. Some ageing deer heads were fixed to the walls, along with a few ceremonial swords, Scottish bagpipes and some kilts. We followed the notices for the 'Private Party', not that we needed to as there were armed Mujahideen standing at intervals in the rooms leading to the snooker table.

Groups of Mujahideen milled around the snooker room. Thick plumes of cannabis hung in the air. Kalashnikovs were neatly placed in the corner. The snooker-playing commanders wore Afghan hats and had their shalvars above their ankles, revealing their Nike trainers.

'The little fat long-haired bastard with the kind smile is Commander Zaman.' Cousin Habib stepped out of earshot of the snooker players and said to me, 'He is Gul's main man here.'

We leaned against the wall and watched the snooker match.

Zaman eyed up the cue ball for a while, aiming to pocket a red at the far end of the table. The red ball was perched on the edge of the left corner pocket. He lifted his leg, put his stomach on the table and bent forward awkwardly, checking the angle of the cue ball in relation to the red. One of his feet was just touching the ground, the other half of him on the table. He pushed himself off and walked around the table doing mental calculations; he went to the red and eyed up the cue ball from its position. He chalked the cue and then placed his hand on the table and spread his fingers. He took aim and struck the cue ball to the applause of the sycophants. The cue ball missed the red, but the force of it touching the cushion so close to it made the red drop. He turned towards us and waved a hand towards a table overflowing with food, took another shot and missed again.

Along with a few bottles of whisky, American beer was chilling in buckets of ice all along the floor at the base of the table. Putting my hand into the icy water, I pulled out two beer bottles. I was rummaging around the table for a bottle opener when I heard a familiar accent.

'Bah gum me ol' flower. As yer sen this? Is owt more noble then suppin' from the bucket of those destined for paradise?' The Pir emerged from amidst the throng of dope-smoking Mujahideen. Shaking my hand, the Pir said, 'Duraid Shah told me you were from Bradford. He sends his apologies for being late. He is doing something for the Sheikh, but please enjoy.'

Cousin Habib opened a bottle of beer with his teeth and passed it to me as I laughed and asked the Pir, 'Pir Saab, tell me, are you French or British or American?'

The Pir said in English with a French accent, 'Could a Frog speak broad Yorkshire, like?' He switched to an American one, 'And we Yanks would not know the difference between "by" and "bah",' he laughed.

I was searching for an appropriate reply when loud Pushto music burst into life outside. The Mujahideen let out a joyous roar.

The Pir turned around and followed by the Mujahideen went outside. Cousin Habib bit open another bottle of beer and passed it to me. 'You'll crack your teeth,' I cringed.

Biting open the next beer bottle, he mumbled, 'Punjabi!'

'Something big is happening here,' I said.

'Something big happens here every night,' Cousin Habib said.

'I think we should not drink too much,' I said.

'No. You are right, cousin,' Cousin Habib said, downing the bottle.

Duraid Shah came in followed by four burqa-clad women, who walked gracefully into the room. As though to command, they took their veils off and tossed them in the corner onto a double settee. Two of the women had plaited hair, one had hers tied in a knot at the back of her head and the fourth had her hair loose. They wore silver bells on their hennaed ankles. Two of them wore ankle-length red skirts with gold stripes and the others were also dressed in multi-coloured skirts. Their tops seemed tightly glued to their bodies. They looked around the room, making eye contact with everyone. They stepped out of their shoes, placing their adorned feet onto the ground and bent slowly down, showing their cleavages. They touched the ground with their hands, kissed their hands, touched their foreheads with the tips of their fingers and walked past us out into the garden. A moment or so later there were shouts of approval, interspersed with celebratory gunfire.

'It is a merciful God indeed who forgives this,' I said.

'Saleem Saab, you sin all the time just for pleasure,' the Pir said. 'But tonight is the last night on this earth for many of these boys. And tonight you have had the honour of seeing our Martyrs' Brigade. Tomorrow they will be in paradise. Today they have whores, tomorrow hooris. No sin can they commit that can impede their entry into Paradise. Such is the promise for us jihadis.' He was standing behind me. Two armed Mujahideen stood behind him. I had not seen him arrive.

The Pir glared at me for a moment and then went into a room behind me.

Duraid Shah was about to follow the women out when Cousin Habib bit a bottle open and passed it to him.

'That was a pretty stupid thing to say, Saleem Khan, stupid,' Duraid Shah said sternly.

'It just came out,' I laughed, trying to make light of the incident.

The music stopped.

One of the Mujahideen was called into the room to which the Pir had gone. He opened the door a few moments later and the Sheikh stepped out majestically. His shining cowboy boots clicked on the marble floor. He was closely followed by Pir Daniel J. Steigler and a Colonel P, from the Inter-service Intelligence of Pakistan. I had seen Colonel P leaving Duraid Shah's office once or twice. He had a round brown face with a flat nose, under which was a neatly cut moustache. He had straight black hair which was perfectly parted in the centre of his head. He scanned me with his cold piercing eyes.

The three men nodded at us. We stood up and shook hands with them. As they walked away the Pir said, 'And I, too, am answerable for the Stingers.'

'It is my men who are being martyred because of you not honouring your promise, Mr Steigler,' the Sheikh said.

The Pir said to the Colonel, 'Colonel P, this is a very serious matter and needs to be resolved quickly. The Stingers cannot just disappear.'

'I am looking into this, sir,' Colonel P replied, looking suspiciously at us.

The Sheikh smiled and clapped his hands. One of the Mujahideen and Duraid Shah went out. A little while later, the music started again. Cousin Habib and I stood around in uncomfortable silence until Duraid Shah came back with the dancer with the loose hair. She bowed respectfully to the Sheikh and went into a room, closing the door behind her. The Sheikh stood up, waved his hand over the table and nodded to us as he followed.

As the Sheikh shut the door, Cousin Habib said, 'And may I be punished with the sins of the Sheikh.'

The Pir and Colonel P took a beer each and went outside.

Duraid Shah knocked back two very large vodkas in quick succession and a short while later started to predict, sorrowfully, that soon the Soviet Union would be defeated and the Americans and their Pirs would leave Pakistan, at least till the next Afghan surprise.

'What about Kala, my driver?' Cousin Habib asked Duraid Shah. 'The bastard has six children. They'll be at the Adda soon.'

Duraid Shah looked at me bewildered. 'So I will have to go for Murree vodka, then. But who can say that the Peshawar water damage can be repaired? There was dhal on my plate once and Chambail Chacha's bastard cockerel knocked my whisky bottle off the table and smashed it.'

Cousin Habib and Duraid Shah were now engaged in a deep conversation about Chambail Chacha's cockerel and I went out onto the lawn. The air was filled with the overpowering scent of the flowers of the queen-of-the-night. I leaned against a tree and stood at the back of a large gathering of Mujahideen. The Pir, along with Commander Zaman, was on the stage. A dozen or so young men wearing green headbands stood to attention in front of him. The atmosphere was pregnant with expectation.

The Pir walked forward and spoke into the microphone. He started with an Arabic prayer for the martyrs and then said a few words in Pushto before switching into Urdu, 'I bring you the blessing of Ronald Reagan, the President of the United States of America. He has sent this message: "You gentlemen, you who have taken up the sword of freedom are the moral equivalents of America's founding fathers. I have met with freedom fighters and a brave man whose wife was killed in front of his two children. And someone who lost his brother in a tunnel in a village in which 105 people were massacred. The free world is watching what is going on in Afghanistan. We have seen Afghans massacred at weddings, villages and cities bombed from the air, and the throats of babies slit by the claws of that bear. I promise you, in the name of the people of America, we will stand by you in your march to freedom and in years to come we will be there with you to ensure your blood has not been spilt in vain. May God bless you in your Jihad against the foreign invaders. America salutes you!"'

The Pir paused. His words echoed around the grounds. He waved towards the young men with green headbands and said, 'The blood of these martyrs will free the world of tyranny. You who are about to embrace martyrdom, I salute you.' The young men responded with chants of 'Allah O Akbar'. Soon the grounds resounded to this chant. A few guns were fired into the air. The Pir pointed behind the audience where the Sheikh was now standing. He was accompanied by Colonel P. The chanting got louder. The Mujahideen spectators moved apart, leaving a clear path to the stage for the Sheikh, who took slow deliberate steps forward, his keffiyeh lifted softly by the wind.

Taking the microphone from the Pir, the Sheikh recited a prayer in Arabic. Cameras flashed. The Sheikh turned to the men on the stage and said, 'From every drop of your blood will rise an army of martyrs. Enjoy your last night on this earth and look forward to an eternity of peace.' The Sheikh embraced and kissed each of the young men on the stage, saying, 'And the Almighty bless you with martyrdom and drive the occupiers from Muslim lands.'

I had seen enough and wanted to go home to my flat. Duraid Shah was stooped over, empty glass in hand, snoring. Cousin Habib was mumbling something passionately to him.

The next morning, Duraid Shah phoned us in the Adda. There was an issue over the delivery by driver Kala. Not only had the truck turned up late, but it had also broken down in Bannu. We weighed our options. We were not keen on going to the tribal belts of the North-West Frontier Province. They were unsafe badlands at the best of times and at that moment, with so much fighting across the border in Afghanistan, they had become extremely dangerous. On the other hand, we were duty bound to go and sort out the problems of our driver. Duraid Shah gave us a new order to deliver two more trucks to the Jamaat compound in Charsadda, Peshawar.

The journey to Charsadda was a two-hour drive. I sat in the beautifully decorated cabin of a Bedford truck, listening to Pushto songs. Next to me was a small boy in stained clothes who continuously lit cigarettes for the driver, a big fat man with a multicoloured cap on his wild curly-haired head, swearing at anyone who overtook him, pressing on his deafening pressure horn and singing along with the songs in between.

The inside was padded soft leather and painted with gold-coloured flowers. Tassels and small bells jingled to the movement of the truck. Cousin Habib climbed into the open-air cabin at the top of the truck and tried to sleep, every now and then banging and shouting down for the music to be turned down. The driver ignored him.

The compound we were going to was on the side of the GT road. A number of trucks from our Adda had come here for deliveries, but this was my first visit. An outer wall, where regular armed guards sat in the flimsy shade of eucalyptus trees, ran for a few miles just off the GT road. Our driver parked the truck in the shade of a building alongside a convoy of vehicles flying the flags of the Jamaat. Not far from us, in a classroom, a European man was giving instructions to attentive students on how to dismantle a weapon. Teams of young men were undergoing military exercises in a huge yard. Convoys of other organisations, with their respective flags fluttering in the wind, were parked around the exercise yard. A man wearing khaki shorts with the emblem of the US on each buttock walked past us, stopping to take photographs every now and then.

Cousin Habib and I got out and the truck moved off into the compound. A young Mujahid was waiting for us and he led us to a car where another man was waiting for us with blindfolds.

'You have to put these on,' he said.

'No,' I said. 'Those American's don't.'

He pointed the barrel of a Kalashnikov at me. 'Put these on.'

'I am not going anywhere,' I said, turning away from him.

The other one cocked a pistol.

'You will cover your eyes and get in the car,' the Mujahid with the Kalashnikov said. 'We have little time.'

'Just do it, yaar,' Cousin Habib said. 'Let's get Kala and go home.'

We drove blindfolded for a few hours along dirt roads. Hot air burnt my nose and I could taste the dust. We came to a stop by the side of a mountain, where our blindfolds were taken off. Kala's truck was parked nearby. It was fully loaded. Commander Zaman was giving instructions to a group of Mujahideen by drawing on the ground with a twig. The Mujahid with the pistol stayed with us while the other went up to Commander Zaman and whispered something in his ear; he looked at us, nodded and waved for us to come over.

'And soon the Kafir will feel the wrath of those destined for Paradise,' Commander Zaman smiled, shaking his shoulder-length hair as we got closer. He had fiery eyes. Adjusting his Afghan cap, he said quietly, 'May the Almighty bless you for taking the trouble to come out here.' He pulled chilled bottles of Coca-Cola out of a cooler, gave them to us and said, 'Drink, the journey ahead is long.'

'Commander Zamanji,' Cousin Habib said, nodding back at the truck, 'we don't actually load the truck, as you know. We only give a bilti for it, but it seems to be still fully loaded. What is the problem?'

128

'We need a trusted driver,' Commander Zaman said.

'Where is Kala, the driver?' Cousin Habib asked.

'He went to help the Mujahideen but was captured by the infidels.'

Cousin Habib threw me a worried look, thought for a while and asked, 'Is he alive?'

'Life and death are in his hands,' Commander Zaman said, pointing upwards. 'But death is sometimes better than life for those who are captured by the Kafir.'

His voice became cold. His eyes tightened. The car that had brought us here went back. Commander Zaman waved at the Mujahideen, who scrambled around quickly collecting things and boarded the truck.

'May the Almighty protect you on your mission,' I said. 'We came to inspect the truck, and as everything is in order we will take your leave and go back.'

Cousin Habib was frozen to the ground. He clearly understood things I didn't.

'We have no driver for this truck,' Commander Zaman said.

'I cannot drive a truck,' I said.

'He can,' Commander Zaman nodded to Cousin Habib, 'and you can carry.'

A Mujahid was standing by the passenger door waiting for us to get in.

'Cousin, keep your mouth shut. This is not Valaiti,' Cousin Habib said. 'Just get in.'

We had only driven a short distance when we were joined by four jeeps with flags of different Mujahid organisations. Our convoy drove silently along rocky tracks and somewhere crossed the Durand Line into Afghanistan. The Jeeps split into two different groups and went off along different dirt roads. We went on for a few miles and when the dirt road ended were met by men with mules.

Commander Zaman opened my door and said as the guard jumped out, 'God will reward you for your courage.'

'We have done all you asked, Commander Saab,' I said. Cousin Habib dug his nails into the side of my leg and I stopped mid-sentence.

'I would not wish to see you martyred here,' Commander Zaman said, turning away.

When Commander Zaman was out of earshot, Cousin Habib hissed, 'I've told you. Keep quiet. Can't you see all those men loading the mules? Do you think they don't want to go home?'

I kept my composure the best I could and watched the mules being loaded. We were given a rucksack each to carry. Commander Zaman smirked as he went past us. When he was out of earshot, Cousin Habib whispered in my ear, 'The bastard is making us carry the explosives.' He could see I was terrified and added, 'But don't worry—this is their most valuable thing. They will protect us.'

'Why are they making *us* carry them, then?' I asked.

'Just in case they go off. They don't want to lose fighters, do they?'

We walked on a path along a ridge carved out of the side of the mountain, below us a greenish-blue river. An eagle circled above us. It swooped below us towards the river, changed its mind and went back up again, soaring as before against a beautiful blue tranquillity.

There was some distance between the main body of the fighters and Cousin Habib and me. Two armed men were behind us. We must have walked for more than an hour when we were ordered to stop. I was exhausted. I rested my ruck-sack against the side of the mountain and went a few yards further on to rest.

Cousin Habib used his as a pillow and said, 'Stop worrying about it going off. You'll only feel a buzzing and hear a bang.'

I did not answer him and watched a man from the main group of fighters. He was a tall strong man with a bow and arrow. He took aim at a tree on the other side of the ravine. The arrow flew across. A string was tied to it. It snaked after the arrow. Someone on the other side pulled the string. It got thicker and thicker until a nylon rope was pulled over to the other side. Tied to the rope were thicker ropes. The eagle flew down, went under the rope and flew back up again. Slowly, a rope bridge began to get wrenched into place.

Waiting for everyone to cross, I thought back to how Carol and I had walked across a rope bridge in Kalam. She had laughed and cried with fear when we were halfway across and it was moving from side to side. Her voice was drowned out by the roaring waters of the river below. Once on the other side, we had gone to a hotel where the tables were set by the cold waters of a mountain stream.

I closed my eyes and dreamt of Carol. 'You should be home with me,' she was saying. 'You don't belong in all that chaos. Just come home.'

Someone kicked my foot and said, 'You can go home to sleep when you've finished.'

Before I stepped onto the bridge, a nylon rope was tied round my waist.

'See, even if the bridge collapses, they won't let you fall,' Cousin Habib smirked, stepping in front of me. He turned around and said, looking down, 'And don't look down.'

Holding tightly to the sides of the ropes, I stepped gingerly out. The bridge moved to and fro each time I took a step forward. My heart pounded in my chest with each gust of wind. Sweat gushed down my back. Cousin Habib let out a big sigh when I stepped off the bridge at the far end.

On the other side, the fighters split into smaller groups which went along separate tracks. We went up and down so many mountain tracks that each new track looked much like the one before. The path we were on suddenly came to a dead end amidst some bushes on the mountainside. The mules in front of us kept moving forward, unconcerned by the fact that the path was blocked and there was no way for them to turn around without falling into the river way down below us to our right. As we got closer, the bushes were pulled apart and the path led into a cave. Inside the cave, the mules were unloaded and the Mujahideen took their packs and went deeper into a number of tunnels.

Commander Zaman came out of one of the tunnels and said, 'Our destination is not far from here. We are going to liberate one of the main camps of the Russian 40th Army. God willing, we are going to capture camp Jalalabad and slaughter the infidels so that they understand why this will become the occupiers' graveyard. As the Sheikh says, we will bleed the bastards to death.'

We followed Commander Zaman through a labyrinth of tunnels, some natural, others man-made. We crawled up a slippery path towards some light and squeezed out through a narrow opening crisscrossed by roots and came out on the side of a rocky hill covered in wild bushes. From the outside, it was impossible to see the tunnel from which we had come.

The Russian camp was clearly visible below, set in a dusty clearing away from the hillside. Though it was faint and muffled by the wind, I could hear music from the direction of camp. As my eyes adjusted to the light, I could see there were many men with rockets aimed at the camp. The Pir was lying on his stomach looking down through a pair of binoculars. He beckoned me towards him. I crawled in his direction, holding my breath. He passed me the binoculars and I focused them on two Russian soldiers dancing outside the main gate, behind destroyed tanks.

Two Mujahideen fighters looked through the telescopic sights of their rifles. They adjusted their sights ever so slightly.

'Rock 'n' Roll,' ordered the Pir.

Two shots rang out, one after the other. Bullets streaked towards the dancing soldiers. A moment later, one dropped to the ground, then the other.

'Wow, the prototype M90 is a babe,' the Pir said, punching the air. 'Rock 'n' Roll!'

Amidst chants of 'Allah O Akbar', the hills boomed into life as rockets and missiles shot out and rained down on the camp.

The pounding from the mountainside suddenly stopped. Waves of men carrying rockets and guns emerged out of the sand near the camp and ran towards it discharging their weapons. An eternity or so later, a roar of 'Allah O Akbar' rang out from the hills as the Mujahideen flags went up in the camp. Every now and then there was a burst of small arms fire. The air was filled with the smell of battle.

Vultures flew high above the camp. One landed not far from me.

Cousin Habib was holding his hands over his ears and staring down at the camp, a ghostly look on his face. The Pir stood up, nodded to us to follow and hopped effortlessly down over the rocks.

We had cleared the hills and were out in the open. Bullets ripped into the ground all around us. A plume of smoke rose from behind the broken wall of the camp. A Russian tank crashed through the wall. It turned its barrel in our direction. I could hear Cousin Habib shouting something. I turned around and saw him coming at me, running out of the dark mountainside behind. He flew at me screaming, 'Down cousin, down!' He pushed my head into the hot sand. We rolled over and slid down a small incline. A missile went past me and slammed into the tank. The tank stopped moving. Thick black smoke began pouring out of it. A burning soldier crawled out. He fell to the ground. The tank exploded.

'I couldn't move, Habib,' I said. 'I just couldn't.'

'Ssh! Keep still.'

We stayed as still as we could until the fighting stopped. Commander Zaman marched up to us, threw a spade into the ground, nodded towards two dead men nearby and said, 'Bury them.' Turning to Cousin Habib, he said, 'You saved his life. We could do with men like you.'

'It is my duty,' Cousin Habib said.

'We need more trained men like you,' Commander Zaman said. Turning to me, he laughed, 'And in England don't they teach you not to put your chest out to a Russian tank?'

'I didn't ask you to bring me, and I am . . .' I said, clenching my fists in anger.

Cousin Habib pressed my hand. Commander Zaman turned towards the camp, saying, 'Hurry up with your supplies and lose the spade.'

We took turns digging and made a ditch just big enough for the bodies to fit in, and as quickly as we could we covered them with whatever rocks and stones we could find. Burying the dead, I said to Cousin Habib, 'I owe you my life.'

'What is it with you Britishers?' Cousin Habib said, patting down the sand into the shape of a grave, 'you have to insult a brother for doing what he should.'

'You could have died,' I said.

'For a moment I became a soldier again,' Cousin Habib said.

'You are so brave,' I said. 'Not like me.'

'Inside, I am scared, cousin. Really, really scared! I just want to go home. I want out of this hell, but we can't without these bastards telling us to.' Helping me with my rucksack, Cousin Habib said, 'I should never have got you into all this. You had a good life in England.'

'I didn't know it would come to this,' I said.

'Cousin, you westerners are not meant to die in this war,' Cousin Habib said.

Two vultures were perched on the outer walls of the camp while their comrades swarmed overhead. An emaciated dog stared greedily at the broken remains of a soldier. Cousin Habib held his nose as we stepped through the stench of burning flesh and over a charred body. We went into the camp and our rucksacks were taken off us.

The smell of explosives and burnt flesh hung in the air as a hot wind blew sand into our eyes. We stepped into the dust storm and came out in a square courtyard of the camp.

Some buildings were smouldering, others had been completely gutted. Inside the courtyard, white paint on the ground marked out a rectangular football pitch with goal posts at either end. The body of a short dark man dangled off one of the posts. The Mujahideen were throwing the naked bodies of Russian soldiers on top of each other into a big pile in the centre of the football field. A vulture swooped down, pecked at a body and then jumped out of the way as another corpse was tossed onto the heap.

Nodding to the body, Habib whispered, 'Kala.'

Two Mujahiden holding a naked dead soldier by the ankles dragged the body past us, his guts spilling out. Cousin Habib sat down and vomited.

'You wouldn't be so upset if you went to the village of Kana-khel. The Russians even killed the chickens there, roasted the elders, pissed on young dead men and took all the pretty women,' said one of the Mujahideen who was dragging the soldier past Cousin Habib.

A gust of wind blew open a door near to us. A human head still wearing spectacles, the eyes wide open, rolled out in front of us. The glasses were tied to the back of the head with a cord. I too vomited.

'This is the fate that awaits all invaders,' said Commander Zaman, coming up behind me and kicking the head towards the pile of bodies. Placing his hand on my shoulder, he said, 'The best way to get over this is to slit a Russian throat.'

I cried.

'This is war, Saleem Khan, holy war,' Commander Zaman said.

We went a few yards further and turned right past a burnt-out building. A woman wearing a multicoloured skirt but naked from the waist upwards was being pushed towards us by a Mujahid, who prodded her with his rifle each time she slowed down. She held her arms across her breasts. A bed

136

sheet was sticking out of the remains of a window close to us. I snatched the sheet and shouted to the woman, 'Here, take this.' She looked back at me with defeated eyes. Her face was stained with blood and dirt. Her hair was matted. I stepped towards her. The Mujahid who was pushing her turned towards me, let out a burst of fire into the ground in front of me and said, 'She is ours.'

Cousin Habib snatched the sheet from me and ran forward screaming, 'Shoot *me*, you bastard!'

Commander Zaman placed his hand on the Mujahid's weapon and whispered something. Both of them laughed. Cousin Habib held the sheet out for the woman. She took the sheet, turned around, spread the cloth on the ground, lay down on her back and pulled her skirt up. Cousin Habib gripped my arm with his trembling hand.

I thought of Carol at the airport as she was leaving Pakistan. I should have said I love you, I thought. I don't want to die here, not here, Carol. I don't belong here. I should have listened to you and gone with you. I have a house and a life. What am I doing in this hellhole?

Cousin Habib let go of me, held his face in his hands and wept. He went up to the woman, wrapped the sheet around her and helped her to her feet. She looked at me with vacant eyes and said something in Pushto.

Cousin Habib said, 'She asks if you knew what her mother's cow gave birth to?'

Before I could reply, Commander Zaman said, 'We do not have time to discuss with whores of Ruskies what cows give birth to. The commanders are waiting for us.'

'What do I say to her?' Cousin Habib asked.

'It was a female,' I said.

He told her. She smiled as the Mujahid pushed her to follow Commander Zaman, who went and sat behind a desk next to another commander. Behind the commanders, men stood guard holding the flags of their respective organisations. The Pir snapped photographs of a pile of watches, wallets and other valuables. Colonel P surveyed a stockpile of weapons and ammunition casings which was continuously added to by the Mujahideen. The Pir sat down to take a close-up of a wristwatch. Commander Zaman pointed us towards two chairs. We sat down. An overturned box was placed in front of us and two glasses of juice were put on it. The juice was the colour of blood.

A young Russian soldier was dragged in front of the commanders. The Pir turned and photographed the soldier. The soldier was bleeding from the left leg. He waved a photograph towards the commanders, who looked at each other and nodded. A Mujahid pushed the soldier back, who said, stumbling, 'Baby.'

The Pir stepped close to the soldier, looked at the photograph and said, 'Very pretty wife as well, you Ruskie pig.'

The soldier smiled nervously. The Pir nodded at the commanders and someone tossed the soldier a bandage. The soldier put the photograph in his pocket and tied the bandage around his bleeding leg.

The Pir, accompanied by Colonel P, came up to us and said, 'Gentlemen, drink this first-class pomegranate juice. Drink to the glory of the coming of the Mujahideen. Drink and observe how this evil empire is bleeding to death here in the quicksands of Afghanistan. The graveyard of empires.' He paused and glared at the commanders who were arguing passionately with each other. Their respective fighters pointed

138

their weapons at each other. Colonel P, and the Pir clinked their glasses and the Pir said, downing a glass of juice, 'It is always like this when they find a woman.' He paused for more juice and said, 'They will settle the distribution of the weapons and the booty after a bit of good old-fashioned bargaining, but when it comes to women they can easily get into a fight,' he laughed. 'Such is the way of the warrior.'

Suddenly a fierce dust storm sent sand grains stinging into my face. Colonel P gave an order to the commanders and the guns were lowered. Commander Zaman emerged from the dust storm and said, pointing to the heap of dead bodies, 'Russian mothers will know what fate awaits the invaders of Muslim lands.'

Commander Zaman did not wait for any reply but turned around and left. The dust storm was getting stronger when the Pir indicated we should leave. Cousin Habib looked as though he was in a trance. I held his hand and we followed the Pir and Colonel P. Four Mujahideen escorted us out of the gate. One of them held a rope tied to the neck of the Russian soldier, who limped along as best he could. The woman, now wearing a Russian shirt, walked in front of the soldier. The Sheikh, accompanied by a dozen or so men on horseback, raced by and melted into the hills. By the time we reached the foot of the hills, it was just getting dark. The Pir raised his hand and we stopped. The wind lashed the bushes. The Pir tilted his head and listened to the wind, which carried a faint mechanical noise.

'Helicopter gunships,' Cousin Habib whispered to me.

The Russian soldier pointed to his mouth. His lips were parched. The Pir gave him some water and asked, 'M11 or M14?'

The soldier took a few gulps of water lowered his eye, showed his photograph to the Pir and said, 'Pretty daughter. Two. Very pretty.'

'M11 or M14?' the Pir asked again, listening to the wind.

'M14,' the soldier replied meekly.

The Pir took the photograph from the soldier, looked at it and returned it to him, saying, 'Very pretty.'

The soldier smiled. The Pir nodded to Colonel P and snatched the tag from around the soldier's neck. The Pir shot the soldier in the head with his pistol, saying, 'We have less than five minutes to get away.'

At first they looked like black dots, just like vultures. Then I could see the outlines of the M14 helicopter gunships. Four of them were flying towards the camp. Two MIG fighters boomed overhead. A moment later the camp lit up in flames. Three of the gunships shot into the camp and the fourth came at us.

The Pir grabbed Colonel P by the shoulder and said, 'Look Colonel, look at the fate of our Mujahideen. If we only had those Stinger missiles we gave you. Where are they now when we need them?'

Colonel P looked sheepishly away.

'Now *move!*' The Pir ordered.

Oblivious to the thorns, we scrambled up the hill with the roar of the gunship getting louder and louder and slid into a hole through an opening hidden by rocks. Two of the Mujahideen led; two remained behind to guard the entrance. The ceiling of the tunnel was so low that it cut into my head each time I raised it a little. We crawled as fast as we could. The ground was jagged in places, slippery in others and water dripped on our heads. We came out into a wide opening close to a pool of water. The two Mujahideen who had led the way overturned a rock, pulled out some plastic, wrapped their weapons in it, jumped into the pool and disappeared. I was waiting for them to come back out of the water when Commander Zaman emerged from it.

The Mujahideen who had stayed behind came running in. One of them was holding a detonator and the other wires. The barking of dogs echoed through the tunnel. Pointing to the pool, Commander Zaman said, 'Take a deep breath and go towards the light.'

'Cousin Habib can't swim,' I said.

'He can walk, it's not deep,' Commander Zaman said.

The barking of the dogs got louder as the Pir stepped into the pool. Commander Zaman took hold of the woman by the hand and led her into the pool. Cousin Habib and I took a deep breath and followed. I could see no light. Cousin Habib tried to pull me back, but I dragged him forward. The ground underneath me gave way and we fell into deeper water. The ground shook to the sound of an explosion behind us. I could see some light ahead. People were shining torches into the water.

On the other side of the water, the cave opened up. A river ran through the middle. We boarded three canoes and raced downstream, ducking under ridges, hands stopping us crashing against the walls, until we came to a larger cave. A rope net prevented the canoes from going any further.

The cave was well lit, powered by a generator. Light from dangling bulbs bounced off the water and flickered around us. There were men with weapons everywhere. The inside had been cut and carved so that sleeping quarters were dotted around all over the place. We were led towards some curtains, behind which blankets had been spread out on the ground on top of some rugs. I lay down and fell asleep.

When I woke up, a Mujahid was standing nearby, his thumbs tucked into the sides of a chain of bullets that crossed his chest. I asked him, 'Are we in Pakistan?'

'Deep in the heart of the earth, where the Kafir can't find us,' he said. 'Come outside and join us in celebrating this historic victory.'

Four musicians were sitting and playing on a platform made out of slates. The Pir and Colonel P were sipping vodka and chatting to Commander Zaman who was smoking a hooka. Groups of men perched on whatever support they could find, drinking tea and sharing hookas. The air was thick with the smell of cannabis. Cousin Habib and I followed Commander Zaman and sat close to the Pir and Colonel P The Pir poured two shots of vodka for us. Cousin Habib shook his head.

The Pir said, 'One would think we were enemies.'

We took the vodka and sipped it.

The cave began to resonate to shouts of joy. The woman from the camp was walking towards the stage. She was dressed in bright clean clothes, her hair neatly plaited. A green dupatta was pinned to the back of her hair. She looked blankly in our direction and bowed. Red lipstick shone on her lips and her eyes were decorated with eyeliner. She walked gracefully towards the makeshift stage.

'What a prize you got, Commander Zaman,' the Pir said.

Commander Zaman raised his hand, lowered his head in gratitude and said, 'If we had had the Stingers, we would have lost fewer men today.' He clapped his hands for the dance to begin.

The musicians bowed their heads respectfully and stopped. The drum player tightened the ropes on his drum and the one playing the harmonium lifted the lid off his instrument. The cave echoed to the chatter of voices and then the music suddenly broke out again. The woman began to dance to loud applause and cat calls.

As the dancing was reaching a climax, a young man came up and gave the Pir a piece of paper. It had a few lines of typed text on it, but the Pir stared at it for a long time and then said angrily to Colonel P, 'The Iranians have shot down one of our aircraft, Colonel, with a Stinger. The only Stingers unaccounted for are those we have given to the ISI.'

Commander Zaman's eyes lit up each time the word Stinger was mentioned, but as he did not understand English he quickly went back to smoking the hooka and enjoying the dance.

Colonel P lit a cigarette and inhaled deeply. His face turned pale. The Pir continued, 'How can a Stinger fall into Iranian hands, Colonel? How?'

'I don't know, sir,' Colonel P shook his head.

The Pir pointed a finger at Colonel P and said, 'Let us get the rules of the game straight, Colonel. We pay you. We need answers. All our weapons land at Karachi and you guys take direct control. They are taken to your base at Ojhri camp in Rawalpindi. You and you alone bring them to Peshawar, and you can't even pass the buck to the GHQ as you are answerable to General Zia himself.' Pointing to the piece of paper, he said, 'They know the Stingers were sold.'

Colonel P looked away from the Pir and did not answer.

The Pir, standing up, announced, 'I have to send a report immediately.' After the Pir left, Colonel P kicked Commander

Zaman on the sole of his foot and the latter immediately stood to attention.

'Choose your words with care next time,' Colonel P said.

'Ji, yes, sir,' Commander Zaman replied.

Colonel P went off in the direction of the Pir. After they left, Cousin Habib turned his back on the dancer and said, 'I can't watch her do this.'

'What was all that about Stingers and Iranians?' I asked Cousin Habib.

'I went to see her when you were asleep. Her name is Gulzarina. She comes from a village fifty miles south of Kabul. The Russians captured her and her sister four years ago, or maybe five. Her sister shot a Russian officer with his own gun as he was getting dressed and then she shot herself. Gulzarina had a husband, but he was killed in the Russian raid. She had been tending to her mother's cow when they were raided. She has a little sister as well. Gulzarina belongs to the Hizb for now. They paid a big price for her. They will use her until we get to Pakistan, where she says they have promised her she will be freed.' Cousin Habib looked around and whispered, 'She doesn't know Zaman has already sold her.'

A tray of naans and dried meat was put in front of us. As we were eating, Commander Zaman leaned over and said, 'You leave in half an hour.'

Three Mujahideen led us through a winding maze of tunnels and caves. We were blindfolded for the last leg of the journey through the caves. When we came out into the open, I felt the pleasant warmth of the sunlight on my face and was about to pull the blindfold off when one of the guards touched the barrel of his gun to my face and said, 'You will be told when to do that.'

We were loaded onto a truck soon after coming out of the caves. Once or twice, I tried to take off the blindfold but the prod of a gun stopped me. I tried to peep out from a slit at the bottom of the blindfold but could make no sense of where I was from the flashes of the green of trees or the rugged hillsides.

The blindfolds were removed when we got close to Peshawar. We were dropped off near the main bus station. Cousin Habib flagged down a rickshaw and said, getting into it, 'You go. I will be back as soon as I can.' I was looking for the bus to Rawalpindi when a rickshaw stopped in front of me, covering me in the fumes of its exhaust. Cousin Habib jumped out of it and asked, 'Do you have any money?'

I searched my pockets and shook my head. He gave me four 500-rupee notes and got back into the rickshaw, which then left the bus station.

I bought a bottle of mango juice from a stall close to a barber's shop. I was so thirsty I drank another mango juice before walking towards a row of shops. Here I bought some new shoes and a ready-made shalvar kameez and went to a barber's shop for a shave.

The shop was deceptively large on the inside. There were five chairs in front of four mirrors. Four of them were occupied. A pink bald man, who had just been shaved, was having oil rubbed into his head. Next to him a man with a fat wobbly face smoked a cigarette while a little boy lathered his face, stopping for the man to put his cigarette into his mouth and take it out again. On the other two chairs, men were having their hair cut. Looking at myself in the mirror, I realised why everyone was staring at me. My hair was covered in dust, my face was dirty, my clothes were stained and my eyes were bloodshot.

'I want a wash,' I said in Urdu, showing him my bag of clothes.

The owner of the shop was sitting behind a table reading a newspaper. He screwed up his eyes and said, 'This is not a mosque,' and went back to reading.

I showed him a 100-rupee note. He raised his eyebrows. A young boy with an old man's face popped out of somewhere, handed me a towel and asked, 'Shampoo, Saab?' I nodded. He gave me a small container of shampoo and led me to the back of the shop to a cubicle with a bucket. There was a bar of soap on a small wooden stool close to the bucket.

I sat down on the small wooden stool and threw some water over my head. Kala's dangling body flashed in front of my eyes. All sorts of faces, living and dead were going round and round in my head and no matter how hard I rubbed the soap into my hair they refused to leave me. I threw more and more water over me until the bucket was empty. I opened a small brass tap which stuck out of a mouldy wall and tried to re-fill the bucket. Just then the boy shouted from outside, 'One bucket per customer, uncle.'

I changed into the new clothes, left the old ones hanging on a nail on the door and sat silently through my shave, not recognising the man in the mirror, and then went back to the bus station where I caught a blue Lahore-bound bus. I got off on the GT road close to the Adda.

The Adda had not been swept since we had left and there was dust everywhere. My eyes suddenly felt heavy. My body ached and I slumped down on the mat on the floor. As soon as I closed my eyes, I could smell burning flesh and hear gun fire and explosions. I pushed myself up off the mat and after sweeping the floor, I went through all the accounts to make sure I was on top of the paperwork. I was still working when Cousin Habib came to the office.

'We promised to pay the stone-crushers over a month ago and have still not done so,' I said to Cousin Habib. He did not answer but disappeared into the back of the Adda and went to sleep. It took me four hours to get through all the paperwork and then I went out to get some kebabs.

When I came back with the kebabs, Cousin Habib woke up.

I opened the newspaper in which the kebabs were wrapped and placed them on the table. A fly came and sat down on a stain of grease in the newspaper.

'There are fifteen trucks that have not paid us,' I said, breaking a piece of kebab.

'They said her sister was in Pindi,' Cousin Habib said.

'And the payment from Duraid Shah is late,' I said, wrapping a piece of kebab into a roti and putting it in my mouth.

'If she is here, I will find her and take her to her mother,' Cousin Habib said, standing up. He rubbed his bloodshot eyes and pressed the temples of his head with his hand for a moment. His blue kurta was torn and stained.

'Have a shave and clean yourself up before you go,' I said.

He stared at the wall behind me and then quickly turned, snatched a cheque book out of a drawer and went out.

After he left, I went to the barber's and had another shave. Truck drivers came and went from the Adda. I told them we had no orders and made no attempt at having conversation beyond that which was necessary to get rid of them. Kala's wife came and squatted silently on the ground, waiting for me to give her some news about her husband. I ignored her and continued with my paperwork.

Cousin Habib came back the next day in the early evening. I was going over the figures for the umpteenth time. He stood at the entrance of the Adda. Behind him, life roared by up and down the GT road.

'I saw Kala's wife just now. I told her he was in Karachi. That's what I told her,' I said.

Cousin Habib sat down on a chair, lowered his head and cried. I poured a glass of water and held it out for him.

'I found her sister.'

'Whose?'

'Gulzarina's.'

'A hundred thousand congratulations, cousin!'

He looked at me and then lowered his heavy eyes.

Cousin Habib took the glass from me and sipped the water. The telephone rang. He grabbed the receiver. I heard a man's voice say hurriedly, 'Habib Saab, Gulzarina has arrived in Rawalpindi. She has been bought by the Gulmahari group.'

Throwing what remained of the water in his glass across the room, Cousin Habib said, 'I failed her. Her sister was sold. Her legs and arms were broken and she was made to beg.'

'Come on now, yaar, how do you know this? How do you know it is her sister?' I said, flicking the light on. There was load-shedding and no power.

'Many of the children that are bought in Afghanistan and brought here have the same done to them,' Cousin Habib said, pulling his legs up to his chest.

'Is that where you went last night?' I asked. 'Looking for a dancer's sister?'

Cousin Habib curled up even tighter.

148

'How many dancers have you seen, yaar?' I asked. 'They all have sisters.'

Cousin Habib sat up, 'I failed in my promise. I looked for her sister in all the bazaars. I have talked to the ghoondas and child smugglers and do you know what one of them said?'

I shook my head. Cousin Habib continued, 'He said, "Take any one you like! You can have one with one broken arm or two, smashed hands or sliced tongue or gouged-out eyes. Or I can make one to order. It is cheap in this war."'

Cousin Habib left before dawn. We had slept in the Adda again. By the time I woke, Yasmin and driver Kala's wife, along with his children, were waiting for me. They were sitting on the ground near a truck not far from the sewer. I gave her some money and told her to go away until I sent for her. Yasmin glared at me and then her eyes melted. She looked broken. She took the money but did not move. I wanted to tell Yasmin and her auntie that I had seen his dangling body. A part of me wanted to fall at their feet and beg for forgiveness for sending him to his death.

The fruit and vegetable market had already surged into life. I went to the barber's and had a shave and shower. As the barber rubbed the soap brush onto my face, I looked at the rising foam in the mirror and tried to work out what to do about Cousin Habib. My thoughts kept flickering back to the body dangling on the pole in the Russian camp. The head rolled by in the back of my mind. The barber put the radio on and started humming to an old Noor Jehan song. I thought of Gulzarina dancing in the cave. I closed my eyes and pushed the memories out of my head. Cousin Habib was paying no attention to the business and if this continued for a few more weeks, then we would lose the contract with Duraid Shah.

149

Maybe that would be a godsend. I could go back to England and send back some money for Cousin Habib so he could set up some other business.

When I came back to the Adda, Yasmin and Kala's wife and children were still there, just as I had left them.

'For God's sake, Yasmin, are you deaf?' I said to her. 'Go home and take her with you. I will send for her when I hear something.'

Yasmin looked at me, stony-faced.

'Go feed the children.' I stepped forward and handed Kala's wife a 50-rupee note.

She did not move. I gave her another 50 rupees. She gave that to the eldest boy. He ran off towards the market.

I went inside and phoned Duraid Shah. He spoke quickly, 'Yes, Habib did come to see me. I gave him some money, much less than he asked for. But I have it now. Shall I send it to you right away? There are lots of dancing girls here, Saleem Saab, lots and lots. Saleem Saab, this is Pakistan! Saleem Saab, go all the way to the link road, just past the dump where your trucks pick up from. Turn right, go down the hill for about three miles and past the old village until you see four houses on the right-hand side. Park the car there and go on foot to the camp of the Hizb. It is across the stream. You can't miss it.'

I put the receiver down and the phone rang immediately. The line was crackling. I said in Pothowari, 'Line is no good. I can't hear you. Phone later,' and put the receiver down. It rang again. Someone was shouting down the line, 'Hello, hello, Habib Saab. Speak louder—it is a bad line.'

'Habib is not here,' I shouted down the telephone.

I slammed the receiver down and it rang again. I picked it up and said, 'Ring later for God's sake—'

'Saleem! Is that you?' It was Carol.

'Oh, God, Carol, it's really a bad time to talk,' I said.

'Is there ever a good time for me?' Carol went quiet for a moment and then said, 'Just come home. I need you.'

'I went to Afghanistan . . .'

'You don't belong out there, you belong with me. I love you.'

A boy in bedraggled clothes said something to Kala's wife. Yasmin was staring at me with burning eyes. I looked away from her.

'You didn't tell me about the parking ticket, Saleem,' Carol said.

'What parking ticket?'

'Before I came to Pakistan, you got a ticket for speeding. Why didn't you just pay it? Now there's a warrant out for your arrest. I've paid the ticket but the warrant is still out.'

'I have to go now, Carol. I just can't talk,' I said, putting the receiver down. I went into the back of the Adda to pick up a folder with details about Kala. As I lifted the lid of the wooden trunk in which the records were kept, I heard a rumbling sound in the distance from the centre of Rawalpindi. It sounded like the collapse of a big hill. It was followed by the unmistakable sound of a massive explosion. I ran outside, past Yasmin and Kala's family.

'Bomb blast!' someone said, pointing to the sky. Rockets were snaking up from the centre of Rawalpindi.

I ran back to the Adda, rushed up some steps and went to the roof of the building and looked around. Traffic on the GT road had stopped. Dozens of missiles were going up, leaving behind plumes of smoke and snaking off in different directions. Some fell back down in fireballs. Others dropped a short distance away. One wriggled through the air towards us, screaming like a firework. There was a deafening explosion from one of the houses near a hotel at the back of the Adda. Duraid Shah's white Toyota Corolla pulled up behind driver Kala's wife. I went back down to the Adda. The telephone was ringing. I waved at the driver of the Corolla to come in and answered the telephone. The line was so crackly I could not make out who was on the other end.

'At your service, Saleem Saab,' Chambail Chacha said, walking into the Adda. Then he nodded outside and added, 'I will reverse the car.'

Chambail Chacha beeped the horn a few times in anger at driver Kala's wife who stood in front of the car staring at us, her children either side of her. The sky above her was filled with streaks of missiles and smoke from burning buildings. Chambail Chacha swore at her to move. She walked toward me, throwing down the money I had given her, screaming, 'Where is the father of my children?'

Chambail Chacha revved the car. I looked away from Kala's wife's impassioned eyes. She touched my chin, pulling my face towards her with rough cold fingers.

'Is he alive or dead?' she asked.

I looked into her dry eyes. Yasmin turned her back to me. Tears were burning in the corners of mine.

Chambail Chacha spat some residue from his mouth out of the window and drove past Yasmin, speaking quickly, 'A big missile landed on Duraid Shah's house. He wasn't there. I was with him in the office when this happened. He had just given me money for you and told me where to find Habib Saab.'

'May God help us,' I said.

What should have been a short journey took hours. The closer we got to Rawalpindi, the more people were running away in every direction. All manner of vehicles and carts were streaming out of the city. Every now and then there was a crackle of bullets, a thud or a bang, followed by plumes of smoke. Small dark clouds were rising from many different places across Rawalpindi. A missile screamed past us. Chambail Chacha stopped near a smouldering car. Smoke was rising from the wreck and its dead passengers. A buffalo ran madly in our direction. On the other side of the road, a bus was ablaze and burning passengers were trying to climb out of the windows. A policeman was running close to the buffalo, holding his bleeding chest. Four men were chasing the policeman. A missile screeched and snaked towards us. The policeman dived to the ground. The buffalo was parallel to the burning bus. I felt the heat of the missile as it flew over us. It turned and dropped towards the ground and through the stomach of the beast, slammed into the bus and exploded.

'Heat!' Chambail Chacha screamed, pulling me out of the car. 'They go for heat, Saab, heat!' As we scrambled into a gutter, I caught a glimpse of the buffalo. It stopped, let out a cry and fell into a pool of its own blood. The policeman scrambled up. He was close to us.

'Stop him, in God's name, stop him!' someone shouted in a hoarse voice.

Chambail Chacha grabbed the policeman's arm as he went past. The policeman stumbled and fell. His eyes were filled with terror. One of the men chasing him was carrying an axe.

The policeman joined his hands together and begged, 'Forgive me, in the name of God, forgive me!'

The man with the axe tore open the policeman's shirt. The policeman had been hiding a woman's arm. There were gold rings on the fingers and gold bangles on the arm.

'He cut her arm off with this,' the man said, raising the axe. 'She was still alive.'

'I have a wife and four children,' the policeman pleaded.

'She got married only yesterday,' the man with the axe said.

'In the name of the Prophet!' the policeman cried.

'She was my sister. My only sister,' the man with the axe said.

'You bastard!' I shouted at the policeman.

Smoke from the bus, filled with the smell of burning flesh, drifted towards us in thick dark waves. Chambail Chacha pulled my arm. I tried to free myself from him. He shook his head. He yanked me away just as a huge explosion shook the ground. We dived into the gutter again. As the smoke cleared, my ears were still ringing. We got up. The crowd had vanished. The policeman lay decapitated.

We got into the car and drove on towards Duraid Shah's house along the main road. Cars were coming and going in every direction. We had been driving for a few miles when Chambail Chacha pulled off down a side road, cursing the traffic police who had deserted their duties. Two young men were standing in the middle of the traffic island directing the traffic. A missile slammed into the island and they, too, were gone.

The road to Duraid Shah's house was littered with the wreckage of charred trucks. Though they were beyond recognition, some of these must have included those I had sent from the Adda. Duraid Shah's house overlooked the metaled parameter of the Ojhri camp from which the missiles were rising up with decreasing frequency. When we got to Duraid Shah's street, Chambail Chacha put his hands over his ears and cried, '*Toba, toba, toba*. May God forgive us.'

Houses adjoining the camp had been reduced to husks and many of those on the other side were burnt or blown out. The street was deserted. We went into Duraid Shah's house, stepping over the ruins of the outer wall. I half expected his black and white bull terrier to come barking at me, as it usually did when I came round. But there was no dog. Duraid Shah was kneeling on the ground rubbing his hands on broken pieces of glass. He was dressed in a shirt and neatly ironed trousers. He was sitting by the foot of the stairwell that led to the first floor. He lifted his hands. Debris was stuck to his palms. I placed my hand on his shoulder. He shooed me away.

Chambail Chacha picked up an upturned water cooler. It was half full. Duraid Shah shook his head at me and rubbed his hands on the ground again. He leaned forward and pulled out a tiny shoe. He kissed the shoe and pointed to a smudge on the ground where he was rubbing and said, 'This is where my son was martyred, Saleem Khan.'

I put my hands on his and tried to help him up, but he remained sitting and said, 'He was playing here. He always played here before breakfast. He was here calling the dog. My wife was cooking. A missile came in through the wall and exploded in the kitchen. They came and took all the bits of my wife and son. Look there, Saleem Saab,' Duraid Shah pointed behind him with a jerk of his head. 'What is left of my world?'

The roof of Duraid Shah's house had been blown off. The upper portion had caved in and crashed through to the ground floor. A gaping hole with a few jagged bricks stood where a wall had once been. One of the L-shaped cement pillars that had held the barbed wire was broken on the ground. Beyond the broken fence were row upon row of burnt-out trucks.

'Did you get all the payments that I had cleared for you? I need to go to the bank and get some money out; my wife wants to buy clothes for her brother's wedding. She will spend so much; doesn't ever think about how she is spending,' Duraid Shah said in a matter-of-fact voice.

I lifted my hands and looked up.

'Chambail Chacha, take Saleem Saab through the back into the camp and tell General Ashraf I sent you. He was the last one to see Habib.'

As we were about to leave, Duraid Shah's dog came out of the rubble and stood in front of us. It looked at me with a sorrowful questioning gaze. I felt the dog was asking, 'Why?' As we went past it, the animal slowly turned its head and continued looking at us. Then the dog lowered its head and stepped aside, letting out a cry as human as any I had ever heard.

Chambail Chacha picked up some bricks and placed them in a line across the barbed wired for us to step on. We had gone a short distance when two Pakistani soldiers on a motorcycle raced towards us, shouting at us to stop. We stopped.

'Just speak in English and, if you can, sound American,' Chambail Chacha said.

'You tell them we are here to see General Ashraf,' I said.

'Saleem Saab, in the name of God, speak in English,' Chambail Chacha whispered.

The soldiers dismounted a few yards away and walked towards us with pointed rifles. I said loudly, 'New York. Washington DC. McDonalds and Ronald Reagan eats cookies.'

The soldiers stopped and lowered their guns.

'Where is General Ashraf?' Chambail Chacha asked. The soldiers pointed towards a Pakistani army officer who was standing just past the last charred truck. He was surveying the scene.

The soldiers followed us on the motorcycle. As we got closer to the officer, Chambail Chacha said, 'He is a Brigadier General, is he not?'

'How do you know?' I asked.

'Just speak to him in English as well, Saleem Saab, English. When they are drunk or angry, officers all speak English.'

'I am a friend of Duraid Shah, General Saab, I have just come from his house over there,' I said pointing behind me. 'What is left of it.'

The Brigadier General looked at us and then looked away again.

A missile screeched out of the rubble and shot up into the air. It snaked in the opposite direction from us.

'That was the first in twenty minutes,' the Brigadier General said, looking up at the smoke trail of the projectile.

He turned towards us with pursed lips and nodded in acknowledgement. He was a tall clean-shaven man. The name Ashraf was tagged onto his uniform. He had sharply cut features and thick short hair. Sitting down on an overturned crate, he pointed to a couple of others. He looked at his wristwatch, picked up a transistor radio from beside him and started to tune it into a station. I took a crate and sat opposite him. A newsreader was speaking on the radio:

'The Indian Intelligence Agency Research and Development Wing, or RAW, in collaboration with Khad agents from Afghanistan, was responsible for the terrorist sabotage at the

Ojhri ammunition dump. This has caused some damage to the twin cities of Rawalpindi and Islamabad.'

He turned the radio off and placed it back on the ground. He took a miniature Quran out of his chest pocket, kissed it, touched it to his forehead and read a few verses in a melodic voice. He paused and said, 'Indians could not do this,' and continued reading the Quran.

The ground below us shook to the sound of muffled explosions.

'Americans, *they* know who did this,' he said, nodding in the direction of the army helicopter that was hovering above the camp, 'and now the motherfucking president, general Muhammad Zia-Ul-Haq, has come to see what mess his men have made.'

General Ashraf stopped reading, kissed the Quran and put it back in his pocket. He picked up a twig and turned it in his hand and said, shaking his head, 'RAW. Khad. Russians. Bullshit!'

He gave us a cigarette each, offered us a light first, lit his and said, blowing smoke out of his nose, 'These missiles, especially Stingers, they cannot just fly around. Some of the shells can take off but these missiles, they cannot. They have to be primed and fired. I cannot prime them. I don't know how to and I am a military man.'

He stopped. There was an explosion underground. The ground shook. An anguished look crossed General Ashraf's face. 'There are thousands and thousands of them down there.'

Chambail Chacha looked at me with fearful eyes.

'This dump was not under GHQ control. ISI ran this place. And they are answerable directly to General Zia himself and they sold the Stingers to Iran.' General Ashraf cleared his throat and said slyly, 'And you know Iranians, they got their hands on them alright and shot an American helicopter out of the sky. And when the Americans asked how the Stingers got into Iranian hands, what has ISI to say? They blew up my home city, just to hide their crime from the Americans.' General Ashraf looked up into the sky and cried, 'Almighty, forgive us for what we have done.' Turning to me, he said, 'But you have not come here to listen to this.'

'I am looking for my Cousin Habib. I was told you talked to him earlier,' I said.

Without answering me, General Ashraf summoned the two soldiers who had followed us there. They ran forward and stood to attention.

General Ashraf gave me a set of car keys and ordered the soldiers, 'Go with them in my car to the Hizb camp.'

The soldiers stamped their feet and went back to the motorcycle.

'I will return the car as soon as I can, General Ashraf Saab,' I said.

'Leave now,' General Ashraf said.

Chambail Chacha drove, following the soldiers out of the Ojhri camp. We followed them up a winding road and then down a dirt track near the end of the city overlooking the Nala Lai, a wide-open sewer. They stopped outside a small gate. Two bearded guards were playing Ludo, their rifles leaning against a tree nearby. One of the soldiers said something to one of the guards who was shaking dice in a cup. He looked across at us for a moment and then swirled the dice onto the Ludo board.

'We should pay them,' Chambail Chacha said.

I took out a bundle of rupees and handed them to Chambail Chacha. He put the money in the inside pocket of his vest and said, getting out of the car, 'Saab, you just stay here.'

As Chambail Chacha went towards the guards, the soldiers rode back the way they had come. Chambail Chacha sat down with the guards and spoke to them as they continued their game. After some time, one of the guards stood up and took Chambail Chacha round the back. They were gone for a short time. When Chambail Chacha returned he said, sorrowfully raising his eyebrows, 'It is in His hands.'

'Is Habib alright, Chambail Chacha?' I asked.

'We have to wait and see,' he replied.

'For what?'

'A man by his name was caught with a dancer woman,' Chambail Chacha said. 'She is being sent to another camp and he is done with. That is what they said.'

'Oh, God, no!' I cried.

'We may be just in time,' Chambail Chacha said, reversing the car past the guards and driving back out the way we had come. 'They are going to take him and the woman out of the camp soon, in a van. This will be our only chance. The van will stop just before the bazaar.'

Chambail Chacha parked the car and adjusted the mirror. He gave me a pistol and said, 'Saleem Saab, you will have to be quick.'

'I have never used one,' I said, taking the gun. 'You keep it.'

'I have mine,' Chambail Chacha said, proudly pulling another pistol out of one of his vest pockets. He asked, 'And what can you Englishmen do?' Unclipping the safety on my pistol, he laughed, 'Kill only chickens?' He paused for a moment and then dropped a few more words, 'Even cockerels!' He waited for me to say something but I kept quiet, hoping he was only guessing.

'You English are really strange people, Saab,' he said.

'What are you talking about, Chambail Chacha?'

'You have never mentioned anything about that day, but Duraid Shah told me everything and Habib Saab was so sorry for stealing my cockerel and begged my forgiveness. Can you believe that? He begged forgiveness of me? Me, a guard!'

I felt ashamed of myself and kept quiet.

Chambail Chacha stuffed some snuff in his mouth and started the car. A van was coming from the direction of the camp. The guard who had taken Chambail Chacha away was driving. We followed the van out towards the main road that led to the bazaar. The road was blocked by a funeral procession. Chambail Chacha said, 'Now, Saab.'

'This is not the bazaar,' I said.

'Saleem Saab, they are stuck.'

''How do we know Habib is in there?' I asked.

'Someone is,' Chambail Chacha said, getting out of the car.

I followed him out. The driver of the van was shouting to someone in the back, telling them about the funeral procession. One of the back doors of the van burst open. Cousin Habib was on the floor in between two benches, blood dripping down over his eyes. Two men moved towards him. One of them was holding a knife, the other a gun. Gulzarina was sitting in the furthest corner. Cousin Habib kicked the other door, screaming, 'Gulzarina, run!'

Chambail Chacha shot the man with the gun in the head. His gun dropped to the floor of the van and he fell back. The knife dropped out of the other one's hand. The van jerked forward violently. Cousin Habib fell out of the van, knocking the gun out of Chambail Chacha's hand. Gulzarina jumped out after Cousin Habib. The other guard went for his gun.

'Stop him, stop him!' Chambail Chacha screamed.

I ran forward, grabbed the knife and lunged at the guard in the van before he could shoot. I felt my hand touching his stomach. I pulled my hand away. He tried to grab my hand and I pushed the knife into him again. This time he screamed, holding his stomach.

A missile slammed into the side of a house on the other side of the road from the funeral procession. Just then the wheels of the van screeched as it turned sharply away from us.

Gulzarina went to sit in the front passenger seat as Chambail Chacha quickly put Cousin Habib in the back of the car. I placed his head on my lap. He was bleeding from the stomach. He turned his face to me. He had no eyes. Someone from the funeral procession gave us some water.

'Which hospital shall we go to, Saleem Saab?' Chambail Chacha asked.

'No hospital, cousin,' Habib said in a voice straining with pain. 'It is too late, for me. Take me home to the village. I want to die there.'

'Don't talk like that,' I cried. 'You are going to hospital.'

'Valaiti babu,' Cousin Habib squeezed my hand, 'give me Gulzarina's hand.'

Chambail Chacha stopped the car. We were on the GT road now, close to the military hospital.

I tapped Gulzarina's shoulder. Cousin Habib lifted his hand up. Gulzarina took his hand as he said, 'Now, cousin, this is my wife and she is, with the grace of God, with child. You must look after my child as you would your own, cousin.'

Gulzarina turned her face away and cried. Cousin Habib said, 'If I should die before I get to the village, you must tell them. She is my wife and she is with my child.'

'I will,' I said. I bent down, kissed him on the forehead and whispered in his ear, 'No one will ever know.'

Cousin Habib smiled and said, 'And cousin, God willing I will have a son and you must name him. And you will have a daughter. And I hereby name her Aisha. And cousin, will you give my son your daughter's hand?'

'I will, and what if I have a son?' I asked.

'He will be my Habib,' Cousin Habib said, 'and you must find two brides for them, and marry them on the same day.'

I could feel his heartbeat getting fainter.

'Do you know the way to our village?' I asked Chambail Chacha.

'I have taken this chicken thief there many a time, sir.'

A smile slid across Cousin Habib's lips.

'Leave me here,' Gulzarina said to Chambail Chacha, 'I am not worthy.'

Cousin Habib's heart beat faster.

'Sister-in-law, you have a husband to take home,' I said.

Habib closed his eyes, breathing slowly.

Gulzarina placed her head in her hands, sobbed for a while and then told us what had happened.

'They had bought me and brought me to the Hizb camp,' she said. 'They brought me here in a big army truck with other women. They used me here as they used me there. I asked God the same thing here as I asked Him on the day

I was captured by the Russians, "What crime have I committed? Have you not seen what the Russians have done to me?" But God did not answer me there and he did not answer me here. And your cousin, he found me. I don't know how he found me here, but the angel did. He came to my cage. He told me he had bribed the guards to free me. He told me he had found my sister. He showed me her photograph. I kissed the photograph and thanked him, even though it was not my sister. I did not tell him it was not my sister. The guards double-crossed him. They took me and your cousin in front of Commander Zaman. He came here personally to resolve the issue. He had sold me and he felt it his duty. They tied your cousin to a tree and whipped him. When they stopped beating him, he said, "I have seen your jihad." Commander Zaman said, "Then you will see no more." He opened the front of a car and poured some water out of the battery. He had your cousin's eyes forced open and put a needle into each of his eyes and poured the water from the car battery into them. Your cousin fell to the floor screaming in pain, holding his face and kicking his legs like an animal.'

Cousin Habib managed to hang on to life until we got to the village. With his dying breaths, he told his mother that Gulzarina was his wife. With his last breath, he said to me, 'Go back to England, but save the child.'

Gulzarina stood on her own in the middle of the path beyond the fence of thorns, away from the other women, in the blazing heat of the sun, and listened to Cousin Habib's funeral prayers. Yasmin went up to Gulzarina and held her hand. After lowering Cousin Habib into his grave, I looked back but Gulzarina was gone.

When I got back from the graveyard, the women were being fed in the large courtyard of Cousin Habib's house and the men in mine. I went to see if Gulzarina had eaten. She was nowhere to be found and no one had seen her.

'Where is your daughter-in-law, Auntie?' I asked Habib's mother, who was sitting on the floor among a throng of women reciting prayers, keeping a count of them by making small piles of beads close to them and picking more beads from a large heap in the centre. My auntie's head was resting on the carved leg of the bed on which Habib used to sleep. Her dupatta was tied around her head, her tear-stained face ghostly pale.

Yasmin sat next to my auntie, threw a fiery glance at me and continued praying.

Auntie looked accusingly at me and cried, 'What did you do to him?'

'Where is she, Auntie?' I demanded.

'There is no place for that Pathani here,' Auntie said, suddenly standing up. Her eyes raging. Her fists clenched.

'Don't you dare say that about my cousin's wife, Auntie!' I shouted, and ran out of the house to look for Gulzarina.

Someone said they saw a strange woman walking towards the graveyard. I ran to the graveyard, but she was not there. Someone else said a woman was walking on her own through the old stream that led to the road which led to the hill of black rocks close to the GT road. I ran to the stream, but she was not there either. There were footprints in the mud, but too many footprints. I was then told that a woman was lying across the rail track under the bridge and that she was dead. The bridge was not far, but as I stood frozen with fear a Karachi-bound train whistled in the hills behind me. It would take ten minutes at least to get to the bridge and it was doubtful that I could reach it in time. But I ran. And the train kept whistling as it made its way round the hills. I saw it approaching, curling around the last bend. There was only one more hill for it to pass behind and then it would cross the bridge. From this distance, it still looked like a big toy. I ran towards it and waved with both my hands. It whistled louder and louder. It went behind the hill. I screamed.

When I reached the track under the bridge, many passengers had got out of the train and were shaking their heads. I rushed through them. A woman was leaning over Gulzarina. The woman turned and asked, 'Does anyone speak her language? It's Pushto.'

Gulzarina was delirious.

'No, it's Dari,' someone said.

'It's Tajik and she speaks English.'

Someone else said, 'I think she's speaking Russian.'

My path was blocked by people. I tried to speak but my throat was so hoarse that no one could understand me.

'Who are you and where are you from?' the woman leaning over Gulzarina asked, pouring some water onto her lips.

'My sister,' I said, pushing through the crowd.

Gulzarina opened her eyes.

'Is he your brother?' the woman asked Gulzarina, who nodded.

The woman covered her head with her own dupatta and helped Gulzarina off the railway tracks.

Gulzarina went silently with me back to Cousin Habib's house. My aunt was standing at the gate, blocking our path.

'She will eat her husband's funeral's roti,' I said, brushing past my aunt, who stared at me with tired eyes.

Gulzarina squatted on the floor near the edge of a bed.

'On the bed, sister-in-law,' I said to Gulzarina. I told my aunt, 'Get me the Quran.' She did not move.

I went inside and came back with a Quran. I placed the Quran on my head and said as loud as I could, 'As God is my witness, I witnessed the marriage of my cousin to Gulzarina. And if there is no one here who objects, then I will take her as my wife.'

Gulzarina stood up, slapped both her hands to her face and screamed, 'No. In the name of God, no! I have called you my brother.'

My aunt held Gulzarina's hands and stopped her slapping her own face. She hugged her and said, 'Come, daughter-in-law, eat your husband's roti.'

Yasmin stood up from among the women, walked up to Gulzarina and hugged her. Turning to me she asked, 'Have you eaten?'

'I am not hungry.'

Nodding to a manji bed under the shade of a tree, she said, 'Sit over there. I will bring you some food.'

I went and sat where she had asked me to and watched Gulzarina being led inside. A few moments later, Yasmin gave me a glass of water to drink and then brought me some food.

I stayed awake most nights. Sometimes aimlessly climbing a hill or lying on a manji gazing up at the sparkling sky and smoking dope, sometimes talking to the wind or, when I did doze, at times talking in my dreams. In the mornings, Cousin Habib's mother would bring my breakfast and sit watching me silently. I had nothing to say to her and she rarely asked me anything. After breakfast, I went to the old banyan tree just outside the village near the edge of a cliff under our shrine. I played here as a child and sat in the tree's shade with Habib flicking stones into the pond below its dangling aerial prop roots. The hollow of the trunk was much wider now, so wide I could stretch out in it. I sat here smoking dope, slipping in and out of dreams.

The postman came to see me. 'I like to put the letter in the hand of its owner, but I have not been able to find you, sir,' he said, handing me three airmail letters. The letters were all from Carol. I looked at the postmark on the first letter. It had taken six weeks to get here. I opened it. There was too much written in it. I read the first line, 'I have lost count of how many messages . . .'

'Your world is too far from me,' I said.

I ripped open the second letter. Carol wrote, 'Why didn't you tell me about Habib?'

I saw an image of Cousin Habib flash through my mind—he was stumbling about, his eyes gouged.

I drifted off again, remembering the day I was unable to take my hands out of my trouser pockets. Then, he still had his eyes. We were in a truck with driver Kala going down the GT road towards Lahore. Cousin Habib was drumming on the dashboard, singing, 'You need to get out of this dream.' I sat up, half expecting to see him.

'You need to stop dreaming, Valaiti Saab.' Abbi was smiling at me. Placing a small axe against the side of the tree, he squatted next to me and looked out at a deep pool of rainwater.

A nightingale was singing somewhere above me. A buffalo with a nervous little bird perched on its back came out of the sunlight and stepped into the pool, in which dangled the gently swaying roots of the banyan tree. Abbi threw a small stone into the pool. It created magical ripples across the water. The buffalo sat down in the middle of the ripples, flicking its ears.

'Is it English weather that makes you lot so cold?' Abbi asked, tapping a cigarette in the palm of his hand.

He emptied the contents of the cigarette into one hand by pressing and rubbing it between his fingertips. Filling the emptied cigarette with a mixture of dope and tobacco, Abbi said, 'You need a woman to take your pain away.'

I laughed.

Passing me the cigarette, Abbi said, 'And you used to love Yasmin, and for a massalan she is pretty.' Blowing smoke out of his mouth, he sniggered, 'Not like gorees, but pretty, eh?'

He stayed with me for a while, smoked a few cigarettes and left.

The buffalo in the pool had only its head out of the water. The little bird was now perched in between its ears. The buffalo shook its head violently. The bird hopped off, hovered and settled back down where it had been.

'Snakes can't sting Love—isn't that so, Saleem Khan?' Yasmin said, stepping out of the sunlight. She was drenched in sweat. She tied her hair up with her dupatta, threw it over her shoulders and stepped into the pool and prodded the buffalo with a stick. It stood up and left the pool, water dripping off its body. Yasmin walked behind it, looking in my direction every now and then.

When I wasn't sitting under the banyan tree I went to Habib's grave, always stoned, and rubbed my hands through the soil, smelling it, clearing weeds out of it and talking to him. If someone tried to talk to me, especially when I was with Habib, I became abusive. After a while, people just shook their heads when they went past me.

The nights frightened me the most, especially when I closed my eyes. It was the smell of my dreams that most terrified me. The smell of Habib, the smell of the explosives and the smell of burning flesh and rotting bodies were so strong I could taste them on my tongue and would wake up drenched in sweat, trembling.

I lived in a trance, where things flashed in front of me but didn't stay too long.

Yasmin brought me food, usually when I was by the tree but sometimes to the grave. She always left it in front of me, disappeared and re-appeared to take the food away. Once, as she put the food in front of me she said, 'Saleem Saab, you must shave and cut your hair.'

I threw the food at her.

'Habib would want you to do this?'

'Who are you to tell me what to do,' I hissed at her.

'Just your servant,' she replied, stepping back.

She came back a little while later with fresh food, placed it in front of me and said, 'You have a guest, sir.'

'Send them to hell,' I said.

She melted into the sunlight at the edge of the tree and re-materialised a short while later with Chambail Chacha. He held his hand out to me. I shook it. He came down, held my hand in both of his, kissed it and sat down silently beside me.

After some time he said, 'And life must go on, my son.'

'Do you still take nasvaar, snuff?' I asked.

'Do you want some?'

'No.'

'I still take nasvaar.'

'How many chickens do you have?'

'I am only interested in one, now.'

'A cockerel?'

'Yes, a cockerel. It is Valaiti,' he said.

'Ha, what else could it be?' I asked. 'Russian?'

'This one has lost himself.'

'Doesn't he like hens?' I laughed.

'He doesn't like life,' he said. 'He won't eat.'

'Where do you keep it?'

'I don't?'

'Where is it then?'

'Here.'

'You brought it to my village?'

'No, it was already here,' Chambail Chacha said, breaking a piece of roti. Dipping it into some dhal, he held it up toward my mouth saying, 'In life there is death.'

I took the food and after a long time I felt a taste of the spice and roti.

'Where are you working nowadays?' I asked, eating more.

'I have gone back to the village,' he said, holding a cloth bag in front of me, 'but today I have come to give you something.'

I opened the bag. It was full of money.

'Duraid?'

Chambail Chacha nodded.

'Why?'

'It was owed to Habib,' he said.

I took out a handful of notes and held them out to him.

He shook his head, saying, 'I am a poor man. What would I do with so much?'

'Take it,' I insisted.

He stood up and said, 'God helps me.'

'Come eat some food before you go.'

'I have just eaten.'

I stood up but felt dizzy. Chambail Chacha bent down, kissed me on the head and left.

Throughout this time, Yasmin stood silently out of earshot. I waved to her to come to me. She did.

'Give this to Gulzarina. Tell her it is from Habib,' I said. As she was leaving, I called her back. She came back.

'Why did you come back?'

'You called me. Who am I to refuse?' she said.

'I am tired, so very tired.'

'I will always come if you tell me to.'

'Then come when your work is done.'

After she left, I filled a few cigarettes with dope and chain-smoked them until sunset. I staggered home. Gulzarina was waiting for me along with my auntie.

Handing me the bag of money, Gulzarina said, 'What is this?'

'It is yours,' I said. I was beginning to hallucinate. Cousin Habib was crying. Tears fell out of the empty sockets of his eyes.

'I will take it on one condition,' she said.

Habib danced on a bed of flowers.

'What?'

'I want my brother-in-law back.'

My auntie came forward, rubbed her hand through my hair and said, 'Enough, now, my son.' Nodding towards Gulzarina, she said, 'And you have a child to raise.'

'And I need a sister-in-law,' Gulzarina said, pressing on my hand. 'Clean clothes are hanging in the bathroom.'

Sometime that night, Yasmin came and started pressing my legs.

I continued to smoke and live in a daze, punctuated with hallucinations, the passing of time and people, just colours and sounds in my world. And somewhere in this world, I married Yasmin. And sometime after that, when I was sitting in the hollow of the banyan tree, chain-smoking dope-filled cigarettes and listening to a nightingale that had kept me company for I don't know how long, the postman came and gave me a postcard from Carol. It said: *Congratulations and best wishes for your future.*

The nightingale stopped singing. A strong wind swirled through the leaves of the tree, its twisted roots trembling around me. A branch of the tree cracked and dangled ominously. I raised my hand to protect my face. My fist did not open. I forced it open. A peacock's feather flew out of my hand.

'Don't sit in there too long, Saleem Khan,' Abbi said, floating past me, 'snakes hide in these places.'

I saw myself running to the graveyard. Pulling away at the overgrown grass, I said, 'I have to go back to England now. Look what I have done.'

'Why did you betray Carol?' Cousin Habib said inside my head. 'How can I go back after what I have done?' I asked.

I stood up and came out of the hollow of the tree. Abbi was not there. The cracked branch broke off the tree and swung down above my head, knocking against the trunk with such force that I felt the ground below me vibrate. There was a mechanical buzz in the air.

BOOK II

Gulzarina

The hiss and buzz of a helicopter somewhere nearby chases away the memories of Pakistan. The helicopter has been hovering over my house in Longsight for quite some time now. I thought I was dreaming, and kept trying to go back to sleep. Police sirens fade in and out of the creaking groans of my empty house. The helicopter *is* close by. I rush downstairs as quickly as my legs will allow me, expecting the front door to burst open. My heart flutters in my chest. I stop in my tracks. The kitchen door is ajar. The hands of the wall clock have just passed seven. The waistcoat laden with explosives is still hanging on the back of the chair and the trolley bag is where I left it.

Perhaps they know of my plan, I think. No. How could they? I try to reassure myself, staring at the yellowing net curtain that keeps the world from entering and disturbing the musky aroma of my kitchen. My worn-out old trolley bag leans against the kitchen wall, next to a large radiator from which greyish-white paint is flaking into small piles on the floor. I have placed two mobile phones in the bag of the trolley. The numbers have been primed to wireless detonators. These sit in the outer pockets. There are two large bibles inside the bag, one on top of the other, both secured with masking tape. The pages of these have been cut out. Each hole contains half a kilo of plastic explosives. The spines of the bibles contain four small flat batteries linked together. A thin wire dangles out. It is wrapped in a fine cloth and its end has a paper cross that acts as a page marker. It is also an aerial, primed to a third mobile phone which I carry in my pocket. That number will activate the bibles, shredding the bag to smithereens. It is also connected to the plastic explosives around my chest. But there is a two-minute delay with this. Once the timer starts, my fate is irreversible. All I will be able to do is witness my last deed, moments before my own extinction.

I have made a small pile of things I will take with me in the trolley bag. I look at Carol's stone for the last time, turning it around in the palm of my hand and then place it next to the bibles. There is also the first passport I came to Britain with in 1965; it is now a faded green. And that photo of a young man with short hair, wearing a tie for the first time in his life, goes next. I pause on another picture of myself, this time with shoulder-length hair, in the Pakistani passport I held before I got my British one. This goes in as well. After putting my daughter Aisha's photograph into the inside pocket of my coat, I zip up the trolley bag.

I stand up and go into my front room. There is no bulb in the main socket in this room; it fell out of its rusty casing and smashed on the floor many years ago. Now the room is lit by a lamp in the corner, above my desk with my letter to my daughter, near which two clocks hang on the wall; one gives the time here, and the other the time in Pakistan. I have typed this letter. The A4 sheets of paper are piled neatly next to an open envelope addressed to her, on the back of which is written: A *father's love never dies*. It lies close to a photograph of her.

~

I think back to just before I took the picture. Aisha was eight years old. She had turned her back on me and continued playing the violin. I offered her a chocolate bar, but only if she turned around and played. Then, just as she turned, her mother came into the room and said to her, 'Loose hair is not for good girls. How many times have I asked you to tie it back?' Turning to me, her mother had said, 'You are letting the devil sing out of the hands of my daughter.' After I took the picture, Aisha walked up to the window, threw the violin out onto the road and then ran upstairs to her bedroom. She came down a short while later, holding a pair of scissors. She had cut her hair. She picked up a box of toys, threw them across the floor, folded her arms across her chest and looked at me.

'Clean this mess up right now,' I ordered.

'I hate you!' She shook her head.

I pushed her. Yasmin ran to try to break Aisha's fall, but Aisha fell backwards and cut her lip. It wasn't a big cut. I was so upset with myself for hurting her that I started crying. Aisha freed herself from her mother, gave me a great big hug and said, 'Abba, it was an accident. It doesn't really hurt.'

That night when I put her to bed, I told her her favourite story of how, when I was a boy, I had once played with a real black cobra. After the story, I played her a sammi on my flute and watched her drift into sleep. As I was wiping the flute, she whispered sleepily, 'Abba, sing it for me.' I sang the sammi for her until I was sure she was asleep. As I was tiptoeing out of the bedroom, she said, 'Abba, why are you seeing the other woman?'

'What are you talking about?' I snapped.

'I can smell her on you, Abba,' she said from under her quilt. 'And I know who it is.'

'Who?'

'Her, that goree. That white woman. Mummy told me. Mummy said she is called Carol and you go to see her every time you come home smelling of sharab, Mummy said. And I know where . . .'

I didn't let her finish and walked out of the room. I could not believe she knew Carol's name. Yasmin stepped away from Aisha's bedroom door as I went past.

A bedroom door slamming shut makes Aisha's smiling face flash in front of my eyes, freeing me from memories, and I say to Aisha's photograph, 'Why, when I was in love with a white woman, did I marry your mother? I should have answered you, but I could not. Forgive me, Aisha, just like you did for cutting your lip.'

I pick up my letter to Aisha and hold it against my pounding heart.

I have read and read the letter so many times that the words are ingrained in my mind.

My dear beloved daughter,

I have transferred all the money I have to you. It will show up in your account a day after I die. It will see you through life. And this house is yours now; this too has been transferred into your name. A solicitor will contact you in the next week or so and, Aisha, everything in it is yours as well.

And yes, you were right to be angry with me for what I did to your mother. You are right to be angry with me, but now all I ask is for you to forgive me. Just like you forgave me for cutting your lip.

And why did I end my life in such an act?

First let me tell you, how I loved the moments when you used to come to see me.

I never knew when you would come, and when you came, I never wanted you to leave, but you just never stayed long enough. I wish I had been a better father, and watched you grow and not just seen your youth go by me. But I can't go back now. I can't get to understand you, apart from understanding what I did to you was wrong.

In the pages that follow, I have talked you through the wounds which have brought me here, to this moment.

There are some things I could not write in English, which I wanted to say to you in my own language, your language, so I have left you a long message at www.thelastactofsaleemkhan. com. The username is my village name and the password is your middle name.

The words are too painful. I block them out of my mind. I turn the paper over, but Aisha's smile beams out through the blankness.

As I put the letter down, away from the golfball-sized jagged stone, I knock my ambulatory heart monitor onto the floor.

A fly buzzes somewhere close to the window. It is a painful, desperate cry. I scan the curtains for movement. They are still. The fly is trapped in a spider's web that runs from the edge of the window across to the corner of the other wall. The web quivers. The fly struggles for life. A shadow stretches along the wall towards the fly. The fly is silenced. One of the mobile phones bleeps four times. This is the first of the pre-programmed detonation alarms.

~

A dream is pushing itself into my mind. I am standing looking down at an old man asleep in a hospital bed. He is holding a small rock in his hand. Streaks of dried tears run down his face. I stretch a hand to wake the old man up, to get me out of his dream. He is beyond reach. A white pigeon falls out of the sky. It is on fire. Tony Blair is on the television, laughing. Al Qaeda attacked us, he says, over there in America. He starts dancing to the beat of Punjabi Bhangra, chanting: Saddam-Hussain-is-insane, ABCWMD, in the North, South, West, East, or the sea. He nods to my neighbour, Sarah Ann, out walking her dog. It is an old, unhappy mongrel. It squats and shits on the pavement. It is a hard, constipated black turd. Sarah Ann nods encouragingly at the dog, saying, 'Good boy.' She turns to me and smiles.

'Did you not see the war plane, Sarah Ann?' I ask.

'Luvly day, in'it,' Sara Ann says, scooping the dog shit into a plastic bag.

Tony Blair runs towards me. He is coming through a dust storm. British soldiers are clapping. A bomb goes off in the middle of them. Two hands fly through the air, still clapping. A soldier holds out what remains of his arms. Tony Blair says to the soldier: 'This is where the future of our civilisation is going to be decided, right here in the deserts of Kandahar.' The desert rises and falls like a sea wave. Gulzarina, her hair loose, rises out of the grains of the waves.

I am about to hit Tony Blair with Carol's rock when she says from somewhere, 'It won't do anything to him.'

'Carol, my love,' I call out. 'Help me!'

A stinging pain ripping through my arm wrests me out of my dream. I must have swung my arm whilst sleeping and hit something.

I shaved today. I don't know when or why I shaved my armpits and my pubic hair but when I finished, I thought of my dead wife Yasmin's refusal to have sex with me the first night after her arrival here until I became clean, like this.

I have become as clean as any jihadi and the shaved patches on my chest, where the nodes of my ambulatory monitor should rest, are itching a little, reminding me of the discarded unit.

Should I draw the curtains of this room, I think? But what need is there to keep the eyes of the world from a place I will no longer be in? It has been dark in this room for many months. Someone in a car is doing handbrake turns on the street outside. A helicopter is hovering somewhere. Through my cracked window frames, I can smell bacon being grilled.

There are loud knocks on my front door. I smile at the thought that Aisha always knocked twice and had come to see me. I open the door, but there is no one there.

The scent of the burning bacon reminds me of the open-air festival in Piccadilly Gardens, where I had seen Aisha with John. She was then twenty-one. I was about to get onto a bus. It was around midnight and the city centre was brimming with teenagers and revellers going home at the end of a warm summer's night. Some police officers were encouraging drunken youths onto buses; other officers just stood around. Aisha was with a group of white lads. She wore a low-cut pink top and a matching short skirt. She staggered about, giggling, and bumped into an old woman, who held on to her and stopped her from falling. The old woman had her back to me. She said something to the lads, who laughed back at her. Aisha looked across at me. I lowered my head and tried to walk away but she shouted over to me, 'That twat, over there, with the cap, is my Dad.'

I turned around. One of the lads, a tall boy with dark brown hair, had his arm around her, his hand over her breast.

'This is John, Dad,' Aisha said, 'me boyfriend.'

'She's just a slut who's had more pricks in her than a second-hand dartboard,' John said, raising his shoulders.

The lads laughed. Aisha whimpered, 'You're horrible, John!' She bent forward and vomited.

'That's gross,' John said, stepping away from Aisha. 'Go home, bitch.'

'You know I love you, John,' Aisha said, wiping her mouth.

The old woman sat down beside Aisha, keeping her skirt off the ground and gave her a tissue.

John and the other lads boarded a bus, laughing and slapping each other. Aisha tried to stand up but fell. The old woman helped her onto her feet, whispering into her ear.

Aisha hissed, 'I'll be on the job at the end of your road, Dad, just you watch.'

I turned around, went towards the railway station, stopped when I was sure she could not see me and waited till I saw her board a bus. I went home and fell asleep. It was late into the night by the time I woke up and as I opened my front door to go out to for a drink, Aisha was standing on my doorstep, smoking. Her hair was matted. A puddle of water had formed at her feet.

I stepped back from her. My lips quivered as I saw her mother's frown on Aisha's forehead. I was overwhelmed with feelings but was unable to say anything for some moments and when words came, they were not what I wanted to say.

'In anger, you are just like your mother was when she was happy.'

She turned her face away from me and cried, 'You killed her.'

A car drove past. Throwing the cigarette into a hedge, she stepped inside, shutting the door behind her, walked past me into the back living room, brushed against my coffee table knocking my overflowing ashtray onto the floor, drew the curtains and opened the door into the garden.

She stood looking out on the garden. An image of her mother, kneeling face down into an open Quran, in a pool of her own blood, her wrists slit, flashed in front of my eyes.

Aisha turned around, glared at me and said, 'It was because of you I became motherless at twenty.'

'She should have left a note for you, maybe that . . .' Even as the words were coming out of my mouth, I knew I should not have said what I did.

'Yes, she could really have done that, couldn't she?' Aisha mocked, sitting down on my single settee, tucking her hands in between her knees.

She looked much smaller now than she was; as tall as me. She had my family's square ancestral chin, but she did not have my eyes. Hers were dark brown, just like her mother's. Her nose was thin, not stubby like mine, or short like her mother's. It was much closer to my mother's, and, like her, Aisha too had freckles on her face. But Aisha's hair was curly, her eyebrows plucked and her eyeliner ran down her face.

I went into the kitchen and came back with some water and held it out for her. I was about to tell her not to smoke, especially in my company, when she said, 'I don't need you to get me water.'

I put the glass down on the arm of the settee next to her.

Flicking ash into the water, she said, 'And I'll smoke if I want and if you can't handle it, it's your problem.'

'I am glad we are getting on today . . .'

'Getting on today,' Aisha said calmly. 'How fucked up are you, old man? You think I'm calm. I'm always burning. Burning away! And I am here to send you to hell if I can.'

She grabbed the glass of water and flung it at me. It missed me and smashed against the wall behind me. She stood up, laughed, pushed me out of her way and walked out of the house, repeating, 'Wait and see.'

I didn't see Aisha for nearly a year after that. I shut my ears to the rumours that my friends had seen her standing on street corners in the red-light areas of Whalley Range. But she left no room for mistake and sent me cards telling me how much she was charging her clients, especially if it was anyone I knew.

I began to dread the mornings when the post came. For a while, there was a card from her virtually every day. I couldn't read them and tore them up as soon as they dropped through the letter box and cried, begging her forgiveness. And then she stopped writing. Even then, I dreaded the mornings.

Once or twice a week, along with Mangal Singh, I started going to a Punjabi club in Ashton. The club was famous for hiring Polish girls as barmaids. Mangal Singh and I sat down. A scantily dressed young woman took our order and a few moments later Aisha came back carrying a tray of our drinks.

Mangal Singh looked at me, lowered his head and cried.

Placing the drinks in front of us, Aisha whispered, 'Twenty quid for a blowjob in the back and thirty for a surprise, boys.'

We left the club and drove back to Manchester in silence.

The next time I saw her was March 2003. It was the day after a mosque in Manchester had been razed to the ground. Aisha knocked on my door. She was wearing jeans and a dark brown T-shirt. Her hair was tied in a long plait behind her head. Her lips were swollen and she had dark bruises under her eyes.

'Dad,' she said. 'Look at me, Dad, look.'

'Who did this to you?' I said, stepping towards her.

She put her hand up at me and said, 'No, Dad, stop.'

I couldn't remember the last time she had called me 'Dad' and the sight of her, and me not being able to go near her, made me feel so weak I felt my legs giving way.

'It was John,' she said. 'He wasn't really my boyfriend, Dad. I got into some bad things.'

'It's not your fault,' I said, opening the door wider for her to step inside, but she didn't.

'I don't know what I was doing, Dad. Honestly, I don't,' she said. 'They were all right usually, but then yesterday they were out in the city centre, we'd all drunk a lot and they had bought some bacon sarnies. And I never eat bacon, I just can't. And we were just messing about when they saw a couple of Muslim lads, and I don't know how it started but John and his mates started swearing and shouting at them, calling them terrorists and all sorts of things. And then they started beating them. I tried to stop John and he turned on me, swearing. He pushed some bacon into my mouth and I spat it out. And he hit me and did this to me, Dad. I'm really, really sorry, Dad.'

'What are you sorry for?'

'For what?' she cried, stepping back. 'And you know all those cards I sent you, it was all lies. I just lied to you. You must have heard the rumours about me. All I did was just stand around making sure your mates saw me. I just did it to hurt you.'

'Come inside.'

'No.'

We stood quietly for a moment. She turned round and ran off.

'Stop running, Aisha,' I called after her. But she didn't stop.

A week or so later, Mangal Singh and I were walking past the Territorial Army base in the Birch near Birchfields Park on our way to the Wilmslow Road to join an anti-war demonstration, which everyone we knew was going on.

Looking at the Territorial Army base, I asked Mangal Singh, 'Yaar, what I don't understand is if so many people in this country are opposed to war, then why do we have all these military bases all over Manchester? There's a huge one in Ardwick and one in the town centre and . . .'

'They have these all over the country in nearly every town,' Mangal Singh said.

'I mean, why don't they stop these soldiers from going out to war?' I said.

Mangal Singh laughed, 'It's a game, old man, just a game. To do something like that means they have to pay a real price, not just get a sore throat.'

We joined a huge colourful demonstration moving through Rusholme, snaking towards the city centre. Aisha was there with a group of girls. She walked right past me. I am sure she saw me, but she did not say anything.

A few years went by. I heard nothing from her. Then one Friday afternoon when I was alone at home watching Tony

Blair and Jack Straw on television insisting that they had not misled the British people, there were two loud knocks on my front door. It was Aisha. When I opened the door she was standing on the doorstep wearing a black Niqab.

I was taken aback. We stood silently looking at each other for a moment.

'You do not have to cover your face in front of your own father.'

'Tell me, and tell me truthfully. Did you ever make me eat pig?'

'No.'

She did not believe me. I felt her eyes ripping into me. The veil in front of her mouth kept lifting up from her short angry breaths. You are right, daughter, I thought. My lack of belief in God was not important in a house that needed Him.

'What did I learn from you, nothing. Nothing, you sad old man! You taught me nothing and what did you do to my mother? She would be alive if it was not for you. You killed her.'

Believe in your God, Aisha, I thought, looking at her moistening eyes. It was his will. Believe it child. It will ease your pain. I am here for you. Just give me a chance.

But why should she? She is right again, I thought. I wanted her to belong to my past, my village, my memories.

'Are you going to tell me it was the will of Allah, is that it?' Aisha asked.

I shook my head, 'You are all I have left . . .'

'What did you ever do for me?' Aisha asked.

'I never left you wanting . . .'

'You sent us money, yeh. You did that, and left us alone so you could be with your goree, and your booze, and that's what you did. Were you there for me? Never! You are . . .'

I was expecting obscenities from her, but she locked the fingers of her hands and cracked them and said, tightening her eyes, 'I don't need you anymore. I have found who I am. I know what I am. I have found myself in my God and in my Prophet, May Peace Be Upon Him. And by God I know now why you in your godlessness failed in everything, everything! I don't know why you left God, but you didn't have to force me into your world. You think I don't know how you tortured my mother. How you humiliated her, how you told her she was just an ignorant village woman who understood nothing of what she read. She may not have, but she understood what she felt; she felt it from the rhythm of the language in which God had spoken.'

Aisha stopped and waited for me to say something.

What can I say to you, daughter, I thought. Where is all this coming from? I just want you. Come back to me, come back to me with God. Just come back. I don't care.

'You don't care what I think, do you?' Aisha asked.

'I care for you, my daughter.'

'I don't care if you care or not.' Aisha said. 'Do you want to know where I have been all this time?

'Tell me.'

'I go to meetings and I read about my religion and my history. I have my teacher. You don't need to know who it is. Who knows who you will go and tell when you are pissed? And let me tell you how lucky I am to be here, for it is from here that they go and destroy our world. But let me tell you, we will win. We will have a dictatorship, a dictatorship of believers instead of this godless fraud of democracy. And your cruelty, your law, your rules, your orders opened the door to truth for me,' Aisha said, turning around to leave.

'Please daughter, come inside.'

Waving a hand in the air, she said, 'Remember. You may be my father, but you are not my God. I have said what I came to say. I will never see you again.'

After she left, I sat down in the hallway, leaned against the door and recited the Kalima: there is no God but Allah, Muhammad is the Messenger of Allah. Maybe I had been wrong? I cried. 'How could she throw her mother's words at me? How? God, I need your help.'

There is no God to be found in tears, I thought. If he is anywhere, he is not with you old man. If he is anywhere, your daughter has found Him and to find you daughter you have to find Him as well.

The next Friday, I went to the Victoria Mosque. I picked up some prayer beads from a basket by the door and sat down next to a pillar, leaning my back against it. Moving the beads along with my left thumb, I nodded here and there at surprised faces to whom I had sworn my unbreakable allegiance to atheism in the past. When I prostrated, I tried to recite the prayers in tune with those coming through the mosque's loudspeakers, but all I could say inside my head was, 'I have never asked you for anything. If you exist, give me back my daughter.'

On a bright, dry but bitterly cold day, as I was leaving the mosque, Aisha went past me, her face covered with a black shawl. She turned around and threw me a burning look. As she went past, I asked, 'How are you, my daughter?'

She stopped, but stood with her back to me for a moment and then said, 'It has got so cold today.'

'It's supposed to snow heavily tonight.'

Looking up into a clear sky, she said, 'Not a cloud in sight.'

I looked up. There were only the streaks of white from passing aeroplanes.

'It's up to Him,' Aisha said, 'but I don't think it will snow.'

'Here take this,' I said, holding an envelope in which I had been carrying around five hundred pounds for her.

Her right hand trembled.

'It is for Eid,' I said.

She turned her head slightly towards me, let out a slow angry breath and said, 'Give your money to those who need it.'

'I know you are not working,' I said.

'You know everything, don't you, Dad?' Aisha cried, running away. But she stopped by the mosque's gate.

As I went past her, she started walking next to me but said nothing. I turned towards Longsight. She crossed the Birchfields Road with me, in silence, and then said, 'I am sorry I was rude to you in the Masjid.'

'It's alright,' I said.

'I should not have spoken to you in that tone, in there,' she said.

'You were not rude,' I said.

'I was,' she said.

'No, you just didn't take the money.'

'I wanted to take the envelope,' she said.

'You can have it now,' I said, putting my hand in my pocket.

'I wanted to rip it up and throw it in your face,' she took hold of my hand, 'right in front of everyone in the mosque.'

'You can do that,' I said, giving her the envelope.

'I get by well, honestly,' she said, taking the envelope.

I wanted to ask her to come round on Eid, but said, 'You can buy some nice new clothes for Eid and maybe something for your house.'

'I am all right, Dad, really,' she said wiping her eyes. 'I have a tenant now.'

She gave me a quick hug and then crossed the road and ran for a bus heading towards the city centre.

It suddenly became even more chilly and started to drizzle. By the time I got home, I was soaked. But it didn't snow that night.

Warming my hands on my hissing gas fire, I smiled at the thought that she was right; it didn't snow. I watched the rain slide down the windows overlooking my back garden. I waited for the time to pass and went outside to go to her house in Chorlton.

The lights in her front room were on. The yellow curtains were drawn. Behind them, a woman was standing, her hair tied in a knot on top of her head. She undid her hair and threw it over her shoulders. It was a young woman and it had to be Aisha, I thought. She was talking to someone, who must have been sitting in a corner. Maybe I should just knock on the door and ask her for a cup of tea. I took a deep breath and went to knock on the door, keeping my eye on the window. Aisha went out of the room. I stopped. She came back a few moments later with something in her hand. She bent down and put it down.

Why was I intruding in her private life? I felt ashamed. I panicked and rushed home.

I went to the mosque every day in the hope of seeing my daughter but only ever saw her on Fridays, when after prayers she would walk a little way with me, then hug me, cross the road and go into town. One Friday, as she was leaving, I asked her, 'What's the name of your tenant?'

'Auntie Elizabeth,' Aisha said, looking across the road.

'Can I meet her?' I asked.

'My world, Dad,' Aisha said, looking at me with flashing eyes. 'Stay out!'

That night my telephone rang at around at 3.00 a.m. I jumped out of bed as at this time of the morning calls were usually the harbingers of bad news. It was Gulzarina.

'I have not been able to sleep for days, brother,' she said as soon as I answered.

'Is all well, Gulzarina?'

'My Habib is showing interest in some girls.'

'It's what happens,' I laughed with relief.

'No. This will not happen. We made a promise. I need your answer. He is destined only for Aisha.'

'I will ask her when I see her next but, you know, it's not like Pakistan. She doesn't listen to me.'

'The Almighty will help,' Gulzarina said.

The next time I saw Aisha after prayers she asked, 'Dad, tell me something about Mum.'

My chest tensed. I felt cold. My ears began to burn. 'Well, you know,' I said, 'both of us come from the same village . . .'

'Come on Dad,' Aisha interrupted, 'I mean what was she like?'

What was she like, I thought? What was she like? What did you do to that woman who would come to see you on the roof of your house in the middle of the day, in the pouring heat of the summer, barefoot? I saw myself waiting on the roof, sitting in the corner under the shade of a tall tree. She walked up the stone steps holding something behind her. As she stepped onto the roof, the call to prayers burst out of the loudspeakers of the mosque.

'Listen to Raju Jat giving the Azaan,' Yasmin said, nodding towards the mosque. 'Not even donkeys are safe from him.' She got closer and I stood up. Throwing the water from a cup at me, she laughed, 'You men have the same thing on your mind. Mullahs and . . .'

'Yasmin, have fear of God,' I interrupted her.

'And you are standing up to pray are you?' She looked me up and down, knitting her eyebrows.

'Dad, is that so difficult?' Aisha asked, chasing away the memories of her mother. 'Go on. Do tell me something about *her*, Abbaji. Tell me, did you ever love Mum?'

'Love her!'

Aisha looked at me.

Did you ever love her, Saleem Khan? I thought. My stomach knotted. Or was it all a dream? Or was it just a lie, left behind somewhere, in between there and here? I would like to tell you the story, the beginning of the story of your mother and me, and you, but how can I do that when you know the end?

I was coming back from work. I had come home early this day. It was a hot day. I was thirsty. I was close to our village's well. I could see women at the well and stopped under the shade of a tree, waiting for them to leave, but they just kept on filling their pitchers and spilling the water and refilling them, every now and then, looking back at me and laughing among themselves. Eventually they left and I went to have a drink. When I got there, Yasmin was sitting at the base of the outer wall of the well, next to the overflow, holding her right ankle. I was taken aback. I thought no one was here. She looked at me. Her foot was stuck in a mud gutter, into which the overflow from the well water fell.

'I have dislocated it,' she said.

I stepped around her water pitchers and bent down and helped her pull her foot out of the mud and then poured water on it and cleaned it. It was not swollen. I held her foot by her ankle in the palm of my hand, and asked her to move it side to side. She did. I asked her to wiggle her toes. She did, all the while oofing and aahing in pain.

I told her, 'It's not dislocated.'

'But, it hurts,' she said.

'You might have cracked a bone or something,' I said. 'If it hurts tomorrow you should go see a doctor.'

'I'm sure it's broken,' she said.

'I'm sure you will be fine,' I said lowering her foot down on the ground.

'It really hurts now,' she protested. I stopped and she sighed, 'That's better.'

'Shall I call someone to carry you home?' I asked.

'No, no. It is getting better,' she replied, taking her foot out of my hand, 'but, you didn't stop because of me, you must be thirsty.'

'I am,' I laughed.

I went up to the top of the well and pushed the bar of the wheel of the well a few times, and helped her refill her pitchers. When I came down to help her lift them I asked, 'Why did your friends leave you?'

'They, just did,' Yasmin replied with a mischievous smile.

I helped her to lift the pitchers onto her head, one after the other. Each time our fingers touched. After she placed the second one on her head I asked, 'Will you be OK, with all this weight?'

'Watch me.'

And I watched her limp away towards the village and then drank my fill.

That night I could not help thinking about her. I kept seeing her foot. At the time, by the well, I didn't notice it had been decorated with henna. I kept seeing her foot in my hand and I kept seeing her mischievous smile and hearing her last words, 'watch me.' I did watch her walk out of view, limping away on her left foot.

I took a deep breath and said, 'I did once love her.'

'*Her* had a name, Dad,' Aisha cried.

'She had a name,' I murmured.

'Say *her* name, Dad.'

'Yasmin.'

'Now tell me you loved her.'

'Yes, once I did love Yasmin.'

Aisha turned towards me, looked at me with bloodshot eyes and asked, 'Then what happened, Dad?'

'England,' I said. 'I came to England.'

Aisha went quiet for a while and then asked, 'And that white woman, was she worth leaving my mother for?'

I thought back to when Aisha had told me she could smell Carol on me. I tried to suppress the memories of going to see Carol.

Aisha's sigh chased Carol out of my mind, 'Oh, Dad, come here.'

She put her arm in mine and we walked up the road towards Platt Fields Park. A flock of pigeons glided over the entrance of the park and disappeared behind the trees.

'Why did Mum commit suicide?' Aisha asked. 'Did she ever say anything to you before, I mean, did you ever think she would do it?'

'One day when I came to see you, it was a few days before she died, the house looked strangely empty. You were in your bedroom and refused to come down and see me. I sat down in the sitting room and asked your mother . . .'

'Call her by her name, Dad, please.'

'I asked Yasmin to go and call you down. As she was leaving, she said to me, "I want you to look after my daughter after I am gone." I laughed at her, "Are you going to your village?" She'd said, "I'm leaving forever."'

'She came up to see me and told me you were downstairs, but I hated you so much I swore at you and told her to go down and tell you what I said. And she'd said, "He is all you have left." She stood looking at me strangely for a while. She asked me to come to her room. I went with her and her clothes were neatly packed on the bed. Everything was ironed and folded. She asked me if I wanted any of her suits. I said, "Girls in Manchester don't wear village suits." She'd laughed and told me she was giving them all away. "You going to become *modern* Mum," I'd said. She smiled, shook her head and went downstairs.'

'When Yasmin came downstairs she told me, "You need to learn how to be a father to your daughter. Leave now and come back in three days' time. She will need you," I didn't know she would be dead in three days' time, I swear I didn't.'

As we crossed the road, a car going in the opposite direction swerved and came directly at us. Aisha quickly pulled me out of the way. The car turned suddenly towards the city centre. A young man from inside the car lobbed a beer can at us, shouting, 'This is England.' Beer from the can made an arch as it flew towards us. The can missed us and hit a parked car nearby.

'Aisha, are you OK?' I asked.

'Our England,' she said, laughing.

Walking into the park, I thought she laughs just like her mother used to at her age. Just like her mother.

'Was Mum always quiet, Dad?' Aisha asked, breaking a leaf off a tree.

'What do you mean?' I asked, trying to hold back memories of Yasmin, from before I came to England. She was so loud, you could hear her long before you saw her; no wedding complete without her leading the women singing and dancing.

'I just don't remember her ever shouting, or saying much.' Aisha thought for a moment and said, 'Or ever laughing, like normal people.'

An image of Yasmin in our house in Manchester flashed through my mind. A ghost who I hardly ever talked to, sitting in the living room, a Quran in her hand, reciting, rocking backwards and forwards, with me deliberately sitting in the same room drinking whisky. Sometimes the ghost caught fire and argued with me for sending too much money to Gulzarina, saying, 'You care more for her son than you do for your own daughter. You have to save the money. She will grow up and we will need the money.'

'I will raise Habib's son as I promised him before he died . . .'

And to hurt me, she would say: 'You never think about your own.'

These fights usually took place at the end of the month, when she knew I sent money to Gulzarina, or after I talked to Gulzarina on the telephone or when she sent me photographs of young Habib, which I would look at for ages, searching for that which I knew was not there, an image of my dead cousin.

The thoughts of what I had hidden stirred inside me. I stopped them by saying to Aisha, 'She was a good woman your mother was, Aisha.'

'Thanks Dad, you really know what I want to hear, don't you?' Aisha said bitterly, looking at a discarded cloth stuck in the thorns of a bush close to her.

'Oh, you asked was she always quiet . . .'

'It doesn't matter, Dad. It really doesn't matter anymore, does it?' She pulled the cloth out of the thorns, straightened it and tied it around a small branch.

'Why did you tie that cloth around that branch like that?' I asked, remembering her mother doing this in a shrine in our village.

'I just did.'

Aisha flipped the front of her veil off her face and lifted her head towards the sun, which had just come out.

The branches of the trees swayed gently. Birds called out to each other. A little child cried somewhere behind some bushes, crying all the louder on hearing its mother calling back.

I felt a warm pain deep inside me as I recalled how, on the day before I came back to England for the first time, Yasmin had insisted that I go with her to the Shrine at the top of the hill, beyond the never-drying lake in the jungles of my village, to tie a strip of green cloth to the old peepal tree under which a holy man had once sat. She had wished aloud, 'Peer baba, grant every wish to my Saleem Khan and make sure he is not enticed by white flesh when he goes to England.'

Why are you thinking about the day when she arrived in England, I asked myself inside my head, trying to suppress the unwanted memories. I thought of her coming out of the airport, dressed in green, a dupatta over her bulging stomach. She followed me silently to the car, opened the back door and got inside as I put her suitcase in the boot. As we were pulling out of the car park I asked, 'When is the baby due?'

'When God wills.'

In the driving mirror, I looked at her looking at me. Her face was swollen. She looked quickly away when she saw me looking at her. Leaving the airport car park, I thought of Carol and saw her jeering at me, saying, 'You're just like the rest of 'em. You got your little village girl, didn't you?'

I was about to run into the back of a car in front and slammed the breaks as hard as I could. Yasmin screamed as she smashed into the back of my seat. The driver behind me pressed hard on the horn of his car. I waved an apology to the irate driver and then turned to Yasmin, who sat back in the seat pressing gently on her stomach.

'Is the baby OK?' I asked, driving off again.

'Thanks be to God,' Yasmin said.

Aisha looked at the time on her mobile, bent down to the ground, picked up a twig, snapped it and threw it in the air, watching it twisting and turning.

When she looked down I said, 'Aisha, whatever has happened? I am still your father and I do have a duty towards you, like fathers do.'

She looked away from me at a bus that was going down the road. The bus stopped, but Aisha's head was a little tilted, as though she was looking past the hospital where she had been born, down past the university where I had dreamt she would go one day and into the city centre, where she would soon disappear.

'I had been wondering when you would say all this, Abba,' Aisha said.

'Your Auntie Gulzarina called me this morning from Pakistan . . .'

'And she wants me to marry her goatherder son, eh?' Aisha said, putting her arm in mine and walking up the road with me.

'He teaches at a university in Islamabad,' I said. 'He is a good-looking man as well.'

'Well, now you've really got me, Dad! A good-looking man in Pakistan,' Aisha said. 'They're all the same, Abba. They come here and crap on their wives before running off with white women. But you know all about that, don't you?'

Aisha's words sent a chill down my back. She's a child, I thought. She doesn't know how much she hurts you.

Pretending I had felt nothing, I pulled a photograph of Habib Junior from my pocket and showed it to her.

She laughed and said, 'I like the hero pose and the hero haircut, Dad, and the hero moustache . . . they just take my breath away.'

'I made a promise to his father, your uncle . . .'

'Dad, if I marry, I will do so for myself, not for your promises.'

'Aisha, don't be angry with me.'

'I am not,' Aisha said.

'Will you think about it?'

'I will think about it.'

'I'll knock on your door and let you know if I want to,' Aisha smirked, 'but tell me before I go, did you and Mum have an arranged marriage?'

I shook my head.

'Mum said she was low-caste, a massalan. Is that so Dad?'

'Yes. But I never believed in this.'

'But you're high-caste, aren't you? Mum said you were Jats who called themselves Khans.'

I nodded.

'Mum said high-caste men took low-caste girls, massalan girls, and raped, ravished and beat them whenever they wanted, and no one cared or did anything.'

'Sometimes this happens, but nothing like this happened in—'

Aisha interrupted, 'That's not what Mum said.' Turning abruptly towards me, she asked, 'Was she just your massalan, your low-caste bit?'

'Stop it now, daughter,' I pleaded, 'enough.'

Aisha kicked her foot through some dead leaves and asked, 'Did Mum ever meet your white woman?'

'No,' I said.

'At least you spared her one indignity.'

It snowed that night. Watching my garden fill with snow, I remembered the first snowman Aisha had built, when she was about five. She asked me for a carrot so that it could have a long red nose, but there were no carrots in the house and she became angry and threatened to break it up. I went in and brought a fat kerala out. She hated this vegetable. She grabbed my hand and led me outside, pointed to the neighbour's snowman and said, 'See Abba, snowmen have to have red noses.'

'Ours can have a green nose,' I said, walking back and pushing the kerala into the face of the snowman.

Aisha shouted at me, 'No snowman has ever had a green nose, and I hate kerala. They're horrible and yucky.'

I spent the whole night falling in and out of snow-filled dreamy sleep, fighting my urge to go past Aisha's house, promising myself to respect her privacy.

In the morning, I went to Aisha's house. I reached her street around eight o'clock. My feet hurt from the cold. I could feel it biting into my hands through my gloves and my ears were burning. I had a carrot in my pocket. The snow had stopped falling. Children on their way to school were throwing snowballs at each other. One landed at my feet. Another exploded on my back. Some kids laughed somewhere. A snowball whizzed past and hit a woman not far from me.

I had come with the intention of knocking on Aisha's door and asking her to build a snowman with me. I hid as much as possible behind parked vans and cars. The snow had been shovelled away from Aisha's door to the pavement. The front door opened. I stepped back and hid between two cars. An old woman came out of Aisha's house. She had her face turned away from me. I heard Aisha say something to her but all I could make out were the words 'Auntie Liz.'

The old woman turned slowly in my direction. I tried to steal a glimpse of her but her face was turned away from me. She was a short woman, well protected against the cold. As she set off, I stepped back onto the pavement and called out, 'Carol.'

She stopped. It had started to snow again, with big flakes. She turned. She lifted her head and looked at me. The blue of her eyes moved like a flame, and then became misty. Her face tightened. Her lips opened. A big snowflake hit my eye.

'You have no right to be here,' Carol said.

'And you do?' I asked.

'She must not see you here,' Carol said, looking back anxiously. 'Not with me.'

'Carol,' I said.

'Yes.'

My mind went blank for a moment and then I asked, 'Can I walk with you?'

'Can I walk with you, he asks?' Carol said. 'At the end of a lifetime he asks, "Can I walk with you?"'

It was a beautifully crisp snow-covered world through which I walked with Carol towards the centre of Chorlton. Her back straightened as she crossed the main road breathing steam out of her mouth.

A car coming towards us down the Wilbraham Road skidded on some ice and bumped into the back of another one waiting at the traffic lights. The driver of the stationary car got out, stood in the middle of the road blocking traffic going in the opposite direction and started shouting at the driver of the car who had bumped into him. Irate motorists started blowing their horns. I laughed.

Carol turned to me, with a flash of blue across her eyes as she said, 'Someone could have got injured!'

I tried tightening my lips to stop myself laughing. Her eyes softened. Her lips were moist now and beautifully red.

'I swear you look younger now than you did on the other side of the road,' I said.

'Oh, *now* he thinks I have become younger!' Carol said, blowing steam through her hands.

'What's happened to your wrinkles?' I asked.

'Are you trying to chat up an old woman?' Carol laughed, taking hold of my hand.

I felt a wedding ring on her hand and pulled mine away.

'I am sorry,' she said, stepping back a little.

'It's my fault,' I said. 'I'm sorry. I didn't know you were married.'

The motorist who had been bumped into was now swearing at the car driver he had blocked. Others beeped in a frustrated frenzy. The snow fell thick and fast, scattered by a chill wind which blew it off the tops of cars.

Carol put her hand over her wedding ring and smiled, 'And why should you know? It has been twenty years since you left me.'

'It wasn't like that, Carol,' I said.

'Just a white whore,' Carol said.

'Carol, please stop.'

My stomach knotted. My throat dried. I could hardly see through the held-back tears.

A police car had now arrived. The irate motorist inspected the back of his car and then drove off quickly. Carol walked into a café a short distance away up the hill. I followed her in and went to the toilet to wash my face. When I came out, Carol had bought me a tea.

'Is it still one sugar?' she asked, as I sat down.

I shook a small plastic bottle of sweeteners at her.

'I should have guessed,' she said, switching cups around. 'I like it sweet sometimes.'

'Who did you marry then?' I asked, sipping the tea. Her hair had greyed but the curls moved with the same beauty as they had done the last time I had seen her.

'He wants to know who I married!' Carol tutted, adjusting her chair. She put her left hand on the table and said, 'See.'

I looked down at the ring on her hand. It was a small silver ring with diamond shapes cut into it. I recognised the ring. I had gone to the Sadar Bazaar in Rawalpindi and bought Carol the ring and silver earrings.

'I told my mother I was married in the eyes of God,' Carol said.

'You didn't believe in God, Carol,' I said.

'But you go to the mosque nowadays,' Carol said, handing me a tissue.

'Oh, that's just that,' I said, blowing my nose. 'Why did you move in with Aisha?'

'I came to see the house where we used to live. I was walking past the post office when I saw a notice in the window asking for a woman to house share. It was our old house. I recognised it in the photo. I knocked on the door and Aisha opened it. I knew at once she was your daughter. She had your chin and the forehead. I rented a room and after a while she tried to sell the house. I bought it and asked her to live in it until she found another one. The house is still hers in my will, but she doesn't know it and you must never tell her.'

'No,' I said.

'Never tell her I am Carol. She hates the woman her dad left her mother for.'

'I understand,' I said, looking away from her. 'You waited all these years for me.'

'You waited all these years for me, he says!' Carol threw her head back, laughing. 'No, Saleem, I didn't wait for you. I didn't want another man.'

'I never stopped loving you,' I said.

'He never stopped loving me, he says,' Carol said, stroking my hand with a finger.

'I still love you,' I said.

Carol went quiet for a while, and then pushed her chair back and said, 'I must be going now.'

Walking out of the café, Carol said, 'I'm going shopping tomorrow. Do you want to come along?'

My heart pounded erratically.

'Do you want my number?' I asked.

'I have it,' Carol said. 'It's our old one, isn't it?'

I nodded and said, 'My mobile, I mean.'

'Aisha has it stuck on the kitchen door,' Carol said.

'I didn't know she had it.'

'There is not much you do know about her,' Carol said, turning her face away. Her words suddenly became cold. 'But, then, you did desert her as well.'

'I did,' I said. 'And I can't go back and undo anything, can I?'

Carol turned around, squeezed my hand and left.

I whistled and sang all the way back to my house, an old man's blood beating a youthful rhythm. I cursed myself for not contacting her all these years. What had gone wrong with me? How hard was it to pick up a phone, or go to her house in Bradford? Why had I not phoned her on her mother's death?

The next morning, I got up earlier than usual and looked at myself in the mirror.

'What's she going to do with this face?' I said to the mirror.

'Shave it then,' the man in the mirror said mischievously. I had not seen him so happy in over two decades.

Rubbing my hands through my hair, I said, 'You need to get this trimmed, you old scruff.'

The man in the mirror blew into his hands and said, 'And she doesn't want to smell your dirty breath, either!' I spent the morning wandering about the house waiting for the hours to pass. I had made three cups of tea, one after the other, but forgot to drink them. After many years, I drew back all the curtains in the house and opened the windows. The cold air no longer dug itself into my bones. I relived yesterday with Carol, savouring the minutes, thinking back over the way she lifted her hand when she talked to me. I smelt the hand over which she had rubbed her finger and could still see the white flash of her teeth when she threw her head back laughing, and her bouncing hair, still full of life.

We met in the centre of Manchester in Market Street. I was there an hour early by the entrance to the Arndale, looking for her through the waves of people coming and going. She came down from the bus station wearing a blue-striped skirt and a brown coat. She looked much slimmer than yesterday. The buttons of her coat were unfastened. She smiled when she saw me. She stopped to let a woman pushing a baby in a pram pass. The woman was pushing the pram with one hand while trying to drag an obstinate boy along with the other. Carol said to the woman, 'Wait.' The woman looked puzzled and stopped. Carol went over to the ice cream seller, bought an ice cream with a chocolate flake stuck in it and offered it to the boy. He looked at his mother, put his hands in his pockets and lowered his head.

'At least say "thank you" to the lady,' the mother said.

'Thank you, lady,' the boy said, without lifting his head up.

'Well, take it then,' the mother said.

The boy's face lit up. He took the ice cream saying, 'Thank you, lady,' again and ran off into the crowd of shoppers with his irate mother rushing behind him.

We stood looking at each other and laughed. I tried to hug Carol but she pushed me away and turned towards the Arndale Centre.

'Sorry,' I said, following her.

After a little while I asked, 'Can I hold your hand?'

Carol turned towards me. Her face tensed. The blue of her eyes merged into a raging storm. She said, 'In all those years I was with you, you wouldn't let me hold your hand in public, would you? You never once let me put my arm in your arm, "It's not what we do," you said. "Everyone will think I am white." Well, *I am white*, that's just what I am. You barge into my life and think I'll just have you back. Is that what you think—I am still your little white whore, eh?'

We walked silently towards a bench near the Manchester Wheel.

The storm became a mist and Carol said, 'I am who I am, that's all I am.'

I don't know where the sudden anger came from, but I said, 'You were always white when my mates were around, Carol.'

'How can you say that after what you put me through,' Carol said coldly.

A memory of Carol sitting stiffly with Mangal Singh and my mates from the old mill in a bar flashed through my mind. When she came out with us like this, Mangal Singh often said, 'She's lovely but she's like those goree who like us one to one but just can't stand a group of Pakis when we are together.'

And I remembered translating this for Carol and her snapping back, 'How dare you! Do you know what it's like for a woman to sit in a pub with a load of men—any men!'

What's the good of saying this to Carol? No point going over old pain, I thought, as Carol pressed on my hand.

I smiled at the memory of Mangal Singh eating in my kitchen, with Carol rolling rotis, turning them in her hands and tossing them onto a hot tava, her hair tied behind her and a flowery apron covered in white flour around her front. 'She's more Desi than Desis,' Mangal Singh would say.

'And do you remember how Mangal Singh always used to say I was more Desi than Desis?' Carol said, wiping her eyes.

210

'What you crying for?' I asked.

'Don't know,' she said. 'What you crying for?'

'Don't know.'

'Let's go and shop,' Carol said.

We went into the Arndale and walked around for a while window shopping.

'I'm going to buy me some clothes,' Carol said.

I followed her into a shop. She picked out some tops and went to try them on. She came out and stood in front of me. I tried hard to think of something then touched a top with a paisley pattern that Carol was holding and said, 'I think this colour really suits you.'

'Now you can match colours, can you? When we were together, you never once came to women's shops with me. Below your dignity was it, eh?' Carol said in a sorrowful voice. 'You were never one for anything special, were you?'

She was waiting for an answer. I pursed my lips and nodded. She went in to change. How could I have been such a bastard when I was with her, I thought? She needs to let her pain out.

She came out and did a twirl for me in her new top, her skirt dancing in the air as she turned. I looked on. She said, smiling, 'Well, how do I look?'

I searched for words that would not upset her.

She looked at herself in a mirror on the wall and asked me, 'Come on, how do I look?'

'Delicious,' I said.

Carol grinned, pulled her top straight and said to a young woman going into one of the changing cubicles, 'He thinks I look "delicious" in this top.'

After Carol finished shopping, we went for a meal in a café near Shude Hill. I could find nothing more beautiful than watching her breaking a small piece of naan, dipping it in sauce, then putting it in her mouth and chewing it slowly as she always did before swallowing. The earrings that I had bought her over twenty years ago swayed gently. She sat with her back to the window that overlooked the tramlines. They came and went, as did the customers in the café.

As she was leaving, I tried to hug her again, but she pushed me away with a peck on the cheek, whispering, 'That was in another lifetime, Saleem Khan.'

As soon as I got home later that day I texted her: Can u talk?

She texted back: Yes.

I replied: Can I ring u?

She replied: OMG.

I didn't know what that meant and replied: Yes/no?

She replied: No.

My throat dried and I suddenly felt sick. Maybe I have got everything all wrong, I thought. Just then my mobile rang. It was Carol.

'Is that you, Carol?' I asked.

'Who else would it be on this number?' Carol said with a childish giggle in her voice. 'What's up with *you*?'

'What do you mean?' I said.

'It's you who wanted to talk,' she said, 'then why did it take so long to reply?'

'It was the OMG,' I said.

'OMG?' she asked.

'I didn't know what it meant,' I said.

'He didn't know what it meant!' Carol laughed.

When she stopped, I asked her, 'Carol?'

'What?'

'I want to do something special for you. Will you come over to my house?'

The phone went silent.

'Carol?' I said.

'What?'

I waited for a moment and then said, 'Sorry, I did not mean to upset you. I was just thinking, it being your birthday like, why don't I cook you a meal?'

She was sobbing but did not say anything.

'Well, it is your twenty-first,' I said.

'Twenty-fifth, stupid, that's when we went out first,' Carol said.

'Will you come?' I asked.

'Na. What for?'

'Something really really special.'

'You and something special,' Carol said. 'That I have to see.'

I had tidied up the house, bought some women's magazines to find out what women of her age wanted. I bought all sorts of anti-wrinkle facial creams.

After reading the women's magazines, I was confident I had bought her just the right present, neatly wrapped and already on the table.

I went to the barbers for a haircut and asked him to give me a hot towel shave. He was a man in his late thirties who had taken over the family business after his father-in-law died. Holding my hair in his hand, he said, 'Uncleji, women like young men, and you could look young with some colour on this.'

'What are you talking about, you little bastard?' I laughed.

'Come on Uncleji. Colour this black and you will look

213

years younger. It's not like the old days. It's quick drying now. Modern stuff, uncle. Done before you know it.'

'All right, go on,' I said. 'But there is no woman, you know.'

'No, Uncleji,' the barber said, placing a hot towel on my face.

When I put my glasses back on to see myself in the mirror, someone else was looking back at me.

After I left the barber's, I hurried back. It was another beautiful day. The sun was out. I cooked the chicken and made the dough for the rotis, covered it with a wet cloth and left it to settle.

Carol came in the late afternoon. I stood in the shadow of the hall when she knocked on the door. She stepped inside, looked at me, put a hand over her mouth and said, 'Oh my God.'

I took her coat. She said, 'What on earth made you do this?'

'I just thought . . .'

'A tacky Paki, that's all you are. A beard with henna would complete the picture.'

She walked into the kitchen, saw the presents and said, 'Ah, he did all this for me!'

'Happy birthday,' I said.

She opened the first one and roared with laughter. I laughed as well but did not know what it was she found so funny.

'Saleem Khan, you are so corny. You've been reading women's magazines, haven't you?' Carol said, regaining her breath.

'No!'

'Did you read it somewhere: What every woman wants—*perfume*,' Carol laughed. 'This is the same one you always bought me, when you remembered.'

'It's not, is it?' I said.

'It is,' Carol said. 'And I bet I know what the other present is.'

'No, you don't.'

'I bet *he's* bought me chocolates and I bet it's the "Lady Likes" type.'

She was right. I took an upturned tava off a clean pile of pots on the sink and placed it on the cooker.

'You're making me fresh roti!' Carol said, taking in a deep breath of the scent of the chicken as it warmed. 'And you remembered my favourite dish.'

She kissed me on the lips. I held her tightly and we kissed passionately. We kissed and kissed. Suddenly she pushed me away, saying, 'No, Saleem Khan, no!'

She adjusted her clothes, picked up her bag and left without even looking back at me. I walked around the house, going into each room, and felt like setting fire to it. Why was I so impatient, I thought? It was going so well.

'Well, God, you really are taking the piss out of me, aren't you?' I said, looking up at the cracked ceiling of my kitchen.

I took the bottle of champagne out of the fridge, unfastened the cork, pushed it up a little, then watched it slowly coming up until it popped and hit the ceiling. I poured it into two glasses, one for me and one for Carol, saying, 'Well, here's to another fuck up.' I drank both glasses and was refilling them when there was a knock at the door. It was Carol. She was holding a bottle of wine wrapped in gift paper.

'I had bought a present for you as well,' she said.

I stepped back and she walked in.

'Wine for a mosque-going Muslim?' I asked.

She raised her eyebrows at me as she went past. The kitchen door was open. She looked at the table and said, 'Champagne!' She picked up a glass.

'As the Almighty wished,' I said, raising my glass.

'Who can deny Him?' Carol said softly, holding the tips of my fingers in hers.

She left a little later than she had intended. Her taxi must have only reached the end of my road when I started to miss her. During the night, I tossed and turned, breathing in her scent from the sheets, feeling an unbearable longing for her as I thought over what she had said. She did not want to see me the next day. She wanted some time to understand what was happening. She loved me, had never stopped loving me, but I had betrayed her. Yes, she can forgive, but there was an emptiness inside her, created by my betrayal; a great big void, from which a surge of anger kept on engulfing her, a rage so intense she wanted to tear me limb from limb.

Breaking my promise, I telephoned her the next day. She talked softly back, telling me more than I asked. She was at home she said. She couldn't see me today as she had an appointment at the hospital. She would have to stay overnight and see me tomorrow.

The next morning, her telephone was off. It must have been turned off as she was probably still in hospital, I thought. I texted her to contact me as soon as she was out, but she did not respond. Maybe the battery had gone dead, I thought. I kept trying during the day, but her mobile was off. I didn't know which hospital she had gone to or what the tests were for.

It was dark and I was trying to get myself up to bed, flicking through the satellite channels, stopping now and then on some film I had seen before. I said to myself, 'Saleem Khan, you stupid old git. You chased her away. Why could you not have followed your brains and not—' The buzzing of my mobile cut short my sentence. It was Carol.

'Well, my love,' she said, her voice frail. 'Did you think I had left you?'

'Where are you, Carol?'

'In hospital still, going home tomorrow, inshah'allah,' she laughed.

'What's wrong, Carol?'

'I'll tell you when I see you.'

'Shall I come over now?'

'He wants to come over now!' Carol said. 'It's well past visiting time.'

'Shall I come in the morning?'

'Aisha's picking me up,' Carol said. 'I'll see you later.'

Carol came to see me in the late afternoon the next day. Her face was pale, her eyes sunken. She was a little unsteady on her feet. She had a bottle of champagne with her. She put it in the freezer to chill and then insisted on helping me clean the kitchen, all the time complaining about my dirty habits and how they had not changed in twenty years. She pulled out a cup and showed me the teabag still inside. Then she found another, then another, all with tea bags stuck to the bottom. She took the champagne bottle out of the freezer, touched it to her face and gave it to me to open. As I did this, she rummaged around for some glasses and told me what had happened. She'd gone in for some routine tests and begun to feel very ill when she was in hospital. As the cork popped, she said, 'They've given me three months to live.'

'Oh, God, Carol!' I said, hugging her. 'Couldn't they have got it wrong?'

'Maybe four,' she said. Picking up her glass, she took a sip and put it back down on the table.

'Should you be drinking?' I asked.

She took another sip and said, 'At least I got you back.'

'I don't want to lose you now,' I cried.

'We all have to go,' she said.

I squeezed her close to me. She said, 'Some sooner than others, but we all have to go. And didn't you say there was a phrase in your language about death being something to life?'

'Death is but an excuse for life,' I said.

'And life is for however long it is.' She coughed a little and then put her arm through mine. She picked up her glass, waited for me to take mine and said, 'Tomorrow we are going to Bradford. I want to visit the old tree under which we used to sit and look down on the canal that snaked around the mill.'

As she was leaving later that evening, getting into the taxi, she opened the window and said, 'And don't forget your flute.'

That night, I drank more and asked the Almighty, 'Why did you give me love only to take it away so fast? Are you really the God to whom those in pain should turn or are you the giver of pain?' All night I imagined our trip to Bradford: looking out onto the green hilly fields as the train rumbled along through the beautiful scenery of the Pennines, a journey we had often made in the past, Carol leaning against me, watching the world go by.

The next morning, we caught the first train out. It was a dry day, warm for that time of year. There was not a cloud in the sky. A singing wind brushed some dead leaves off the platform onto the railway line.

In Bradford, the weeping willow under which we had often sat was still there, bigger now, with a wider umbrella of green leaves. A beautiful black cat with erect ears and a long slim body sat in a hollow near the base of the trunk, slowly moving its tail. Carol spread a plastic sheet on the ground and a thick blanket on top of the sheet. The cat stood up. It had a long neck and a shining black nose and the slits of the pupils in its sharp eyes contracted as it focused on our every step. I shooed it away. It did not run, but slowly turned and walked around the back of the tree. I followed it to make sure it had gone. It was nowhere to be seen.

'It really is true, isn't it?' Carol asked when I came back. 'Old men really can't hold it in, can they?'

'I went to see if the cat had gone' I said, ignoring her jibe.

'What cat?' Carol asked.

'The black one.'

'What black one?' Carol asked, leaning against the trunk of the tree.

'Didn't you see it?' I asked.

'Come and sit next to me,' Carol said. 'There are no black cats in these hills.'

We sat under the tree, looking over the dry brick wall down towards the silver waters, shining today under the clear sky. Carol asked me if I remembered the time we went to the shrine on top of a hill across the waters of the stream of my village.

'It was the end of the monsoons,' I said.

The fields had been full of rye. The white building of the shrine had shone in the hills There was a strange stillness in the air. A partridge called out from somewhere nearby, its song echoing in the hills. Another partridge replied from across the brown waters of the river below—waters which had flowed past many hills and many shrines to fall into the river Jhelum and then, coursing through many lands, joined the mighty Indus and raced on to the Arabian Sea.

'There was a poem written in the Shrine. Do you remember it?' she asked.

I did. She asked me to recite it.

Ginaan ishq namaazan paryaan kaday naheen o marday
jay shaq hovay bandya tehnoon vaekh lay devay balday

Those who have prayed the prayer of love, never die come see the lamps burning, if you have any doubt.

'And again', she said.

I recited it again.

'The light of love is eternal, it never dies,' she said.

'And do you remember the photo of you, Habib and me, which we got the waiter to take that day when we were eating in Rawalpindi?'

'I do,' I said.

'And that ridiculous bomb disposal squad!'

'You were sweating with fear,' I said.

'And how furious you were at the bomb squad! One of them had a sledgehammer . . .'

She laughed and I said, 'And the other one was smoking a cigarette. And they looked inside the car and then just smashed the car window and opened the bag inside. You just screamed.'

'It could have been a bomb, couldn't it?'

'It proves there is a God,' I said, stroking her hair. She had curled up against me and putting the flute in my hands asked me to play it. As I played, she gradually drifted off to sleep.

Carol's hands had become thinner. I stroked her hand. She was not wearing the ring. I proposed to her while she was still asleep. I told her I had bought her a wedding ring. I took the ring out of my pocket and held it in my hand.

A small twig fell through the leaves and landed on Carol's face. I brushed it off.

When she woke up, I held both her hands in mine and said, 'Will you marry me?'

She picked up the twig and snapped it.

'You never thought I would propose to you today,' I whispered, 'did you, Carol?'

She smiled again. 'This is our hill and our tree and we are together—is that not enough . . . ?'

We met every day for the next four days, in Manchester. I loved walking around the city centre with Carol, watching the street artists, window shopping and eating greasy takeaways.

One beautiful sunny day we walked down Market Street towards Deansgate. A large circle of onlookers had formed around a young woman playing the violin. Carol squeezed my hand, whispering, 'Come on, Saleem,' and, pulling me by the hand into the centre, held me tightly and forced me to waltz. The violinist nodded at us and people clapped. A moment or so later, a few other couples joined us and before I had a chance to worry about my embarrassment so many people were waltzing that I had become invisible. When the violinist stopped, Carol went up to her and placed a ten-pound note in her bucket.

We walked down, hand in hand, past a man as old as me, who was putting his body through all sorts of contortions to the rhythm of loud rap music blaring out from a CD player nearby.

'I've always wanted to go on the Manchester Wheel,' Carol said, 'with you.'

We stood in a small queue and bought our tickets before getting into an empty glass bubble on the Manchester Wheel. As the doors shut and we swung up, Carol said, 'I wish we had had a child—a girl.'

I looked away from her out onto the street below. A group of Manchester United supporters were waving flags.

'It hurts me too, but I had to say it,' Carol said.

A woman's voice over the Wheel's speakers welcomed us to a 'world-class tourist attraction.'

We looked down at the scene below: some drunks dancing, a big television screen with BBC news on it and shoppers going to and fro. We burst out laughing when the announcer told us about Manchester's reinvention and its place as the confident capital of the North.

'Tell me, Saleem, what was your happiest moment with her?' Carol asked.

'When Aisha was born,' I said. Cousin Habib's face flashed through my mind. 'Habib predicted it.'

Carol laughed, shaking her hair. It moved from side to side brushing across her face. 'Now you're believing all this?'

'Maybe not,' I said, 'but Habib was dying when he predicted he would have a son and I a daughter.'

'Was it really his son?' Carol asked.

I looked down at the big television screen below. Colours were bouncing out of it.

'I'm sorry,' Carol said. 'I didn't mean it like that. I know your village, you know. It's just that I heard what happened to Gulzarina.' Carol coughed. After a pause she added, 'Lovely girl, she is, Aisha.'

'Yes.'

'Lovely girl,' Carol repeated softly, wiping her lips.

When we were at the very top of the wheel, I said, 'You know Carol, doctors can get it wrong. I have known so many people who had cancer and lived much . . .'

'I know.'

We ended our day, as we often did, in a café.

Carol would come to my house in the mornings and stay until early afternoon. Her cough got worse each day and she strained when she walked and was getting more and more out of breath. One morning, she didn't turn up. I rang her mobile many times and left messages for her. It was late in the afternoon when she finally telephoned. She said in a laboured voice, 'Aisha really loves you . . .'

'Where are you, Carol?'

'She has always loved you,' Carol said.

'Carol, can I see you?' I asked. 'Are you in hospital?'

'Aisha is coming today,' she said.

'Can you phone me when she leaves?' I asked.

'She is going to stay the night with me,' Carol said.

She died that night.

Carol's funeral was held two weeks after her death, in Bradford. I went to her wake in Our Lady's. Even though so many years had passed, I recognised Carol's brother, Jack. He was wearing a smart black suit and shaking hands with people as they went in. I hid behind a tree and drank a can of beer. I didn't want Aisha to see me. She came, dressed all in black. Jack hugged her. Jack saw me standing behind a tree looking in his direction. After Aisha went in, I downed the remains of the beer and went towards the church. Jack blocked my way, saying, 'This is private, old man. Friends and family only!'

'She was,' I mumbled.

'You're not family, mate, and I know all her friends,' Jack said. Taking five pounds out of his pocket, he put the note in my hand and said, 'Go have a drink on me.'

I could not move. Jack closed my hand, pressing it tightly, 'It's me sister's funeral, not a place for drunks looking for a freebie.'

I saw Aisha going into the mosque a few days later. I thought she waved at me. I called out to her but she did not reply. I didn't wait for her to come out and went home.

She is alone now, I thought, on the way home. Maybe she will come to me. And she did say she would come and tell me if she were willing to marry Habib Junior. If she agreed, I would arrange the best marriage our village had ever seen. There would be bands and fireworks and lights and singing and dancing. I fell asleep on my sofa dreaming of Aisha's marriage and was woken up by loud knocks on my door. It was Aisha. She walked right past me without saying anything and went into the kitchen. She took off her hijab. There was rage in her eyes. She threw a photograph of her mother on the table. Carol had taken it.

'Remember her?' Aisha asked.

'How could I forget your mother, Aisha?' I said.

'Who took it?' Aisha breathed heavily.

'I did,' I said.

'You fucking liar,' Aisha hissed. 'A nice photo of a servant girl, eh?'

I did not answer.

'You fucked her there and you fucked her up here, didn't you? And look at this,' Aisha said, throwing another photograph onto the table. It was the one of Carol, Habib and I in Rawal-pindi taken by the waiter. 'The bitch had these in an album by the side of her bed!'

'Don't call her that, Aisha.'

'Bitch, bitch, bitch' she cried, throwing some papers on the table. 'This is her will. She left me the house and everything she had.'

I put my hand on Aisha's head.

'You knew, didn't you, *you knew*?' She moved away from me.

'I knew, yes, I knew.'

Aisha's mobile rang in her purse. It had the same ringtone as my landline. She did not answer it. It continued to ring.

'There is us and our past, daughter,' I said. 'This pain will just keep us here.'

A mobile ringing in the street brings me back to my Man-chester of today.

Particles of dust float up in a beam of light that cuts through a gap in the curtains of my front living room. It has lit up the picture of the old woman on the wall opposite. The picture has been with me since the day I moved into this house. The sharp yellow of the lantern, by the light of which she is reading a book, has faded. The darkness sur-rounding her has become a shade lighter. Her silver hair has become more pronounced. The shawl around her neck is no longer a deep-sea blue, but a dimmer green. The pages of the book held in her left hand still look as if they are being softly lifted by a passing wind. She is pointing down at broken letters that had once been words. I had bought this picture when I was in Pakistan and had gone to the local history museum with Carol. It had reminded me of my own grandmother who, like the woman in the picture, also wore large earrings and whose face was also criss-crossed with wrinkles. But my grandmother could not read. I feel a yearning to be a child again, to be with her and to hear her voice singing me a song like she used to on the rainy nights of the monsoons in a language from the valleys of Kashmir, which no one else but her understood and for which she had no name.

'You shall remain as you are,' I tell the curtains.

Turning to leave, I catch a glimpse of the wedding card which Gulzarina had sent to me for Habib Junior's marriage. I pick it up. It is a padded card with silver flowers etched into it. Pressing it softly, I think back to his birth and his wedding that I missed.

Habib Junior was born after I married Yasmin. Back then, in my dope-filled days and nights, other than Gulzarina, I shunned visitors. We rarely spoke to each other. She came every other day, especially after her stomach began to grow, sat on a chair close to me and left as silently as she had come.

I slept during the day under the shade of our tree in the yard of our house. One day I woke up and she was sitting on the edge of my bed towards my feet. Yasmin stood close to her, a glass of water in her hand.

'You can't live like this, brother,' Gulzarina said, brushing a fly off my foot. 'And look how dirty your feet are.'

I sat up. Yasmin handed me the glass of water. I took it and as I was drinking it Gulzarina said to Yasmin, 'Get a lota of water and let me wash my brother's feet.'

'I will do it, he is my husband.'

At the mention of the word 'husband' my body tensed and I spat out, 'Get my sister water. I can wash my own feet.'

Yasmin melted away and came back a moment later with a bar of soap, a small towel and handed a copper lota filled with water to Gulzarina, and went back into the house.

I tried to take the lota but she shook her head, saying, 'My only brother.'

She poured some water over my feet and said, rubbing soap into my foot, 'Don't be so cruel to your wife.'

'I don't want her. I don't know why I married her. She can . . .'

'And I carry *your brother's* child,' she stopped mid laugh.

'When is the baby due?'

Gulzarina went red in the face. The lota dropped out of her hand. Her green eyes flushed with tears.

I sat up in bed, crossed my legs and put my hand under my pillow to find my cigarettes.

'I took them,' Gulzarina said, 'You have to come back to the living.'

'The living?'

'Yes, the living, brother,' she said, standing up. 'Be a man. You need to go back to England and work, and you must have children and remember what Habib wanted of our children.'

Letting out a deep sigh, she said, 'And I know your money is finished, so I have left some for you with your wife.'

'How can I take money from you?' I snapped.

'My gift to my brother,' she said with a wave of her hand, walking out of the house.

'Brothers don't take money from sisters,' I said. And then I said loudly, 'I will send it to you when I get to England.'

'Your cigarettes are in the silver jug with the other thing I threw away,' Gulzarina said as she went out of the gate. 'And I will write to you and you will be surprised at how good my Urdu has become.'

A few days later, I booked my ticket. When I came home after booking my flight, it was late at night and Yasmin was sitting on the veranda. As I went past her, she said, 'When are you leaving?'

'In two days' time.'

She followed me into the room where I kept my suitcase and asked, 'Will I live here on my own?'

I ignored her and went back out and slumped onto a bed.

'Will you call me to England?'

'No.'

It was a damp Manchester I came back to after Habib's death and my marriage. My house was empty of Carol's things, though I could feel her presence everywhere. I started working at the taxi base and as soon as I managed to save the money I owed, I sent it to Gulzarina, along with some for Yasmin.

A few months after I came back, Gulzarina phoned me, 'Congratulations brother, Habib has a son.'

I was suddenly filled with sorrow and happiness.

'Are you both well?'

'Thanks be to God.'

'What does he look like?' I asked, regretting the words as they came out of my mouth.

She went silent for a moment and then said coldly, 'You must name him.'

'Habib. His name can only be Habib,' I said. 'And do you need anything?'

'Yes.'

'Ask anything and I will get it for you.'

'I want you to take your wife to England.'

I went silent.

'My brother!' she pleaded.

A few weeks later I got some photographs of the new baby through the post.

Over the years, Gulzarina sent me many photographs and wrote detailed letters to me of how Habib Junior was crawling, when he caught colds, when he started to walk, about his first day at school and how he was growing up into a beautiful strong young man.

Then one day she wrote to tell me that he was to be married.

The marriage of Habib Junior took place in August. I would have gone to the wedding but for the fact that it was Aisha's birthday and for the first time in many years she wanted to see me on her birthday. We went for a meal on the Wilmslow Road and then, for the first time since her mother had died, I went with her to Yasmin's grave in the Southern Cemetery.

I went to Pakistan three weeks after the wedding. Before leaving, I phoned Gulzarina and told her of my arrival date and asked her to make sure Habib Junior's visits to his in-laws were done before I came. She phoned me back a few hours later and said that she thought it was not a good time for him to visit, but he would be home when I arrived.

I arrived on a Thursday in the middle of the day and got to the village just as the weekly procession to the shrine was leaving; a drummer followed by dancing children. Gulzarina and Cousin Habib's mother were waiting for me at the entrance of their house. My auntie had dyed her hair with henna, two bell shaped golden earrings sparkled on the sides of her face. She placed her hennaed hand on my head and gave me a glass of water to drink. Gulzarina wore a sparkling blue suit, her head covered with a green shawl I had given her. She looked much younger than I thought she would. She was flushed with happiness, holding two large albums of photographs.

It had rained earlier and there was a fresh earthy smell in the cool air.

'So where is the bride?' I asked. 'And why has the groom not come out to greet his uncle.'

'He's still in Afghanistan and on his way back today,' Gulzarina said. Tapping the photo album, she added, 'Just wait till you see how beautiful he looks.'

I felt a sudden chill run down my spine when I heard he had gone to Afghanistan. Stopping the memories of my visit from overwhelming me, I asked, 'And the bride, is she not beautiful?'

Gulzarina let out a hearty laugh. My auntie clapped her hands as she stepped out of the way to let me in.

I took my jacket off and my auntie took it and placed it behind a new wooden chair. A pressed white shalvar kameez suit was dangling off the side of the arm of the chair, below which was a pair of new black leather sandals.

'For you my son,' my auntie said, nodding to the pressed clothes. 'Get out of these silly clothes.'

When I came back after getting out of my Western clothes, Gulzarina was still standing clutching the photo albums close to her chest.

As I sat down she pulled over a chair and sat near me and opened the first page. Habib Junior was standing stiffly in a three-piece cream-coloured western suit, his head tilted up a little.

'This one is the engagement,' she said. 'See how my sons-in-law are standing around their sister, so angry, as if we have stolen their little girl! And this one is with all my son's cousins. They said no one should dance, but you know whose son he is . . .'

She put a hand on her mouth, her face suddenly losing its colour and then her eyes brightened. Gaining her composure, she added, 'Here, see. He is dancing, and with all those girls! And there, that's the henna night. And here we are walking through the street, and how beautiful the flames look. And here, that's me, playing the drum and singing with the women. And this is the wedding; that's his friends firing in the air! They were forbidden, but you know, his father would never listen, so how could his son? And he let them do it! And see these lights—they went all the way from your house to ours. The house looked like a bride . . .'

After a while, the pictures began to merge into each other, but I sat and let Gulzarina talk me through all of them. When she got to the last one, I opened my suitcase and showed her all the presents I had bought for the wedding. First of all, I gave Gulzarina a length of material which was to be made into a special suit for Habib Junior's grandmother. Gulzarina looked it over with admiration before passing it on to my auntie. Then I gave her material for a new suit for the groom's mother. Gulzarina blushed, taking it from me. There were four suits for the new bride and two for Habib Junior. I gave her an envelope with four hundred pounds in it and told her to go and buy the new bride some gold. Gulzarina returned it to me, much to the disapproval of her mother-in-law, saying, 'You have done more than you needed to do.'

'He is my son as well,' I said, pressing the envelope into her hand.

Gulzarina went silent.

I stood up, went over to a manji close by and fell into a heavy jet-lagged sleep, drifting in and out between England and Pakistan. Sometime later I was woken up as Abbi's happy voice boomed, 'Village gamblers are waiting to greet you in Dattay Ni Kassey.' He pointed towards a valley that runs between two hills at the back of the house. He had two plastic bags, one with tools, and the other one he put on the side of the bed.

'With open arms, no doubt,' I yawned, shaking his out-stretched hand.

'With sharpened knives,' Abbi laughed, biting the filter of his half-smoked cigarette. 'We know you Britishers only pre-tend to have no money.' He yanked me off the bed, hugged me and said, 'We sent a young man to England and look what has come back.'

I sat up and looked at him. He had a full head of hair which he had hennaed to disguise its colour. His face had the look of a man who did not let many things bother him. He gave me the plastic bag. It contained a pair of black leather sandals.

'What is this?' I asked.

'I have finally paid back my debt,' Abbi said.

'Debt?' I asked.

Abbi lit a cigarette but did not answer. I remembered. I had just started at the High School for Boys. He used to walk bare-foot to school and I bought him a pair of sandals with my first pay cheque. I took them from him now as I did not want to hurt his pride.

On the way to meet the gamblers, we stopped at my fami-ly's graveyard. The bricks I had ordered were piled up close to my mother's grave. Abbi got to work digging into the hard ground. I joined him as well and broke out in a sweat. He laughed at me.

'Babaji, this work is for us poor ones. You go and sit over there, under the shade of that tree.' I didn't argue—my knees were aching. I got up and sat on a log and watched Abbi digging a small trench along the space he had marked out for my grave, close to my mother's, placing the bricks into the ground along the markings so that they half stuck out.

After Abbi had finished, we went to join the gamblers. They were sitting on rocks in the shade of a tree.

'British bums are soft, Saleem,' one of the gamblers said, standing up to greet me.

I couldn't put a name to his face. Abbi came to my rescue, 'Raju, my elder brother, you still have a tongue that lashes even a visiting friend.'

'Raju, how can I forget you my friend?' I said, shaking his hand. He was a tall man with a warm smile and dark sunken cheeks.

Rolling up a scarf, Abbi placed it on a rock and said, 'Place your backside there, my friend. You Britishers are so used to comfort you cannot even have a simple death!'

I hesitated.

'Sit, sit, yaar,' Abbi insisted. 'When you are young you lot come back to our village to find pretty wives and then, when you are old, you come back to arrange your graves. What has England done to you that you have to have air-conditioned coffins to come back home in?'

'Just play the motherfucking game,' a gambler chided, 'you're wasting time.'

A boy's head bobbed up and down just at the turn of the path. Moments later he was in full view. He was riding on a donkey, shouting obscenities at the beast, striking the emaciated creature with a stick.

'Asif, what more can you get out of this donkey?' Abbi asked. 'You should be carrying the poor creature.'

The boy on the donkey was about to reply when the theme for *Nagin*, a popular Hindi film, rang around the hills. He put his hand into the breast pocket of his Kurta and pulled out his mobile phone. 'Yes, sir. Yes, sir. I am on the way to your house . . . But of course, sir. I have five donkeys with me right now, all laden with bricks. How could I let you down, Raja Saab, you of all people? I will be there in a few minutes.'

'He is a better liar than his father,' Abbi laughed.

Later that night, we sat in our courtyard. Abbi smoked a cigarette, staring into a pomegranate tree. Jackals howled close to the outer wall of our house. Stray village dogs barked back furiously. The night was filled with the song of crickets, and glow-worms flew around in the intoxicating scent of the queen-of-the-night blossom. Suddenly, the loud signature tune of the James Bond movies cut through the tranquillity.

'That's Uncle Jaan's mobile,' Abbi said, blowing smoke rings one through another.

'Why doesn't he answer the bloody thing?' I asked.

'It will cost him if he does,' Abbi replied, flicking his cigarette into the pomegranate tree.

'Does he know what the tune is?' I asked. An image of James Bond flashed through my mind. He was in a powerboat with a scantily dressed woman clinging to his arm. The boat was ploughing through the rising waves of a frothy sea. James was hot in pursuit of some devious delinquent out to destroy the world.

'Uncle Jaan doesn't care what the tune is,' Abbi replied. 'He only cares that half the village knows that someone is phoning him on his mobile.'

Mobile tunes were ringing out from around the village. They would ring a few moments and then ring off after one or two rings.

'Why do they go off like that?' I asked Abbi, who was toying with the idea of another cigarette.

'Unlike you foreigners,' Abbi said, 'we are poor folk. We ring then ring off. It's like saying I am thinking about you, and if you want to hear my motherfucking voice, then you ring me.' He paused to light his cigarette and continued. 'But the most important thing is that we have mobiles now and these have made the mullahs irrelevant for lovers.'

Mobile phones were still ringing all over the village. I made a mental note of the different sounds: James Bond had faded; Beethoven's Fifth Symphony was going strong; an old-fashioned telephone was ringing; a shrieking woman's voice shouting obscenities in English; an old Punjabi folk tune.

'Before the mobile phone, lovers were closer to God. They used to listen to the azaan before they made their way to have a shag,' Abbi said, 'especially the last call to prayers. When the faithful went to pray, the lovers sneaked out of their houses or jumped over their walls and melted into the night and into each others' arms.'

Abbi stopped talking just as someone tapped the loud-speakers of the village mosque, indicating the coming of the call to prayers. I fell asleep listening to the ringing of the mobiles and a less melodious azaan.

I was woken in the middle of the night by Gulzarina. The house was full of people. Gulzarina looked at me with horror-filled eyes. Holding a mobile telephone in her hand she stammered, 'My Habib and my daughter-in-law are no more.'

Gulzarina sat silently in the back of the car as we drove at speed along a dirt road through the winding hills and down into the valley behind the mountains to the back of our village. Abbi sat next to Gulzarina. We raced along a dried-up riverbed that snaked around the valley and reached our destination just as dawn was breaking. Hundreds of people were milling around the burnt-out wreckage of two fuel tankers. The carcass of a bus lay close to the tankers, and behind these was a huge pile of charred bodies. Twisted and mangled limbs: some with bones sticking out of the ash or through melted plastic. Someone approached our car. He had a piece of cloth wrapped around his face. His hair was singed, his face stained with ash.

Abbi unwound the car window and the man pointed to the remains of a minibus and said, 'Habib phoned me to meet him here. He was sitting in the front with his wife. This is a stop and the wagon he was travelling in couldn't go any further because the road was blocked by those tankers. The tankers were on their way to Afghanistan and some Taliban took them and brought them here. The tankers got stuck and the Taliban made people bring their tractors here, but that didn't help so they told everyone to take as much petrol as they could carry. People turned up from all over the place with whatever they could carry petrol in. I went to get some tea for Habib and his wife. The tea stall is just behind there, in that dip, and it was then that I heard them coming. It was so fast. It was NATO planes. I have seen them fly over here before, but never before have they done this . . . At first the air began to fry. Everything became white and my eyes burnt. And then one plane hovered over the tankers, like a helicopter. It went back and went higher and higher and then fired two missiles into the tankers. No one who was out there lived. I saw what was left of Habib Junior and his wife.'

He stopped and pointed to the heap of bodies.

Gulzarina jumped out of the car and ran to the heap of bodies, calling for her son. Her words were drowned out by others calling out for their loved ones as they rummaged through the pile.

Gulzarina pulled an arm out of the heap screaming, 'This is my Habib. This is my son!'

Another man with ash all over his face snatched the arm off Gulzarina, saying, 'This is my brother, Janshaer!'

'Give me my son, you bastard!' Gulzarina swore. 'See, he has a ring, I gave it to him.'

The man turned the arm around. The hand was in the shape of a claw, 'Look there is no thumb, my brother had a thumb. This must be yours, sister.'

'But this is not the ring I gave him on his wedding day. This must be yours.'

Gulzarina went back into the heap. I yanked her back. She stood dazed. Abbi stood next to me. Two men were fighting over a leg. Others were pulling bits of bodies out of the heap.

A young man armed with a double-barrelled shotgun walked towards the bodies, raised the gun and fired into the air. Over the fading sound of the gun, he said loudly, 'We are not animals. This is all that is left of their humanity, but we are alive. All the elders of my village are dead.' He looked around and, raising his voice, asked, 'Who is the oldest here.'

I was clearly the oldest and stepped forward. Two more youths came and stood behind the first. One of these was armed with an axe and the other with a pistol.

'Are you Taliban?' I asked.

'Not until today, uncle,' he said, lowering the barrel of the shotgun towards the ground. 'You, uncle, must help everyone here to bury our dead with dignity. Everyone who has lost someone must go home and have a funeral.'

I stepped towards the heap. The youths stood on either side of me. Gulzarina squatted on the ground. Everyone stood with their heads bowed. Whispers cut through the stench of death.

And they come from thousands of miles away and kill us in our own homes.

Pakistani army, you American whore.

America, how can you sleep at night?

If I could reach you, I would teach you how it hurts.

One voice wailed, another moaned. A bird flew, screeching, overhead.

I lost two brothers.

'Give him two bodies,' I said.

I lost five brothers.

'Five bodies for him.'

I have lost my son and his wife.

'We must wait, sister.'

'There are no more whole bodies, uncle,' the youth with the gun whispered in my ear.

I lost my husband and three of my children.

'Make sure she can have four funerals.'

The armed youth gave her three legs and a head.

Do I only get a hand for my father?

'Be grateful you have something to bury,' I said.

'Is there anything for me?' Gulzarina asked.

I shook my head. A young man going past Gulzarina stopped. He took an arm and a hand out of the sack and placed them down in front of her. She stood up, picked them up and kissed his hands, then turned to me and said, 'The funeral will take place at six this evening.'

Gulzarina's eyes lost their tiredness and she held herself straight like the younger women.

The funeral took place at our family graveyard on time. I had Habib Junior and his wife buried in the space reserved for me. Gulzarina sat silently by the grave all night. I stayed with her a while but couldn't persuade her to come back to the village. She just rocked her body and sang a lament. She did not come home the next morning. The whole village searched for her but she was nowhere to be found.

Each night, someone came to the grave and spread rose petals on it. I spent three nights at the graveside waiting for Gulzarina to come. I did not understand how there were fresh flowers on the grave each morning even though I had sat there all night.

It was around 2.30 in the morning several days later when I was woken up by Abbi. He stood in the moonlight, an axe on his shoulder, one hand on the wooden handle. His shadow stretched towards the veranda where I had been asleep. Even though the night was warm, I felt cold and had a heavy sheet on me.

'I was coming home from the GT Road,' he said. 'When I got to the bottom, near Bataltehri, just past the railway line, a goat ran past me. It jumped out from behind a rock. I tried to catch it. I saw it running down towards the stream where we used to go swimming in the summer. I thought maybe it was thirsty and went after it. It hopped onto a big boulder and then just vanished. And then I heard a woman singing in a language I have not heard before. I went a little further and I could see her. She was sitting on a rock. She had her back to me. Her feet were in the water. She was washing her hair. I swear it could be sister Gulzarina.'

I jumped out of bed and left the house. Bataltehri was two miles or so from my house. We rushed through the sleepy alleyways of my village. Dogs with raging eyes snapped at us. Abbi was in front, holding the axe in his hand. I could not keep up with him and kept stopping for breath. We took a short cut through the fields that overlooked the stream.

I felt cold and dizzy but kept going. I could see the rock that Abbi had mentioned. There was a goat standing on top of it. Abbi stopped, turned to me and pointed to the goat. The water curved away from the rock and turned towards us. The water was deeper the further it was from the rock. The goat turned away from us and lifted its front legs, a shadow fell on it and then it was gone.

Holding my shoes in my hand, I followed Abbi and crossed the water, stepping on slippery rocks. Once out of the water, the sand changed to mud. Abbi seemed to effortlessly pull his feet out of the sinking mud, but I found it exhausting. The muddy ground changed back to sand. After we were clear of the mud, I washed my feet in a puddle of water and put my shoes back on.

At the base of the rock where the goat had stood were unmistakable human footprints.

'Gulzarina!' I called. My voice echoed in the darkness.

'Sister Gulzarina!' Abbi shouted.

I felt my stomach tightening and vomited. I was shivering. Abbi said something. I was sweating even though it was bitterly cold. I was delirious.

The moonlight was so bright it hurt my eyes. Even though I closed my eyes, I could still see the moon. It was falling over Gulzarina. She was pulling her hair out, sitting by Habib Junior's grave, talking to me on the telephone in Manchester.

'My son is going to university,' she said. 'I want to keep my promise to your Cousin Habib and have him marry Aisha.'

'I saw her last week,' I told Gulzarina. 'I saw her on a demonstration in London. We went to stop the war. No, she did not talk to me. She never talks to me. It always rains in Manchester. She wears a tent on her head now. Yes, I will ask her again. She will keep my honour and marry Habib Junior.'

I kept dropping in and out of my life in England. I tried to hold on to the moments when I still had the dignity of the ustad from the High School for Boys, before I became a Paki and a wog. Carol's and Yasmin's and Aisha's faces came fading in and out.

I kept seeing Gulzarina running through the hills holding a gun. There are no pupils in her eyes, only fire. 'If I had wings, I would fly to England and I would fly to you, America,' she said. The hills echoed her words. 'You must bleed as I have bled. No peace, as I have none. Your sons must die, as mine is dead. They should be beheaded and dismembered, so their mothers can see and feel what I feel. Your streets must burn as mine are burning. *Marg bar, Amrika!* Death to you, America! and death to you, England! And to you who hear my words, if you have no bombs, turn your bodies into them! Turn your hands into knives and your nails into claws. And this mother has been killed so many times that she doesn't know how to die.'

'Sing to the Western wind, Habibi, fly to me,' Gulzarina sings. 'Fly, Habibi, fly.' But my arm is stuck in a bush of thorns. I pull it out and raise my hand towards Gulzarina. My hand is bleeding.

Gulzarina holds my hand and says, 'Burn the bastards who burnt my Habib!'

I reply, 'If I live long enough.'

'Sing to the Western wind, the song it understands,' Gulzarina sings.

She chants, 'Allah O Akbar.' I join the hills in reply, 'Allah O Akbar. Allah O Akbar. Allah O Akbar.'

I woke up in a hospital bed. I had a drip attached to my left hand. Abbi was on a chair close to me holding a green shawl in his hands. He smiled at me and said, 'Malaria, Saleem Saab.'

'Was she there?' I asked.

'It was a strange night, Saleem Saab,' Abbi said. 'I swear on my mother's grave I heard a woman crying. I have never heard a cry like that. Her voice kept bouncing around the hills. I could feel it in my heart. I wanted to help her. Then it stopped. I could not move you on my own so I ran off to get some help. When I came back, you had this under your head.' Abbi showed me the green shawl. 'Someone had rolled it up and put it there.'

Abbi spread the shawl out. It was the one I had given to Gulzarina, which she had worn when I arrived.

'Was it her?' Abbi asked.

I just looked at him and didn't know what to say.

Over the next three days I kept slipping in and out of delirium, each time seeing Gulzarina.

'You should have left me to die where I had been defiled,' she kept saying. 'I would not have had a son. I would have died without giving life. Why did you and Habib come? Why? Why? Why?'

'Forgive me Habib for forcing you to go in search of Kala. I should have listened to you. I don't know what I have become.' I begged the ghost of Habib for forgiveness.

Even when I asked for forgiveness, I heard Gulzarina calling out to me to avenge her Habib. I kept promising to do what needed to be done.

After I recovered, I went for long walks in the jungle to look for her, to tell her to her face-to-face what I was going to do when I got back. What have you got to live for now, I thought. Your daughter hates you. Everyone you loved is dead. Why didn't you come back here and look after Habib's son? You asked Habib to go where he did? Why did you do that? He would be alive now if you hadn't. Why Saleem Khan, why? You've lived your life, and what is the point of going back and dying slowly someplace all alone. Before you go, you must make them pay.

At times when I walked in the jungle, I felt she was watching me and I would call out to her, but only my voice echoed back.

I telephoned my bank in England and transferred twenty thousand pounds from my savings into my Pakistani account in two transactions. It took two weeks for the money to show up and when it did I withdrew a large amount in Pakistani currency and went to Rawalpindi to look for Duraid Shah, who I had not seen for many years. I found him in his old house, where I had last seen him. He was thin and frail. Wrinkles crisscrossed deep gorges on his face, some of which ran down his cheeks. He had dark rings under his eyes. The upper story of the house still bore the scars of the destruction. He had left this as it was the last time I had seen it, but the one below in which he lived had been fixed. He was sitting on a small veranda with another old man, who was much plumper and wore a loosely wrapped white turban on his head.

Duraid Shah recognised me as soon as he saw me and said, 'And you are still alive, Saleem Khan.'

The other old man spat into a rusty tin, pressed his hands on his knees and pushed himself up. It was Chambail Chacha. He gently pressed my right hand in both of his, smiling broadly, whilst rubbing his tongue across his teeth.

Duraid Shah was trying to get off his chair. I bent down and hugged him. Chambail Chacha brought a plastic chair for me and I sat down next to Duraid Shah.

As I was sitting down, Duraid Shah said, 'When I heard what happened to Habib's son, I cried an ocean. It was like my own son had been martyred again. I would have come to give you my condolences but I am too weak to travel now.'

'I came to see you in hospital, Khan Saab, but you were in a terrible fever,' Chambail Chacha said, placing a hand on my shoulder.

I nodded, but had no memory of him coming to see me. He stood silently next to me pressing on my shoulder for a moment and then slowly walked off into the house.

When Chambail Chacha had gone, Duraid Shah listened silently to what I said, 'I sent Habib Junior to his death, I did. I had promised his father I would look after him as I would my own son, and what did I do? And who in England knows of his death? England doesn't care. When where I live burns that which I love and returns unrecognisable bones which the mother, a mother I have called my sister, buries in the grave reserved for me, tell me, what is the purpose left in my life? Is vengeance wrong for someone like me? Should I just waste away and wait for my death? Go back to England to die alone in that cold cold place? No Duraid Shah, I want to end my life and take some of those who killed Habib Junior with me. I want to strap explosives around me and destroy those people who bring England's claws here.'

Chambail Chacha returned with a glass of water and waited there until I had drunk it. After he left, Duraid Shah said, 'And you think I didn't bleed after my son was martyred, right here in my very house. And not until the day General Zia paid for what he had done here did I sleep in peace. But that peace only lasted the night of my sleep, the pain never stopped in the day. Your pain will never go, no matter what you do.'

'But I will have gone,' I said.

'And that is what you want?'

'That is how it must be,' I said, handing him a bag with the money. 'Can you help in getting these things to me in England?'

Chambail Chacha came back a short while later with some tea.

Taking a sip of green tea, Duraid Shah asked, 'You have a daughter?'

'I am dead to her.'

Duraid Shah went silent for a while, his unblinking eyes fixed on something past me, something behind me, past the unrepaired wall. Clearing his throat, he asked, 'Why don't you make something yourself in England?'

'Me, make it?'

'I hear it is easy,' Duraid Shah said. 'You know how this Internet works?'

'Yes.'

'Al Qaeda has put things on the Internet on how to make bombs and things at home. They have a magazine called Inspire. It tells you how to do it,' Duraid Shah said.

'I can't read their rubbish. I have nothing in common with them.'

Duraid Shah cleared his throat and said, 'But it is all basic stuff. And you are sure that this is what you want to do?'

I nodded, 'I must. Can you help?'

'I didn't spend my life in the agency for nothing,' he sighed. 'There is nothing that can't reach you.'

'How will you get it to me?'

'There are many Britisher army men here now. Business is done all the time. They and the Americans buy anything they want,' Duraid Shah said without moving his eyes from the wall. 'In Pakistan everything is for sale at a price and it's delivered where you want. Suicide bombers have their prices. Little boys and young men are cheap. A brother and sister, they're more expensive. But I have never heard of an old man . . .' He stopped, looked away from me and asked, 'Is this all you can think of for your life's end, Saleem Khan?'

He looked back at me, with half closed eyes and tightened his lips.

'Why should I live and wait for my end, Duraid Shah, a lonely worthless end, if all I have to live for is to live in torment?'

'And you understand the torment of your grave, do you?' Duraid Shah asked.

246

'They say that the torment of the grave is only understood by the corpse,' I said.

'And you are the grave, eh?'

'No, I am a corpse with dead dreams,' I said. 'Help me.'

Duraid Shah nodded his head.

Pointing to the bag of money, I said, 'I don't think there is enough money here to pay the British if that's what you have in mind.'

'Not everything is bought with money in war,' Duraid Shah said.

A few days after this meeting, Chambail Chacha came to the village. He gave me a bag with money in it, saying, 'You left too much.'

I spent many months searching for Gulzarina. One day I heard of a mad woman throwing stones at passing NATO convoys that went north up the GT road towards Afghanistan. I went there as fast as I could. A Pakistani army helicopter was flying above a slow-moving line of trucks. My mobile buzzed in my pocket. Over the noise of the helicopter, I heard a hoarse voice say, 'If I could reach them, I would teach them.'

'Gulzarina, is that you?'

'How it hurts.'

'I know what I have to do,' I said.

'Allah O Akbar,' she said.

'I want to see you before I go,' I said.

'Allah O Akbar,' she said.

'Where are you, my sister?' I asked.

Her words were drowned out by an explosion.

~

A car backfiring on the street outside my house brought me back to Manchester.

'Come, me ol' flower, this world is not worthy of the likes of you,' I say, buttoning up my long overcoat, sinking my hands into its deep pockets in which a set of keys are knocking against a half-litre whisky bottle. I take a long look back inside the house: all the old wooden doors are ajar; the cracked mirror has slipped off one of the screws holding it and dangles next to the switch.

Holding onto the trolley bag, I walk out of my house. I look up at the helicopter. It is there beyond the web of telephone wires on which rows of starlings are sitting in military formation, unperturbed by the machine above them. The sun plays hide and seek with pregnant clouds. It wins, catching the helicopter in its rays, a monstrous fly trapped against the blue yonder.

The helicopter moves away from our street, hovers a short while, and then arcs towards the city centre. The birds on the wire break formation as if commanded by the movement of the helicopter and fly down, landing on the cracked pavement between dead leaves.

Now Sarah Ann's disgusting mongrel dog, with its tongue sticking out of its mouth and its tail wagging, is coming towards me.

Saleem Khan, you should have waited a bit, I say to myself. I stop on the footpath outside my house and think: 'How can you forget that Sarah Ann takes the dog for its pre-lunch walk at eleven every morning?' The birds, which moments earlier had been unconcerned by my advancing footsteps, scatter.

Sarah Ann will pull the lead in ten seconds, I think. She will cross the road after repeating her habitual greeting to me.

'Luvly day, isn't it?' says Sarah Ann, right on cue.

I nod.

The dog sniffs my bag. It is about to lift its leg when Sarah Ann yanks its lead, saying, 'Naughty boy.'

The dog pulls away and they move on, past the house of George Turner. With his arms folded across his chest like a wrestler, George is glaring at two workers dressed in the uniform of Manchester City Council's Operational Services Unit. George Turner is wearing a smart black suit, which he only wears at funerals. One of the workmen is rummaging through George Turner's dustbins whilst the other is making notes.

'You can shove your recycling policy where it belongs,' George Turner says, kicking over an empty brown dustbin.

The workman who was making the notes steps onto the pavement outside George Turner's house.

'What you going to do, serve me another notice?' says George, waving the paper at him. A few of the neighbours are watching and George reads out, 'Ten bottles of wine! Three clear bottles, four brown and five green.' He steps towards the workman that has made the notes, points at him and laughs: 'That makes *twelve* you ignorant twat, twelve and not ten like you've written here.'

The workman steps back into the road. His colleague stops searching through the dustbins.

George continues, '. . . Two bottles of whisky, one Southern Comfort, fifty-eight cans, two uncooked chickens . . .' he laughs, 'and those certainly weren't mine. I don't waste food! And yep, I put them things in the wrong friggin' bin!'

Doris Mathews from number 45 comes out in her slippers and dressing gown. She says to George Turner, 'And did they find any used ones then, George?'

Before George Turner can reply, Hilda Smithers from number 47 answers Doris Mathews, 'That's one thing he's got no need of.'

'You ought to know, you dirty cow!' Doris Mathews replies.

Apart from the men from Manchester City Council's Operational Services Unit, everyone else bursts out laughing and clapping. George Turner crumples the paper and throws it at the workmen, saying, 'Shuv this up your Khyber and I am *not* going to pay you the 150-quid fine!'

George grabs my arm and pulls me towards his house. 'I've got a pot brewing, Saleem. It'll warm you up,' he says, turning to go inside the house. 'This cold is not good for the bones of old men like you.'

George Turner's kitchen is at the end of a long winding corridor, past a wooden shelf stacked with shoes that have not touched the ground in decades, past ageing umbrellas and an overflowing coat rack behind which there is a mirror that has not seen a human reflection since the death of his wife over ten years ago. By the time I get to the kitchen, he has poured steaming tea into two half pint mugs and is rinsing the teapot in the sink. A small television sitting on a shelf above the microwave is on as ever.

'You could have left the shopping trolley by the door,' George Turner says, drying the teapot.

'You sugared it just right, George,' I say, taking a sip. He had put too much in as usual.

Placing the teapot next to his rusty toaster, George Turner pulls a plastic bag out of a tall glass jar. He stuffs some mouldy bread into the bag, wraps a rubber band on the end, puts the bag of bread down on the table next to me, picks his tea up and steps back a little, saying, 'You've never been good at lying.'

George Turner is a big man with an inflated stomach which pushes the tips of his black waistcoat away from his body. The black tie on his white shirt is curving over his belly button, which due to a long-standing hernia creates a further lump. He is the only person I have ever told about the way in which my daughter has humiliated me at every opportunity. Sometimes I have told him the same story over and over again, and each time he has listened to it intently, as if it was the first time he had heard it, and afterwards he has always replied: 'She has been sent to test you, my friend.'

'Cat got your tongue, Saleem?' George Turner asks, blowing the steam away, 'Not called me to do any of your plumbing lately, old mate. And none of your curries. I've had to make do with takeaways, eh?' He raises his mug in a toast and looking at me cheekily says, 'To Her Majesty's health!'

I do not raise my mug.

He takes a deep breath and picks up the bag with the bread, saying, 'Come on, old friend, let's go and feed the birds.'

'I can't do that today,' I reply.

I think back to the last time I had gone to feed the birds with him. It was on the day the aeroplanes had flown into the twin towers in New York.

It had been a bright crisp day. The birds on the lake in Platt Fields had become restless as George and I approached them. Their erratic movements created ripples all across the water, which pushed dead leaves into the form of a purple arc towards one side of the lake. A flock of white gulls flew noisily towards the island in the middle, their shadows sliding over the leaves as four white swans joined the ducks and geese that swam towards us from every corner. Some birds ran up to us from behind.

'I know you're hungry.' George Turner had dangled the bread bag over the birds.

With the birds noisily following us, we had gone past the empty playground, past the notices from Manchester City Council warning people not to feed the birds and sat down on a bench overlooking the lake.

George broke a slice of bread into small pieces and tossed it to the birds, which went into a frenzy of feeding.

Afterwards, we went to Hardy's Well for a drink. There was a strange silence in the pub. I had gone and sat down and George Turner bought the first round. I looked across at the television screen. All eyes were turned towards it. Images of two aeroplanes flying into skyscrapers were being played over and over again. George and I went and stood behind a group of drinkers. The landlord turned the volume up. An American reporter was saying something about a large transport plane going into one of New York's 'Twin Towers'. The words 'suspected Islamic terrorists' kept flashing from the strapline at the bottom of the screen. I took off my jacket and placed it next to George's on an empty chair and went to the toilet. By the time I got back, George Turner had left the pub. I felt everyone's eyes turned towards me and I too left the pub as soon as I had finished my drink. I was hungry and stopped on the Wilmslow Road for some food. The waiters were all glued to a television in the back. One of them served me food without even his customary smile, constantly looking back at the television.

By the time I had finished eating, it was dark. On the way home I knocked on George Turner's door. He opened it and then slammed it shut again, saying, 'When are you lot going to bomb us then, eh? Keep fucking well away from me!'

The streets were eerily quiet. The next morning, I saw Sarah Ann, but she turned her face away from me. I waved at Dorothy who was looking at me through the window. She drew her curtains. In the days that followed, more and more of the white people on my street stopped talking to me. One night, a gang of youths ran through the estate shouting, 'Muslim Terrorists—Off Our Streets!'

'It's the same old crap all the bloody time now.' George's angry voice swearing at the television pushed the memories of those days immediately following the Twin Towers incident from my mind. A Breaking News headline was showing a report of a terror plot foiled at a mansion.

George turned the television off.

I pulled my trolley towards me.

'You're leaving again, Saleem Khan?' George Turner says, raising his eyebrows at my trolley bag.

'Yep.'

'And you're not coming back again?'

'No, George, there is no way back for me, not this time.'

'When are you going to stop dreaming, me ol' flower?' George Turner says. 'You'll never return to Pakistan.'

'You may well be right, but this time it's for good.'

'And watch that railway bridge before Asda,' George says, 'I got mugged there last week. Not a single person in all those cars said anything. And if it's not muggers, then the pigeons will shit on yer head!'

The bridge is a fifteen-minute old-man's walk from George's house. Under it, a woman is pulling on the leash of a panting pit bull terrier before crossing the road and weaving through frustrated drivers. Above them, an intercity train has come to a standstill. As I come away from the bridge, an automatic text message on one of the primed mobiles vibrates inside the pockets of my overcoat. I stop by the Asda turning to my left and look at the mobile. The text message reads: '8 hours remaining.'

After putting the telephone in the inside pocket of my overcoat, I scratch my chest at the point where the nodes to the ambulatory heart monitor used to go and think back to the day I had been told I had to wear it.

I had shopped at this very store, which I will pass in a minute. I had, as usual, walked home with the shopping in my trolley. Just after I got home, I felt a sharp pain rip through my chest, my heart pounding erratically. It was as if someone was pressing down on my ribcage with their knee. I was out of breath and dialled 999 and, before long, was on my way to Manchester Royal Infirmary in an ambulance.

After the preliminary examinations, I changed into a hospital gown and was taken into a small room. There were two beds in this room. A man on one of the beds was breathing through an oxygen mask. I was lifted off my stretcher and placed on the empty bed. The other patient stuck his thumb up to me and muttered what sounded like 'OK'. I pursed my lips in acknowledgement. He lifted his mask and asked, 'Heart?' I nodded. He placed the mask back on his face and looked away. He was a fat pinkish man, with sharp dark eyes and a newly shaven head. He turned towards me after a little while and mumbled something which I did not understand, but I nodded. He lifted the mask and asked, 'Italian?'

'Pakistani,' I said.

'I thought you were a gora, with that silver chest of yours, yaar!' he said in Punjabi. 'Allah Rakhah from Alam Rock. Came to Manchester to visit my daughter. She just had her first baby and I landed up here. I've had this test and that test. Had things shoved up where things are only meant to come out of!'

'I thought you were a gora as well.' We laughed.

A smiling nurse came into the room and said loudly, 'My name is Sister Deborah. And how are you, Mr Khan?'

'Champion, sister,' I said.

'That's what I like to hear, a positive attitude to life!' She drew the curtains around my bed and continued to talk. As she did, Allah Rakhah was wheeled out. 'We're going to have to stick some nodes on your chest and fingers and do a thorough MOT on that heart of yours, love. Now don't you be going anywhere, I'll be back in a tick.' As she left, I thought that maybe this is how my life is going to end, today or someday, on my own, on a hospital stretcher, or in my house. I wanted so much to see Aisha. I was tempted to ask the nurse to phone her for me and tell her I had had a heart attack.

Sister Deborah was back and was laughing with another woman. I could not see them and guessed they must be close to the door.

'The last two I've had . . . first, a fat pink one, smooth as a baby's bottom, and then this one. He's got so much hair on his chest I'm going to have to use the machine to take the worst off before I can use the razors to create a space for the nodes . . .' Sister Deborah complained. A moment later, she popped her head in from behind the curtain and placed a disposable razor and a hand-held trimming machine on top of a small sideboard, saying, 'Come on, luv, let's get you sorted.' Turning on the trimmer, she said, 'My, my. I've seen some hairy men but you get first prize, you do!'

I grinned.

Trimming hair off the right side of my chest, she asked, 'I mean, what did you do when you went on holiday?'

'I avoided dogs,' I said coldly.

'Dogs, luv?' Sister Deborah asked, trimming the other side.

'In case they thought I was a tree,' I said.

She went red in the face and quickly shaved small patches on my chest. She stuck a node in each and one on my index finger, turned a monitor on and said, 'There you are, Mr Khan, all done!'

I dozed off and when I opened my eyes, Allah Rakhah was smiling at me. 'OK?' he asked.

I nodded.

'They're going to fit you with a monitor, you watch! I've had one of them. Not a good time to wear them, not these days.'

After the tests were finished, Allah Rakhah's predictions came true. I was given an ambulatory heart monitor to wear. Allah Rakhah stared at me with a bemused look as Sister Deborah fitted the nodes to my chest. When I was fully wired up, a red patch was placed above my heart, an amber one at the centre, and a green one to the left. Three coloured wires were connected to the monitor. A thicker wire plugged into a power pack that sat in my trouser pocket. The patches were self-adhesive.

Allah Rakhah took off his mask, sat on the edge of his bed, leaned over to me and said quietly, 'Brother, I know this Bava Shaidu in Coventry. Makes us look young, he does! He wore one of these monitors, but his patches kept slipping. No good these monitors if the patches come off . . . and when the hair grows, it's a problem. Well, he was out one day and he had a problem. So he went to Tesco's, bought himself some disposable razors and went to the toilets. He was in there, shaving his chest, when a gora walked in.' Allah Rakhah looked around and lowered his voice even further and said, 'You know what these goras can be like, so the old man said to him, "Try anything and you're dead!" The gora left. It took the old man a long time to shave and put his shirt back on. As soon as he walked out of the toilet, 'Bang!" Allah Rakhah clapped his hands. 'He was shot in the back with a stun gun. Police pinned him to the floor. There were guns everywhere.' Allah Rakhah took a deep breath and nodded upwards, 'Maybe it's best to leave things to Him . . .' He put the mask back on his face and lay down again.

I didn't believe the story and was about to tell him so, when Allah Rakhah lifted his mask and continued, 'He went back to Pakistan. Said this place was too dangerous.'

The smell of diesel from the exhausts of a delivery lorry chases Allah Rakhah out of my mind.

In the car park of the supermarket, a discarded black bin liner is blowing in the wind, bloated like a corpse. It rises on the breeze, tossing and turning as though in its death throes, twisting towards the railway line, towards a London-bound intercity train. The bag then floats like a hot air balloon above the brambles and a bird shoots out of them. The bag finally rips apart on the spikes of the railway railings.

Taking a short cut past the Longsight Library, I head for the junction of Dickenson Road and Stockport Road. If it were a market day, the aisles between the stalls would be thronged by shoppers; but today there are just a few stalls and cars parked there, and a bored cleaner is washing the ground with a powerful jet spray.

The sun has come out of a break in the clouds, my shadow stretches in front of me.

I should have planned my final journey much better, I think, going through Longsight Market. I should have made a checklist. 'What is there to check, Saleem Khan? You've got your suicide waistcoat on. And you've got your explosives and mobile phones. And you've even got your shadow with you.'

No sooner than it had come the sun had gone, and with it my shadow.

As I get closer, the cleaner turns around, training the jet spray away from me. Five recycling bins are padlocked behind thick metal bars at the back of the market. A crow pecks on a discarded takeaway wrapper. It hops here and there, then takes off and lands on top of a purple signboard attached to the first bin that says 'Paper' on it. Next to this is an orange signboard declaring 'Cans', a black notice 'Clear glass', a brown one 'Brown Glass' and, finally, another one for 'Green'. A silver BMW pulls up. A smartly dressed woman begins to throw her rubbish into the allotted bins, carefully ensuring she makes no mistakes. She gets back into the car which she had left running and reverses out onto the main road before driving quickly away towards Dickenson Road, where the police have blocked the side roads to allow an artistically decorated Bedford truck from Pakistan to slowly drive along the road. It stops close to the traffic lights and a group of young men, mostly white, dressed in shining saffron kurtas and bright green lungis with starched yellow turbans on their heads jump out and form two rows behind the truck. The men in the front row have shehnais and the ones behind them all have a large Punjabi dhol dangling off a belt in front of them. The shehnais blare out a song, 'Tore Punjaban Di', and moments later the drums burst into life. Leaning on a small wall, I watch the truck move slowly towards Wimslow Road with the musicians marching behind. The shehnais suddenly stop. The drummers beat the dhols even louder.

The drummers break formation and walk off in different directions, swinging their shoulders, beating their drums and smiling broadly as they go towards bemused onlookers. One of the drummers, a tall white man with a false beard and a smile that shows all his teeth, comes towards me and then stops, turns towards two young women and swings around on his heels without missing a beat on the drum.

I turn in the opposite direction and cross the road. Empty beer cans are lodged inside a recently trimmed privet hedge. A beeping lorry with its hazard lights flashing is reversing onto the main road, close to the tall spire of St John's Church. The trees in the churchyard shed their leaves as though in agreement with each other, perhaps in farewell to me.

A gust of wind blows an empty can onto the road. It is crushed under the wheels of a passing car. A newspaper, tossing in the wind, is coming towards me. It floats onto the pavement in front of me. It is the front and back page of the *Manchester Evening News* from 5 March 2007. It has grease marks around the edges and a faded yellow stain runs down its middle. A straight-haired woman is grinning under the heading, 'Can You Tell Bev's Age?' In the column next to Bev, the headline reads: 'Help Us Spot the Terrorists, Urge Police'. And the first line: 'They may be living or working alongside you, says top boss.'

This is followed by a series of bullet points:

- Do you know anyone who travels but is vague about where they're going?
- Do you know someone with documents in different names for no obvious reason?
- Do you know someone buying large or unusual quantities of chemicals for no obvious reason?
- Handling chemicals is dangerous. Maybe you've seen goggles or masks dumped somewhere?
- If you work in commercial vehicle hire or sales, has a sale or rental made you suspicious?
- Have you seen someone with large quantities of mobile phones?
- Have you seen anyone taking pictures of security fixtures?
- Do you know someone who visits terrorist-related web sites?
- Have you seen any suspicious cheque or credit card transactions?
- Are you suspicious of anybody renting commercial property?
- Is someone asking for a short-term let on a house or flat on a cash basis for no apparent reason?

Throwing the paper into the graveyard, I cross the road and walk past a poster in a window bearing the words: 'A dog is forever and not just for Xmas.'

Pulling the trolley bag, I quicken my pace a little, wondering why, when I have lived in these streets all these years, I have met no more familiar faces today. Strangers pass me all the way to Birchfields Road. It is full of traffic as usual. On the far side, near the newly built flats, a man picks through a long line of rubbish bins. Not far from him, someone has left some flowers on the spot where, a few days earlier, a young man was executed by being shot in the head. Cars full of men going for Friday prayers turn towards the mosque. A broken umbrella with its twisted body lies in the middle of the alleyway, close to an empty rubbish bin that is chained to a streetlamp. A light wind rustles the dried leaves of the hedge.

By the time I come out of the alleyway, cars of every hue are parked on the pavements and side roads. Even the grass verges have been transformed into a parking lot. Mercedes and BMWs are carelessly strewn across the corners marked with double yellow lines and along the fading zigzags.

The helicopter is back. At first it is only a faint humming sound, almost indistinguishable from the noise of regular traffic along the main roads that run in a triangle around this street, but it gets louder and louder as it comes back in an arc of flight which must have taken it over the city centre. It is much higher now.

Two traffic wardens in crisp new uniforms, riding motorcycles, come around the corner from the crescent that leads to the Central Mosque. They are both white and in their thirties. Their eyes are veiled by sunglasses. They stop in the middle of the road not far from me. The man, wide shouldered, places his feet on either side of the motorbike, holds on tightly to the handlebars and stands guard, revving the engine. The woman dismounts, makes a note of the time and starts taking photographs of parked cars.

She turns her head towards me. I see my reflection in her glasses. She stares at me and steps back. The helicopter passes overhead. The man turns his motorcycle, comes ever so slowly over, and stops close to me. The man shouts something at me but the noise of the helicopter drowns out his words. His eyes are still fixed on me. Behind him there are two engineers from British Telecom working on an exchange box. Not far from these workers are two window cleaners walking leisurely, each carrying a ladder with a bucket dangling off the end. They both wear thick anoraks. I do not recognize these window cleaners. They are not the ones who own the round in these streets. Everyone has their eyes on me. Oh, God, no, it can't end here, I think! I cannot explode here, not *here*!

A repulsive smell of death wafts up from a line of open dustbins behind the bushes. Sycamore leaves, which moments earlier had been slowly undressing the tree, fight with each other in mid-air, twisting and turning as they fall. A large crumpled leaf scrapes along the road and stops by my foot. The tree's branches droop over the road and touch the side of a passing van. More leaves float down. I open the palm of my hand. A leaf yellowed by death falls into it. It is smaller than my shaking hand. It sits there for a moment and slides off. A much larger one twists through the air and hovers in front of me. I catch it by its still green stalk. The green changes to faded red closer to the outstretched ribcage of the leaf. I place it in my other hand and stare at it as I often do at the lines of my own pale hand. It is dark at the edges. Its deep crimson body is being eaten away by black patches.

Tossing the leaf into the air, I watch it float under a car. I take out my tobacco pouch and light a pre-rolled cigarette, saying, 'So here it ends, Saleem Khan, a final failure.'

The helicopter turns and whines away, leaving a stinging silence in its wake.

The man revs the motorbike, looking at me sternly. An order comes blaring out of his radio: 'Go. Go. Go.'

The Telecom engineers stand up and run in my direction with guns in their hands. The window cleaners drop their ladders and rush towards me. They too are armed. Cars and vans with lights flashing arrive from different directions. I cannot press the button here. Not here.

The roads are quickly blocked. The motor cyclist rushes past me, scattering a pile of sycamore leaves. The woman runs towards me, pushes me back against the wall shouting, 'Don't move! Armed police action!'

The helicopter moves off towards my house in Longsight.

The force of the policewoman's push sends me tumbling backwards into the overhanging branches of a privet hedge of the garden of house number 16. The trolley bag slips out of my hand and falls onto its side. As I stumble backwards, I see the policewoman jump over it, run into the heart of the street and disappear into an alley. The window cleaners and the engineers all go in the same direction as the woman.

Were it not for the privet digging itself into me, I would have landed on the rockery. Blood pulsates around my ears. I pull a few broken twigs out of my hair and rub my face before picking myself up and resuming my journey. Taking a last look at the street, I set off for the bench on Park Crescent, close to the Victoria Park toll gates. On Fridays, I usually sit on the bench in the middle of the Crescent and look up at the road that leads to the Central Mosque and wait for the prayers to finish.

The closer I get to the Crescent, the further I am from the stench of the dirty bins. It has all but faded away into the distant marriage of traffic and helicopter. The clouds have aborted their union and have spread across the sky in thinning white streaks. By the time I reach the corner of the deserted Rusholme Conservative Club, the sky is cleansed into an unbroken blue. A chill wind blows crisp leaves across my path. The Conservative Club is squashed between the rear of the end of the Chinese Housing Society and at the back end of the Curry Mile. It is a large building which even in its decay betrays signs of its former glory. A Volvo Estate parked close to the windows boarded with rotten planks has all but rusted away. Though the flagpoles still stand along the club's outer wall, the fence has long since decayed. Beer cans and empty bottles are spread across the road, piling up on the sides of the pavements, trapping dead leaves.

I stop under a local authority notice forbidding drinking in public. It has a red circle with a line over an illustration of a wine bottle and a jar of beer. The order proclaims: *Drinking alcohol or having alcohol in open containers is PROHIBITED in public places in this area.*

Sitting with other drunks on the benches of Park Crescent, I have, in the past, debated the meaning of the order many a time. Each time, we drunks concurred that as we were drinking whisky and not wine or beer, it was legal. On the occasions we drank wine or beer, we argued that the order only covered the post it was stuck to and, as we were clearly three hundred yards or so away, it did not apply to us. There were a few notices closer to us but, as they were on the other side of the road, we maintained that that was the limit of the order and it did not apply to people who sat on the benches, stood near them, or collapsed next to them. Our conclusions were in our opinion correct, as no policeman had ever challenged us to stop drinking on the benches.

The air is heavy with the aroma of the kebab houses of the Curry Mile. I can distinguish between the roasting of kobedas in clay ovens and chicken tikkas and seekh kebabs burning on hot grills. These smells mix with onions being fried in spices to be made into a sauce in which meat, fish and vegetables will all be reduced to the same flavour.

Something moves behind the thick privet of the Conservative Club. A fox, I think. I have often seen it sniffing around discarded takeaways. I stop to see if I can catch my last glimpse of the animal and place the trolley bag upright on its four wheels. It has been feeling heavier as I have walked on. I look down at its wheels. A twig has jammed inside the spokes. I squat down. 'Is that thing holding you down?' I say. My knees click. The vest tightens with explosives pushing against my chest. The end of my coat dips into a pool of water. 'It does not matter how dirty you get now,' I say to my coat.

I break the twig and pull it out in small bits. As I am doing this, I hear the same rustling noise coming from behind the hedge. After taking the twig out, I flick the wheel. It spins. Someone coughs behind the bush. I see a pair of well-worn brown shoes. Steam rises up around them.

'Saleem Khan, why are you dragging that old thing with you?' the owner of the shoes, Mangal Singh, shouts. 'It's nearly as old as you and, like you, well past its sell-by date — and you, you are certainly ready to meet your maker!' He pauses, and buttoning up his flies adds, 'But what would a godless drunk like you know about his maker?'

'I called you, Mangal Singh, and told you I was coming this way and you didn't call back. But then you remember nothing anymore, eh, disease got your mind?'

Mangal Singh laughs, adjusting the blue turban on his head. He steps over the steaming stream he has created and emerges from the gates of the Rusholme Conservative Club.

Placing my hands on my knees, I push myself up. Water drips from the end of my coat.

'Here, take my hand first.' With his right hand outstretched, Mangal Singh steps towards me.

'I am not touching your hand after where it has been!' I shake my head.

'This is the age of remote controls, my friend. With age, you too have to learn how to do these things without the need to wash your hands afterwards!' A pigeon flies over us as Mangal Singh steps in front of me. He smiles, grabbing my right hand and saying, 'That's if your blood is still warm and it hasn't shrivelled up. And I hope you are still wearing that heart monitor of yours!'

'Not today,' I laugh, shaking his hand.

'It is me who is losing his memory,' Mangal Singh says, slapping me across the shoulders with his frail hands. 'Or are you forgetting?'

'What good is wearing that thing now? I have nothing left to lose,' I reply, looking behind him at two pigeons flying out of a crack in the roof of the Conservative Club. They appear like two floating blotches. The birds perch themselves on a branch just above Mangal Singh's head. They rest for a moment and then lift off again. The words of an old song ring in my ear: *vasta ee rab dha, toon javeen vey kabootra, chithi meray veer noon pohnchavain ve kabootra.* 'Pigeon, I beg you in the name of the Lord, take this letter to my brother, oh pigeon.' I think back to our lost friendship.

It was during the summer of 1947, when our childhood had been snatched from us. We had been inseparable, Mangal Singh and I. We were born on the same day, in the same village. My mother gave Mangal Singh his gruthi, his first sweet taste, just as his mother gave me my first sweet taste: a drop of honey dripping into my mouth from the tips of her slim fingers.

As children we had been obsessed with flying. On hot days we would hold out our arms and pretend to fly as fast as an eagle through the winding alleys of our village all the way to the shade of the old banyan tree. Sitting in the tree's coolness, we imagined flying over it, along with the noisy crows, then swooping down like hawks. Sometimes we would just flutter about like the sparrows. Mangal Singh told me that in the next life he would come back as a bird. We spent countless hours deciding on which birds we would like to be. I said we should become eagles, flying over the hills that circled our village; that way we could ensure that no harm came to anyone below.

A flock of pigeons swooping over our heads brings me back to the Rusholme Conservative Club. Mangal Singh is singing the couplet from 'Saif-al-Maluk': *'Baghay andhr hik bulbal aalraan payee see banaani, Ajay na charya thour Mohammad, Ur gaee ay kurlaani.'* He stops singing. 'I do not know if you are here or there,' he asks me.

I do not reply but set off towards the Crescent again. Mangal Singh walks close to me, his shoulder bumps into mine. He coughs heavy whisky breaths.

'You have been following doctor's orders again, eh, Mangal?'

He raises his bushy silver eyebrows by the way of a reply, coughs and spits a mouthful of phlegm onto a pile of leaves.

Mangal Singh's green eyes hide behind the shadows of darkened sockets. He is as always lost, chasing some memory. The wart on the side of his nose now has hair growing out of it. The wrinkles on his face are like the dried banks of the lakes of our childhood.

We stop at the corner of the Victoria Park Hotel and stare at its advertisement: *Non-alcoholic. No TV.*

Mangal Singh is the only person I have ever known who has stayed in this hotel, and that was over five years ago. He was put there by the social services for reasons that have changed each time Mangal Singh has told me the story. I am surprised he has not mentioned it yet. But this does not last long.

'You know, Saleem Khan . . .' Mangal Singh coughs, pauses for a breath and brushes his beard.

'You spent a night here.' I reply. I will have to listen to this story again.

'I spent a night here. And did I tell you? I don't mind the non-alcoholic bit, 'cos all I can take I take before going to bed. I don't even mind the no television bit, can't see much anyway. But it was the way they made me get up at 4.30 in the morning. A young lad, maybe twenty, knocked on my door shouting "It is time for namaaz. It is time for fajr."' I didn't answer the door at first, but he kept knocking until I opened it.

'"What the hell do you think you are doing, waking me up at this time of the morning?" I shouted at him, opening the door.

'"It is my duty," he replied, "and it is yours also, uncle."

'"I don't want to be a Muslim. Now get lost." I told him.

'"If you are staying here, at the very least you must be thinking about converting."

268

"'I have already converted. But all this getting up at 4.30 in the morning, all these thirty days of fasting, praying five times a day and what else have you, I mean, I have become so busy I have no time to commit a sin or enjoy myself! I have decided, especially now, since you woke me up, I want to become a Sikh again. I want to reconvert and I will forever be grateful to you. The one who converted me is surely destined for Paradise, but what will happen to you, eh?"'

Mangal Singh chuckles to himself. A man older than us is riding a bike, slowly, the wrong way round the roundabout. Two cars come in the opposite direction, hooting their horns and weaving past the cyclist who looks at us for sympathy before cursing the cars indignantly.

'You know, yaar, that lad's face that day . . . it went as white as a corpse.'

'Yes, I know, Mangal. You told me.'

'But, you know what he said to me? "Now look, uncle, our faith is not something to be trifled with. Do you know if you leave Islam, you will be joining the infidels, and the only punishment for someone like you is a beheading?"'

Mangal Singh slaps his leg, laughing, 'Pointing down to my thing, I said to the lad, "What sort of a religion have I got myself into? When I joined you made me cut the end of this and now you are threatening to cut my other end off too!"'

I have heard this tale too many times to even smile. But Mangal Singh, as always, is caught up in a fit of laughter punctuated by his habitual cough.

I cross the road and walk towards the benches, dragging the trolley behind me. Mangal Singh steps onto the footpath that runs around the outer rim of the roundabout. Tall oaks, sycamores and birches circle a large grassed area around the old Victoria Toll Gates. We head for the benches which sit in pairs, opposite each other on either side of the gates.

Mangal Singh makes a beeline for the benches, stomping across the wet grass. I follow the outer footpath to another paved section that dissects the roundabout in the middle. Unusually for this time of day, we are the only patrons.

As I walk around the outer footpath, I keep my eyes on Mangal Singh. Will he remember our youth after I am gone? Will someone tell him what I did?

Two of the benches are in sunlight and two are in the shadow of a large tree. Mangal Singh stands in the sunlight. He is surrounded by a flock of pigeons. He lifts his arms calling, 'Shoo. Shoo.' He drops his arms, coughing. Some of the birds jump up, only to land a few feet away. He stamps his feet on the ground. Some of the birds fly a short distance but then continue pecking on discarded naans. My arrival fails to have much impact on the birds either.

The benches close to us are splattered with pigeon droppings. I step through the birds. Some of them coo and look greedily at my trolley. The other benches are in much the same condition. I turn around. Mangal Singh pulls a damp newspaper out of a rubbish bin overflowing with beer cans and takeaway wrappings. Pigeons hop out of his way. He wipes the bench, painting it with a film of pigeon shit.

'That's a grand job, Mangal Singh.'

Mangal Singh ignores me, folds the paper into a ball, walks over to the bin and stuffs it into it. Empty beer cans fall onto the paved centre close to a broken clock. A few panicky birds hop over the remains to their colleagues, for safety.

Placing the trolley carefully at the side of the bench, I sit down, again thinking that my world no longer needs to be

270

clean. Mangal Singh slumps down next to me a moment or so later. All of the pigeons flutter off startled. They fly above our heads, their shadows sliding over us. They hover over the roundabout three times and then land on the other side of the toll gates. Some of the birds land on the outer pavement and some in the middle of the road. A car comes racing around the corner. The birds in the road lift off and land around the discarded clock when it has passed.

A lone pigeon, the only white bird in the flock, lands close to my feet. It looks me in the eyes questioningly. I kick out at it. It does not move.

'Why should it fear two wrecks, eh, Khan?'

'The value of wrecks is only understood by those who question the reasons for their demise, Mangal Singh.'

'Did youth ever question old age, Khan?'

'Does youth need to question age, my friend?'

Mangal Singh does not answer. Like me, he is looking at the white pigeon. It has locked its eyes onto mine. Its left eye has a perfect black circle around it.

Somewhere close to the Xavarian College, someone is playing the musical rendering of 'Saif-al-Maluk' with the very same words that Mangal Singh's father had spoken. A small red car with two boys in it circles around the roundabout before driving away, the song coming loudly out of its open windows.

In the garden a nightingale was building its nest.
Before reaching her destination, she flew away screaming.

The white pigeon with a black circle around its left eye is now perched on top of one of the toll gates, oblivious to the cold Mancunian wind. 'You are a lucky pigeon,' I say to the white bird. 'You were not born then.'

Mangal Singh leans against the bench, his head slumped. His snore gently purrs through his lips, his eyes are half open.

When waiting for her to come by, I always think how she will look: covered in a black chador, her silk robe flowing amidst the waves of men rushing back to their duties after the afternoon prayers.

The pigeons are disturbed. A dark pigeon lands close to the white one, not far from us. The dark bird seems as black as the crows of my village. Its tail feathers fan out and those around its neck puff up. It coos and circles around for a moment or two. The white bird stops, rushes towards the new arrival and pecks it. The black bird lifts off, a feather falls out of its wings, twisting in mid-air in front of the other bird. I am so mesmerised by the flapping of the wings of the black bird that I hardly notice her coming. The bird seems to be flying out of her. It hovers above her before coming down to rest and merging with a mass of birds scavenging on the ground.

She walks towards me. I have not talked to her since Carol died. My heart beats loudly against the explosives. She stops. Another girl runs towards her, out from an expanding wave of men. This girl is shorter. She too has a black shawl draped around her. Aisha says something to the new girl, whose eyes betray a smile.

I take a deep breath. My daughter gets closer to me, laughing falsely. I know the laugh well. It has aged a little, but I recognise the fragrance embedded in it.

She does not turn her head away from me. She blinks as her eyes meet mine. The girls stop laughing and then they have passed. I sit frozen.

'You should just talk to your daughter,' Mangal Singh whispers, without raising his head or opening his eyes fully.

The girls walk away towards Wilmslow Road. My daughter will not turn around. She never does. She stops at the edge of the roundabout. There is no traffic. She is stopping for me, I think. Two bearded Asian youths brush past the girls. One of the young boys is carrying a portable table and the other a box. The girls chat, watching the boys, who quickly unfold the table near the telephone box and set up a bookstall.

A distant thump of loud bass music comes from the direction of the mosque. Mangal Singh raises his head and adjusts his turban. The thumping gets louder and louder. A car comes screeching towards the roundabout. The white boys in the car are singing and shouting along with the music. I can feel the bass hammering against the explosives tied to my chest. The car narrowly misses a parked van. The white boys drive round the roundabout and stop near the girls. I tense and stand up. One of the boys leans out of the rear passenger window and rips the robe off my daughter. She clutches a thin veil to her face. The white boy falls out of the car, to the amusement of his mates.

The other girl pulls Aisha towards her. Before I can get nearer, the white boy has got back into the car, triumphantly waving the cloth.

The girls see me and turn their backs on me. By the time I get to where they are, the white boys in the back of the car are baring their naked bottoms, squashed against the windows. The girls run to the other side of the bearded youths' bookstall. The white boys screech off up Wilmslow Road.

'How can you just carry on selling books?' I ask the bearded youth, pointing a shaking finger. 'You saw what they did to your sisters.'

273

'Allah will punish them,' replies the older of the two, a broad-shouldered man, brushing his long beard. 'They will be held to account.'

He has an unusually sharp pointed nose, thin and arched.

'You just stood there and let them harass our girls! What good is your youth?'

'It is iman. It is our faith that must be protected,' the other youth says, nodding to books on the stall. His eyes shine with the passion of a youthful believer.

'The important question for us to realise, brother, is that we have to cleanse our souls and not worry about the dirt from someone else's mouth or body,' the older one adds, fixing his eyes on me.

'I am old enough to be your father, perhaps your grand-father. Don't you dare call me *brother*.'

'We are all brothers in Islam, in our submission,' he laughs. 'We must accept anything and everything in this world; it is but a test from the Almighty. We must return to the path of righteousness. You want us to be concerned about the doings of these silly little drugged-up boys. They are lost souls. Why must we lose anything over them?'

'Is not the dignity of the living more important . . . ?' I stop mid-sentence. What is the point of this discussion, and especially now? I will be gone soon.

She is still standing by the corner. She has covered her face with a scarf now. The girls are looking at me. Even from across the road I can feel my daughter's swelling tears stinging my own eyes. I lower my eyes and take a laboured breath, hoping the filling of my lungs will give me the courage to walk over to her. But no, I cannot leave this earth with another rejection from my daughter, not on my last day.

274

Aisha has gone. Why did I think she would think any more of me now? I curse myself inside my head. Maybe she will forgive my past when she attends my funeral. And yes, she can fulfil her desire to bury bits of my body wherever she chooses, if she chooses to at all.

'Oh, you stupid old man! You forgot this.' Mangal Singh is gasping for breath, dragging my explosive-laden trolley.

The trolley slips out of his hand and knocks against a passing car. The trolley stops a few feet away from Mangal Singh.

Mangal Singh grabs hold of the trolley, waves at the worried driver of the car and comes towards me, saying, 'You look like a man on some mission, old friend.' Handing me the trolley bag, he says, 'I have a little time to spare. Maybe I could go with you for a while and see what old men like you get up to nowadays. But then I have so much to sort out. Maybe I should leave you?'

Sarah Ann and her dog are coming towards me from the direction of the city centre. She hisses commands at the beast as it pulls towards another dog that is staring at it from the other side of Wilmslow Road. I have lived on the same street as Sarah Ann for over two decades and I have seen her go through many dogs and two husbands.

Sarah Ann's dog shits on the pavement, not far from me. She takes two plastic bags out of her pocket and waits patiently for it to finish. When it has, she puts one plastic bag on her hand as a glove, picks up the faeces, and places them in the other. She is about to throw the dog shit into a bin when she notices me watching her. She takes another plastic bag out of her pocket and puts everything in her jacket.

Mangal Singh is still trying to leave so he can sort his things out. He has nothing to 'sort out', as he knows and I know, yet he always says this after we have been together for a while. He lives alone in a two-up-two-down. I usually ask him to stay a little longer and he ends up spending the rest of the day with me. He is waiting for me to ask him to stay, but my time is almost up now. Taking hold of the trolley, I say, 'Life was good to us. We spent it well together.'

'Spent it well together?' Mangal Singh asks.

'I must go now, my friend. My time is up. May God look after you, Mangal Singh, my old friend.'

Mangal Singh sinks into a thoughtful silence and then asks, coughing, 'When did God get in between us and where is it that you must get to today?'

'Sometimes even atheists have a need of God,' I say, brushing some dust off Mangal Singh's shoulder. 'But this journey I have to do on my own.'

'And Tony Blair is waiting for you, eh?' Mangal Singh laughs.

'You are a canny old fox.' I shake my head. 'There is no space for two where I am going.'

Mangal Singh looks away from me dejectedly, and then a babyish smile races across his face.

I am about to set off towards the city centre. He comes with me. A group of youths get off a bus. They are talking excitedly about a swimming competition at the Aquatics Centre. Mangal Singh asks, 'Do you remember the first time we went swimming?'

'Yes, and only someone as crazy as you could have turned up at my house with two towels and two pairs of trunks.'

'And you said, "No, I can't do that. My chest hair will frighten the gorees,"' Mangal Singh says, his voice rejuvenated.

'And we arrived early enough to make sure we were the first ones in the pool,' I recall.

We laugh so loud that a few heads turn towards us. But I ignore the inquisitive eyes of passers-by and ride along that wave of memory. We had both pretended we were not scared to bare most of our bodies to complete strangers. We had got changed quickly and hurried to the pool and jumped in. I had become horrified at what I had done. I had my back to Mangal Singh. I said loudly to him, 'Yaar, I made a big mistake. I forgot to take off my socks.'

'You are a stupid man,' Mangal Singh had sworn. 'What will these goras think?'

When I turned around, he still had his turban on his head.

'Well at least I took it off before it got wet,' Mangal Singh says now. 'But I must go. I have not watered the plants, and . . .'

'You have a very important appointment,' I interrupt.

'And how do you know these things?' Mangal Singh says, turning away from me.

'And we had a good life, we did, Mangal Singh.' I wave as he walks past the door of a takeaway, onto which a smartly dressed Asian man is sticking a poster with the words *Muslims of Conscience—No Terrorism!*

A middle-aged waiter with newly blackened hair is clearing a table. The waiter laughs, pointing towards something behind me on Wilmslow Road. A man on crutches is standing in the middle of the road. He is waving a poster like that on the door of the takeaway and mumbling, 'Only motherfucking drunks and dead caring sons of Christian donkeys of conscience!' His prematurely aged face is peppered with small cuts. A blood-stained bandage is tied across his forehead. The last time I saw him, about two weeks or so ago, he had been standing in the middle of the road, about the same place he was now, just before the pelican crossing, but that time he had a walking stick which he was brandishing at passing cars and pedestrians. He was a tall man with wrinkled, dark brown skin. When I had seen him last, he was holding a can of extra-strength lager in his free hand.

When sober, he calls himself Syed Abdul Shah Bukhari, claiming antecedents to the Prophet, but the local drunks—and there were increasing numbers of these of all nationalities sharing the common language of intoxication—called him Tommy. I have also heard him call himself Meedha.

One day, just before he lost himself to alcohol, he said to me: 'Uncle Saleem, I have never found a solution in drink and I cannot solve anything without it. Maybe, if it wasn't for those bastards, those bastards in Pakistan who I raised, things would be different. And I raised them in style, Saleem Saab. Like Nawabs. My sister, well, nothing was good enough for her. She would throw away an egg if the yoke broke. She would throw away a suit if a thorn got stuck in it. But still she was my sister. And I was her Valaiti brother who had so much money. And my mother had brought us both into this world, and what means more than a mother? And may the Almighty give her a place in heaven. And then there was my young brother—he who would not wear anything other than western designer clothes and who chose to drive everywhere. Why should *he* work, after all, when he has me for his Valaiti brother? I who had so much money! And, over time, I funded two houses, two palaces, and many shops in Islamabad. Everything I had here, I sent there. But, you know, in Pakistan you have to be really careful, otherwise the estate agents will rip you off. But I still had a little brother and sister to look after. So, I sold one of my houses and remortgaged the other. And then I lost my house here, but I wasn't worried because I thought I could go back to Pakistan and live in one of my other houses there. But when I got there, Uncleji, my sister slammed her door on me. And my brother did the same.'

I sat there listening silently and he continued to talk until his speech became slurred and the glaze of his eyes thickened against the reddening veins. He had knocked back the best part of a bottle of whisky by the time he finished talking. Once completely drunk, his slurred speech became a mixture of Punjabi accents. English and Punjabi words and phrases fell on top of each other in an artistic array of invective.

This same drunk is now walking in front of a lorry which stops just short of hitting him, its pressure brakes hissing, its body juddering as a result of the sudden braking. Pointing at the bewildered lorry driver with his crutch, he says in Punjabi, 'Yes, yes, my real name is Bashtar and I am the first born of a family of motherfuckers!' The driver looks away. The drunk has never much cared about the response from his audiences. He laughs loudly. As the lorry pulls away, he shouts at another driver, 'House of my youth, bastards of my house, family of machouds and dog shit of ego sister fuckers!"

Waving one of his crutches in the air, the drunk thinks for a moment and then straightens up, lifts up his head proudly and chants, 'Allah O Akbar. Shite kebabs and rotten naans!' He repeats the same words over and over again, sometimes emphasising something by nodding, sometimes waving a hand or both his crutches in the air, putting them down just before losing his balance completely. He wobbles around a bit but stops himself from falling onto a red BMW. It is being driven by a woman in her thirties. Her shoulder-length red hair is swaying rhythmically. She tries to drive around him. He stumbles again. She reverses a little. The car behind blows its horn for her to stop. He places one crutch on her bonnet, looks at her for a moment, then rants, 'Shite kebabs and rotten naans.' She swerves away from him and stalls the engine. An oncoming car narrowly misses her. His crutch falls to the ground. He bends down awkwardly, hissing, 'Allah O Akbar, shite kebabs and rotten naans!' Straightening up to the woman, he says in Punjabi, 'Who destroyed my garden.'

The woman shouts into her mobile phone. Two police motorcycles speed towards the drunk. They are wearing protective gear. The drunk points one of his crutches at the police officers and laughs, 'Shite kebabs and Allah O Akbar!'

The redhead jumps out of her car, rushes across the road and hides behind the police officers, crying hysterically. She steps closer to me, speaking frantically into her mobile. 'He has blood coming down his head. He is chanting prayers. Yes. Yes. He is wearing a white bandage across his head. He is cleanly dressed. Oh, my God. Oh, my God, I love you very much and tell my Mum I love her too. Yes. He is still chanting "Allah". Oh, God!'

While she is talking on her telephone, police officers have walked the drunk to the other side of the road. One of the officers comes over to us and says to the woman, 'Can you please get back into your car?'

'Is he safe?' she asks nervously.

'He's pissed,' the officer says. 'Can you please move your car, madam? The excitement is over.'

The woman looks at me apologetically. I smile back at her and say, 'I am a suicide bomber, madam. He is just a broken man.'

She rushes to her car and races away, merging with the rain-drops of a sharp shower which is splattering on my spectacles.

After she leaves, I look at my watch and think, the bastard is here, or about to arrive. If I have calculated Tony Blair's arrival correctly, he will, as usual, soon be addressing the annual Labour Party Conference. I, meanwhile, have fol-lowed the wisdom of the saying: 'The simplest way to hunt a pig is to wait by the watering hole.'

A damp wind pushes discarded autumn leaves towards me. Some shelter behind me, a few scrape across my shoes and two large bony ones, the shape of withered hands, curl on the ground just in front of me. The leaves behind me come out from under the bench, lifted by the wind. They make their way towards me and form a face. The leaves on my shoes move. 'No!' I order, stamping on the leaf by my right foot. It crunches and crumbles. I stamp on the other before it too joins the face. 'No! No! No!' I curse.

The leaf face drifts back and lodges itself against a pedes-trian crossing post.

'Almighty! Which living God talks through faces ingrained in dead leaves?'

He is silent.

'Even as I go to die, I refuse to believe in you.'

I look up. The clouds are thickening.

'Will you send a thunderbolt to stop me, eh?' I ask, looking up. 'Are these believers more valuable than the believers they kill?'

A little brown leaf floats down. Settling on the face, it forms a perfect nose.

'Why you?' I ask the face. It has no eyes. They are hollow. 'You died twenty years ago.'

'I died much before that,' Yasmin replies. Her voice is inside my head. It blocks out all other sounds. It is a crisp youthful voice. 'I died when you put me in the bridal carriage.'

The wind stops. The leaves on the ground are crunched under the feet of passers-by.

Mai ni mein khino akhaan, Oh mother, who do I tell—the lyrics of Shah Hussain's 'Kafi!' sung by Hamid Ali Bela, free me from the leaves. The music is bouncing out of the open windows of a car parked near a police van. An officer close to the car, much to the amusement of his colleagues, starts to dance. A few boys inside the car nod their heads along with the rhythm of the beat. But this song, unlike like the original sung by Hamid Ali Bela, is a violent remix.

'What better way to be carried out of this world than on your words, Shah Hussain?' I say to the music.

The music is turned up even louder as two young women walking away from the college approach the boys. The girls throw them a disinterested look and walk past. The boys reverse slowly along the main road after the girls but move off quickly when one of the policemen raises a finger in warning.

'Ah, Shah Hussain, I wasted my life in this land of bewitching dreams and dread,' I say aloud, my ears straining to catch the last of the fading music. The pavement has become covered in a carpet of leaves.

Holding on tightly to my trolley, I laugh. 'How can an atheist believe in signs written in dead leaves?'

A piercing breeze whips the leaves up again, scattering them across parked cars. The explosives around my chest are getting heavier by the minute. It will take me well over an hour to walk to the city centre. I lean against a wall and think. It is only a ten-minute bus ride to my destination.

'Walk, old man, walk. The bastard won't have finished talking yet!'

The streetlights have come on. My arthritic knees are aching from the damp. A sharp pain is digging into my right leg. The old broken rib is reminding me of its existence and my heart flutters to its own irregular beat. 'Not long now,' I say, tapping the plastic explosive behind which sits my heart. The explosives tighten around my chest. It feels as if someone is pressing down on my ribcage.

'There is no pain you cannot endure,' I say to my heart. 'You must beat until the deed is done.'

My heart quivers.

'Perhaps you are in need of a little warmth?' I say to my heart, pulling a half-litre bottle of whisky from inside my over-coat pocket. As the whisky burns its way down to my stomach, my heart stops fluttering. The pressure of the weight of the explosives around my chest eases.

A pick-up van drives past, loaded with an assortment of bric-a-brac: an old desk, its broken legs sticking up; comput-ers and monitors; some fridges; and an old carpet. It reminds me of all the promises I had broken to my friends of the High School for Boys when I left Pakistan in 1965. I am filled with warmth at the thought of Headmasterji sitting behind a table with three legs, a tree trunk in the place of the fourth. He sat on his pride and joy, the chair, and made sure that you saw the title 'Headmaster' engraved on a large plate before you left his office. Headmasterji never tired of pointing his cane at the nameplate and saying to his staff, 'See, this was given to me in my honour. Work hard and one day, when I retire, I will reward one of you with it.' It never bothered him that it read, underneath the word 'Headmaster': 'To Harminder

Singh Kataria, for services to education, January 1938.' On my last day at the school, Headmasterji had said to me, getting up from his chair, 'We will have electricity soon, I hear; God willing, very soon. And would not this office benefit from a pedestal fan, standing over there in that corner, facing me?' He had put his hand on my shoulder and led me to the window from which he used to watch us being taught our classes under the different trees.

After tightening the top of my whisky bottle, I placed it carefully on the wall outside the ATS garage.

'The bastard must have started his speech by now,' I thought, visualising Tony Blair walking onto the stage in the G-Mex Centre and the party faithful applauding. 'And some of *you* will be joining the swine in hell soon, very soon,' I add. Turning to the whisky bottle, I say, 'Perhaps one last drink from you then?'

The second drink slides effortlessly down, without burning, leaving in its wake a weightless explosive vest.

The dark clouds have thickened, rolling in and out of each other. Their movement towards the city centre seems to have slowed. Were it not for the fact that amidst the changing shapes of the clouds there were thin streaks of light, which somehow fought their way out, it could be night-time right now.

The bus stop is crowded. A row of Stagecoach buses have slowed on their approach to it. They inch forward, ensuring that all the passengers have boarded their buses and no one is left queuing for the vehicle of a rival company sandwiched between them.

The stench of urine from the small alley below the Social Security office clashes with the aroma of roasting meat from the newly opened Afghan takeaway. A few months earlier, it had been an Afghan Cuisine Restaurant. I had eaten there and had had a terrible stomach upset afterwards. It had closed down by the time I came the next day to make a complaint. Its décor is different now. The tables have been rearranged. Where, before, there were two huge pans close to the front door in which the chappal kebabs—a deadly concoction of cheap meat, spice and eggs—were fried, now the grills and ovens have been moved to the back of the shop. One worker is fidgeting with the hood of the extractor. It is making erratic noises. Two other workers are turning skewers, their hands covered in smoke. The front door of the shop is open and the wind stops the smoke from escaping. A young couple are sitting uncomfortably inside. An old white man with a closely trimmed grey beard has his eyes fixed on the sizzling meat. He is unperturbed by the smoke. It is someone I think I recognise. He lights a cigarette. One of the workers points to a no-smoking sign. The old man ignores the worker. He turns his head towards me. My eyes are mistaken again.

The owner of a wobbly wooden trolley, with the words *Lahori Kulfi* written on the sides, is fast approaching. I have never seen him sell a kulfi at this time of day. A waiter with a broad smile entices a group of passing students into the restaurant. The students look at each other. The waiter steps back confidently, the students laugh loudly and walk into the restaurant.

The kulfi seller is now seated outside. He acknowledges me with a nod, pointing to an empty stool next to him. I shake my head.

The police presence begins to thicken as I get closer to the city centre. Two police motorcycle riders are standing under the arches of the railway bridge close to Oxford Road station. Trains rumble on, to and fro, over their heads. The policemen have their eyes fixed on two bearded Muslim youths, who are clearly aware of being tracked and deliberately pose. The ground under my feet vibrates each time a train goes past.

A car suddenly veers onto the pavement and narrowly misses me. I stumble backwards and the trolley bag slips out of my hand and falls into the road. A woman jumps out of the car, grabs my hand and stops me from falling. 'Sorry, luv,' she says. Letting go of my hand, she turns to the police officer and says quickly, 'It's the last train I can catch.'

The policeman nods to the woman.

I regain my balance and watch the woman run towards the station. The trolley bag is on its side in the road. A policeman picks it up by the handle and looks at it suspiciously. I grip my mobile and ready myself for the speed-dial irreversible detonation code. Perhaps this is my end? As with everything else, I have failed.

The policeman walks up to me with my trolley bag, asking, 'What have you got in here?'

My finger is on the speed dial. I need only to press one button and my life is done.

'You'll kill yourself lugging this thing around, mate,' the policeman says.

'I am nearly done with it,' I reply, taking hold of the bag.

Still holding onto the bag, the policeman says, 'It's all closed up there. Where are you going?'

'To the Grand Central for a pint.'

The Grand Central is only a few hundred yards from the railway arches. I can feel the gaze of the policeman pricking the back of my neck as I walk past them up Oxford Road towards yet more police officers who are standing outside the pub.

Heavy rock music is flowing out of the open door of the Grand Central, mixing with the noise of the engines of a long line of buses. A blue bus spews out plumes of smoke from its exhaust. The song 'Riders on the Storm' mixes with the fumes of the bus. Then rain hisses down. And thunder cracks. The rain continues to hiss. Piano notes patter out of another pub. Thunder cracks again. A chill wraps itself around me. The words of the song resonate along my veins: *'There's a killer on the road, his brain is squirmy like a toad. If you give this man a ride, sweet memory will die.'*

'It is surely karma,' I say to the song, stopping close to the door. I smile at the realisation that it was the same song I was listening to when I had the idea of ending my life here.

Leaning against the wall of the pub, I listen to the song and think back to almost a year ago to the day. I had been sitting in this pub, by the window, observing the heavy police presence outside the Grand Palace Hotel on the opposite side of the road.

A man in a studded leather jacket had been at the bar, nodding his head to the song. A woman and a man were sitting not far from me. I hadn't noticed them when I came in. Over the words of the song, I caught snatches of their conversation:

'It was my fault. I should have stopped you.'

'Why didn't you?'

The woman lowered her voice. Looking at their reflection in the window, I strained my ears to catch what she was saying. She looked like she was in her mid-fifties and he looked much younger. Her eyes were bloodshot.

Just then, the music stopped. She threw her hands up and was about to say something else when the man at the bar shouted at the couple, 'You ruined my song.'

The man at the bar was about to move towards the couple when the landlord tapped him on the shoulder and gave him a remote for the bar's audio system. 'Riders on the Storm' was back. This time the music was much louder. The rain was drumming every wall of the pub. The man at the bar was now dancing on his own, shaking his head. His hair lashed his face with each movement. He danced until the song finished and then, with one gulp, finished his drink and rushed out.

Back then, I hadn't noticed the traffic stopping. Police cars had blocked both sides of the road. Armed officers were positioned all around. A group of people were heading towards the mouth of Palace Hotel shouting, 'Murderer! Murderer!' Tony Blair was coming out. He looked shocked at being shouted at.

'One million killed!'

'Liar. Liar. Liar!'

The couple stopped arguing. The woman asked me, 'What's going on out there?'

I pointed to the hotel on the other side of the road and said, 'Tony Blair is coming out of the hotel.'

She ran out, pointed at Tony Blair and screamed with all her might, 'You sent my son to Iraq on a lie, you bastard! You sent him out on a lie and he came back *like this!*'

I followed her son out and stopped behind him. He stood close to his mother, with his head lowered. She held the stubs of his arms up for Tony Blair to see.

Tony Blair was walking out of the Palace Hotel. He was about to get into his car, but stopped and turned towards us.

Policemen and women encircled him. Some armed officers turned their guns in our direction. Police sirens started blaring. Tony Blair took a step towards us. Plain-clothed officers formed another ring around him. He hesitated for a moment and then got into his car and was driven away. Four police officers wearing riot gear strode over to us. While three of the officers stood to attention, their hands on their truncheons, the fourth took his helmet off and said to us, 'It's all over. Go back to your drinks.' Pushing us back towards the pub, he added, 'Come on now, there's no need for all this.'

'He's a murderer and a liar,' the woman cried, placing her arm across her son's shoulders and leading him away from the pub.

'Well, you've made your point,' the police officer said, putting his helmet back on.

Inside the pub, 'Riders on the Storm' started again.

Today, police cars are parked across all junctions within a mile of the G-Mex Centre where, this year, the Labour Party is holding its annual conference. By now I am familiar with the scene as I have been here before during other conferences and have seen him come out of the Palace Hotel and walk up the road to the conference centre.

Security for Tony Blair follows a routine. Just before he comes out, armed officers will get into position and sometime after this he will emerge.

Even though the road beyond the traffic lights is empty, no one is walking in it. The traffic and pedestrian lights in front of the Central Library have been covered with orange hoods.

A tram, the only public transport running in this part of the city centre, rumbles past the roadblocks, beyond which are two rings of wire fencing that leave just enough space for the conference delegates to walk through.

I take a beer and a large chaser and sit overlooking Oxford Road, waiting for my moment.

Not long now, I think, feeling the mobile phones in my pocket.

More and more police officers come and take up positions outside the Palace Hotel. The bastard is about to come out. Soon, you bastard, very soon, it will be *your* blood that is going to be spilt on the road!

Eight o'clock.

I have at least two more hours left on this earth, I think. Almighty, make sure Tony Blair is on schedule, he will pay for his crime and be done and gone, right there by the entrance, within two hours.

'I checked. The film starts at 8.15. We still have time,' a young man says to his girlfriend, hugging her. 'Hope you've got the tickets?'

She looks in her handbag and pulls two tickets out before exclaiming, 'Oh, I forgot to post Mum's birthday card! It's still here.'

'We'll post it after the film,' he replies.

'No, we might forget,' she insists, pulling him out of the pub door.

They have hardly made it out of the pub when a similar thought dawns on me. *How could I forget?*

I have forgotten to post my letter to my daughter. I have left it on the windowsill of my house.

'It's only 8.05,' I mumble to myself, pulling the trolley bag out of the pub. 'I've still got time to collect it and get back.'

'33 Blade Lane, driver, Longsight. And please try to get me back here afterwards as fast as you can,' I hail and tell the driver of a black cab.

'Don't worry, mate!' he replies, performing an illegal U-turn. 'Harry's me name, 'n' drivin's me game.'

'I have to post a letter to my daughter.'

'I'll get you there and back, no need for tears.'

'I forgot to post it.'

'Strange thing, daughters are,' the driver laughs. The taxi has come to a stop at the traffic lights next to the BBC. 'You can never give them enough.'

'I have given mine everything, but I forgot to post her the letter telling her . . .'

'You migrating somewhere, for retirement, like?'

'Just leaving.'

The traffic lights change and we drive slowly past the BBC.

'Don't blame you, mate. This country's gone to the dogs. It was bad anyway and now, with all this security, the city centre's dead. Not a fare in sight. And—pardon my French—it's those fucking private hire lot. I mean, I've nowt against you lot. I'm a minority-white cabbie, I am. But they just don't follow the rules. They'll pick up from anywhere!'

'I had it in my hand earlier today, but I forgot to post it.'

We are now halfway along Plymouth Grove.

'Take a look at that,' Harry says. Police cars with lights flashing are coming fast towards us. 'Something serious is going on. No sirens.'

Harry pulls over to the side of the road. The police cars drive past us.

It is strange how life slows down just before death, I think, looking at the autumn leaves falling in slow motion onto the empty street. The usual cars are parked in their usual places. Everyone is sitting behind drawn curtains.

'What's the number, mate?' Harry asks.

'It's the last house on the left.'

My street curves to the right and straightens up just before my house.

'Stop the car now!'

I thought I saw a shadow move in front of my house.

'Here?'

'Right here!'

Harry stops the cab in the middle of the road.

'No, not like that!' I say.

'OK, mate, keep your hair on,' Harry says, driving half onto the pavement.

The shadow moves again.

'You've got a visitor,' Harry says. 'You sly old fox,' Harry chuckles. 'At your age!'

'It's my daughter!'

'What did I tell you? They never leave their dads. It's just a game they play.' Harry laughs, 'Go on. Give her the letter yourself.'

Harry turns around for the first time. He has a kind smile on his chubby face.

Placing a £50 note in his hand, I say, 'Please wait. I must get back, and you can keep the change, but please wait.'

Returning the money, Harry says, 'You pay when I finish the job, and it won't cost fifty quid.' He steps out of the cab, lights a cigarette and sighs, 'And there's no charge for waiting, not tonight. I've been here meself, I have.'

Aisha turns towards me. My throat dries. The explosives feel so heavy. My hands shake. I find it difficult to pull the trolley. I feel life is draining out of me. My eyes swell with tears. My head feels light.

'I've been standing here for an hour, Abbaji,' Aisha says. 'Let me take this trolley.'

She does not wait for me to reply. She puts her hand into my pocket and gets the keys.

'Why have you got two mobiles, Dad?' Aisha asks. 'And, my God, you are so cold! No more drinking, Dad. It'll kill you.'

'Why are you here?' I ask, blinking against the hallway light.

She waits a moment and replies, 'Why shouldn't I be?'

'I have to go. I only came back to post that letter to you. I have to go. You don't understand.'

'Just sit for a moment, Dad,' Aisha says, taking me by the hand towards to the sofa, 'just for a moment.'

'I have to go. There is no more time.'

'Take your coat off, Dad—.'

'No, no, no. Don't touch it.'

'OK. OK, chill, Abbaji.'

'Why did you come back? Tell me. Why today?'

'I just did.' She is holding my letter, smiling.

'My bag, where is it?'

'It is here, next to you.'

'Where is your purdah?'

She laughs, shaking her shoulder-length hair.

'And I should have gone to your mother's grave . . .'

'It doesn't matter anymore. Do you remember, Dad, when you used to sing to me?' She is stroking my forehead. Her hand is soft and warm. And then she starts singing the only song I ever sang to her.

'Why have you come? Why today?' The second alarm on the primed mobile is going off. I can feel the vibrations.

She runs her fingers through my hair. A thumping pain rips through my head. She strokes my face and asks, 'Do you remember the story of the cobra you used to tell me?'

I close my eyes. The first time I had told her this story, she had sprained her ankle and I was carrying her on my shoulders. I told her how, when I was her age, I too had sprained my ankle and my mother had carried me on her shoulders and had told me the story of how, once, I had played with a King Cobra and survived. Mother had gone to the jungle and left me at my grandmother's house to play with my friend, Shoukat. When she came back, Shoukat and I were sitting in the shade of a wall. I kept putting my hand into a hole in the wall. Inside the hole was a big black King Cobra. Eventually it came out. It was the biggest one in the whole world. When it saw Mother coming towards me it reared up and hissed. She stopped dead in her tracks. Then she turned this way and that way trying to get round the snake, but each time the King Cobra blocked her way. Our whole village came out to help her. But everyone there was too scared to approach the snake.

'Saleem, come slowly to me,' Mother called.

'No. We are playing with my friend,' I said.

'This is a snake and it will sting you,' Mother said.

'It's my friend,' I said. 'It never does that.'

Shoukat's father, Meherban, said, 'Shoukat, get up very slowly and walk backwards towards us.'

Shoukat stood up. King Cobra opened his crown, straightened up, and hissed at Shoukat. I slapped King Cobra on the head and he curled down.

'Run now, Shoukat,' Meherban shouted.

Shoukat ran right past King Cobra.

My uncle came with a gun. But he could not shoot. King Cobra was sitting at my feet.

Mother stepped closer. King Cobra opened his crown again and moved towards her. She squatted on the ground and put out her hand. King Cobra flew forward at her. She pulled her hand back quickly. King Cobra let out a deep growly hiss and moved with every move Mother made, flicking its tongue. Mother, still squatting, moved a bit closer and extended her hand a little in front of her. King Cobra leaned back then struck at Mother with lightning speed. She grabbed it below the head and stood up, the snake twisting in the air.

Still holding the snake, Mother grabbed me by the arm, wrenched me off the ground and pushed me towards my uncle, who was holding his gun and shaking with fear. Mother put the snake into a basket. My uncle aimed his gun at the basket, but Mother stepped forward and pushed the gun upwards. It went off.

'No one will hurt this creature,' Mother said over the echo of the blast from the gun.

Mother tied a cloth around the top of the basket, picked it up and followed by villagers released the snake deep inside the jungle.

That night the dholl player drummed and we danced and celebrated.

'Dad, you're sweating. Take off your coat,' Aisha says.

'The terrorist must not live beyond his last meal in the Grand Central!' I cry in desperation.

'*Sing to the western wind,*' sings Gulzarina, '*the song it understands.*'

The drummer beats the drum faster.

'What are the numbers of the mobile phone, Dad?' Aisha asks.

Now Cousin Habib is talking to Aisha and Habib Junior is saying something to her, also. Aisha is hugging Gulzarina.

Aisha is reading my letter.

'I just never knew you, Abbaji,' Aisha says to me. 'I just never knew.'

My uncle fires a celebratory shot into the air.

'Taxi driver! I have to pay the taxi driver!' I suddenly remember.

'I've paid him, Dad,' Aisha says. 'Shush, now. It is my time to do what has to be done.'

'Why have you come back? Why?' I ask.

'Allah O Akbar,' Aisha chants, reading my letter to her. 'Allah O Akbar.'

'Why have you come back, Aisha, why today?'

Aisha does not reply.

My mother has gone but the dholl player is still there, beating his drum louder and louder, louder and louder, with never-tiring hands. He does not even stop to wipe the sweat dripping onto the hot earth below his naked feet. The beat is thunderous now.

I wake up to loud banging on the front door. I am no longer wearing the overcoat or the explosives. The trolley bag is gone. I call out for Aisha. She does not answer. There is knocking on the door again. I open it. There is no one there.

But there is a note on the windowsill. It is from Aisha. It says: Let me sing to this wind, the song it understands.

Acknowledgements

This novel took over a decade to write. During that time, I received comments and advice from many people, including students and staff at the American University of Beirut. There are too many to mention here. My thanks to them all. In the final throes of composition, I found myself indebted in particular to Amrit Wilson and Phil Griffin. For the painstaking detailed feedback over the decade, thank you, Anandi Ramamurthy, Peter Kalu, Rami Zurayk, Paul Kelemen, and Jawed Siddiqi. The responsibility for any remaining inadequacies is entirely mine.

Tariq Mehmood
Beirut